Discarded by
Santa Maria Library

OMNI
Visions
One

Edited by Ellen Datlow

OMNI Books
Greensboro, North Carolina

Copyright © 1993, Omni Publications International Ltd. All rights reserved.

"The Girl Who Loved Animals," © 1988 by Bruce McAllister
"The Ghost Lemurs of Madagascar," © 1987 by William S. Burroughs
"Stardust," © 1987 by Harvey Jacobs
"Unidentified Objects," © 1989 by James P. Blaylock
"The Gates of Babel," © 1989 by J.R. Dunn
"Hoover's Men," © 1988 by Howard Waldrop
"Phase Change," © 1993 by Joyce Carol Oates
"The Evening and the Morning and the Night," © 1987 by Octavia E. Butler
"His Powder'd Wig, His Crown of Thornes," © 1989 by Marc Laidlaw
"Covenant of Souls," © 1986 by Michael Swanwick

Cover art © Gervasio Gallardo/Jeff Lavaty & Associates

Reproduction or translation of any part of this work beyond that permitted by Sections 107 and 108 of the United States Copyright Act without the permission of the copyright owner is unlawful except brief quotes used in reviews.

Printed in the United States of America

10 9 8 7 6 5 4 3 2 1

ISBN 0-87455-298-2

Omni is a registered trademark of Omni Publications International Ltd. Omni Books, 324 West Wendover Avenue, Suite 200, Greensboro, North Carolina 27408, is a General Media International Company.

Contents

Introduction v

The Girl Who Loved Animals 1
Bruce McAllister

The Ghost Lemurs of Madagascar 21
William S. Burroughs

Stardust 35
Harvey Jacobs

Unidentified Objects 57
James P. Blaylock

The Gates of Babel 75
J. R. Dunn

Hoover's Men 93
Howard Waldrop

Phase Change 103
Joyce Carol Oates

The Evening and the Morning and the Night 121
Octavia E. Butler

His Powder'd Wig, His Crown of Thornes 145
Marc Laidlaw

Covenant of Souls 161
Michael Swanwick

Introduction

Ellen Datlow

Omni Visions One begins a new *Omni* anthology series, a companion to *Omni Best Science Fiction*. The title of this new series of reprint anthologies reflects the attitude of *Omni*'s fiction. In 1981, *Omni* published William Gibson's first Sprawl story, "Johnny Mnemonic," heralding the advent of the cyberpunk movement. In 1983, *Omni* published the novelette by Dan Simmons that subsequently became the novel *Carrion Comfort*. Clive Barker made his American magazine debut in *Omni* with "The Book of Blood" in 1986; in 1988 we published K.W. Jeter's first short story; and in 1990 we published Terry Bisson's first short story.

In addition, *Omni* has assiduously brought those writers who cross genres to the attention of our readers, blurring those artificial boundaries in order to publish the most interesting and diverse fiction available. Thus Patricia Highsmith's fiction appeared in a thematic grouping with Edward Bryant, Pat Cadigan, Whitley Strieber, Gahan Wilson, John Skipp, and Craig Spector. And Jack Cady, Joyce Carol Oates, William Burroughs, Jonathan Carroll, Ursula K. Le Guin, Nancy Kress, Stephen King, William Kotzwinkle, and Karen Joy Fowler have all appeared in *Omni*.

Perhaps most important, *Omni* has encouraged science fiction's growth into a sophisticated literature for adult men and women, not just for adolescent boys. All but one of the stories in *Omni Visions 1* were originally published in *Omni* Magazine between 1986 and 1989. This anthology is a good representation of the diversity of theme, tone, and style of *Omni*'s fiction.

The one original story included, Joyce Carol Oates's "Phase Change," continues the *Omni* tradition.

The Girl Who Loved Animals

Bruce McAllister

Bruce McAllister is the author of the novels *Humanity Prime* and *Dream Baby*—the latter a powerful and moving science fiction work about Vietnam—and of numerous short stories, including two others set in the same universe as "The Girl Who Loved Animals": "The Ark" (*Omni*, September 1985) and "Sister Moon" (*Omni Best Science Fiction One*).

All three stories pose an all-too-believable future in which the few, not yet extinct, wild animals are kept in "arks," a type of zoo, or drugged to make them conform to misguided religious dogma. "The Girl Who Loved Animals" shows McAllister at his best—realistically depicting a near-future society, speculating about a controversial scientific idea, and intertwining both of those strands with several relationships, all reflecting back onto the narrator. The story was first published in May 1988.

The Girl Who Loved Animals

Bruce McAllister

They had her on the seventeenth floor in their new hi-security unit on Figueroa and weren't going to let me up. Captain Mendoza, the one who thinks I'm the ugliest woman he's ever laid eyes on and somehow manages to take it personally, was up there with her, and no one else was allowed. Or so this young lieutenant with a fresh academy tattoo on his left thumb tries to tell me. I get up real close so the kid can hear me over the screaming media crowd in the lobby and see this infamous face of mine, and I tell him I don't think Chief Stracher will like getting a call at 0200 hours just because some desk cadet can't tell a privileged soc worker from a media rep, and how good friends really shouldn't bother each other at that time of the day anyway, am I right? It's a lie, sure, but he looks worried, and I remember why I haven't had anything done about the face I was born with. He gives me two escorts—a sleek young swatter with an infrared Ruger, and a lady in fatigues who's almost as tall as I am—and up we go. They're efficient kids. They frisk me in the elevator.

Mendoza wasn't with her. Two P.D. medics with side arms were. The girl was sitting on a sensor cot in the middle of their new glass observation room—closed-air, antiballistic Plexi, and the rest—and was a mess. The video footage, which four million people had seen at ten, hadn't been pixeled at all.

Their hi-sec floor cost them thirty-three million dollars, I told myself, took them three years of legislation to get, and had everything you'd ever want to keep your witness or assassin or jihad dignitary alive—CCTV, microwave eyes, pressure mats, blast doors, laser blinds, eight different kinds of gas, and, of course, Vulcan minicannons from the helipad three floors up.

I knew that Mendoza would have preferred someone more exciting than a twenty-year-old girl with a V Rating of nine point six and something strange growing inside her, but he was going to have to settle for this christening.

I asked the medics to let me in. They told me to talk into their wall grid so the new computer could hear me. The computer said something like "Yeah, she's okay," and they opened the door and frisked me again.

I asked them to leave, citing Welfare & Institutions Statute Thirty-eight. They wouldn't, citing hi-sec orders under Penal Code Seven-A. I told them to go find Mendoza and tell him I wanted privacy for the official interview.

Very nicely they said that neither of them could leave and that if I kept asking I could be held for obstruction, despite the same statute's cooperation clause. That sounded right to me. I smiled and got to work.

Her name was Lissy Tomer. She was twenty-one, not twenty. According to Records, she'd been born in the East Valley, been abused as a child by both sets of parents, and, as the old story goes, hooked up with a man who would oblige her the same way. What had kept County out of her life, I knew, was the fact that early on, someone in W&I had set her up with an easy spousal-abuse complaint and felony restraining-order option that needed only a phone call to trigger. But she'd never exercised it, though the older bruises said she should have.

She was pale and underweight and wouldn't have looked very good even without the contusions, the bloody nose and lip, the belly, and the shivering. The bloody clothes didn't help either. Neither did the wires and contact gel they had all over her for their beautiful new cot.

But there was a fragility to her—princess-in-the-fairy-tale kind—that almost made her pretty.

She flinched when I said hello, just as if I'd hit her. I wondered which had been worse—the beating or the media. He'd done it in a park and had been screaming at her when Mendoza's finest arrived, and two uniforms had picked up a couple of C's by calling it in to the networks.

She was going to get hit with a beautiful post-traumatic stress disorder sometime down the road even if things didn't get worse for her—which they would. The press wanted her badly. She was bloody, showing, and *very* visual.

"Has the fetus been checked?" I asked the side arms. If they were going to listen, they could help.

The shorter one said yes, a portable sonogram from County, and the baby looked okay.

I turned back to the girl. She was looking up at me from the cot, looking hopeful, and I couldn't for the life of me imagine what she thought I could do for her.

"I'm your new V.R. advocate, Lissy."

She nodded, keeping her hands in her lap like a good girl.

"I'm going to ask you some questions, if that's all right. The more I know, the more help I can be, Lissy. But you know that, don't you." I grinned.

She nodded again and smiled, but the lip hurt.

I identified myself, badge and department and appellation, then read her her rights under Protective Services provisions, as amended—what we in the trade call the Nhat Hanh Act. What you get and what you don't.

"First question, Lissy: Why'd you do it?"

I asked it as gently as I could, flicking the hand recorder on. It was the law. I wondered if she knew what a law was.

Her I.Q. was eighty-four, congenital, and she was a Collins psychotype, class three dependent. She'd had six years of school and had once worked for five months for a custodial service in Monterey Park. Her Vulnerability Rating, all factors factored, was a whopping nine point six. It was the rating that had gotten her a felony restraint complaint option on the marital bond, and County had assumed that was enough to protect her ... from him.

As far as the provisions on low-I.Q. cases went, the husband had been fixed, she had a second-degree dependency on him, and an abortion in event of rape by another was standard. As far as County was concerned, she was protected, and society had exercised proper conscience. I really couldn't blame her last V.R. advocate. I'd have assumed the same.

And missed one thing.

"I like animals a lot," she said, and it made her smile. In the middle of a glass room, two armed medics beside her, the media screaming downstairs to get at her, her husband somewhere wishing he'd killed her, it was the one thing that could make her smile.

She told me about a kitten she'd once had at the housing project on Crenshaw. She'd named it Lissy and had kept it alive "all by herself." It was her job, she said, like her mother and fathers had jobs. Her second stepfather—or was it her mother's brother? I couldn't tell, and it didn't matter—had taken it away one day, but she'd had it for a month or two.

When she started living with the man who'd eventually beat her up in a park for the ten o'clock news, he let her have a little dog. He would have killed it out of jealousy in the end, but it died because she didn't know about shots. He wouldn't have paid for them anyway, and she seemed to know that. He hadn't been like that when they first met. It sounded like neurotransmitter blocks, MPHG metabolism. The new bromaine that was on the streets would do it; all the fentanyl analogs would, too. There were a dozen substances on the street that would. You saw it all the time.

She told me how she'd slept with the kitten and the little dog and, when she didn't have them anymore, with the two or three toys she'd had so long that most of their fur was worn off. How she could smell the kitten for months in her room just as if it were still there. How the dog had died in the shower. How her husband had gotten mad, hit her, and taken the thing away. But you could tell she was glad when the body wasn't there in the shower anymore.

"This man was watching me in the park," she said. "He always watched me."

"Why were you in the park, Lissy?"

She looked at me out of the corner of her eye and gave me a smile, the conspiratorial kind. "There's more than one squirrel in those trees. Maybe a whole family. I like to watch them."

I was surprised there were any animals at all in the park. You don't see them anymore, except for the domesticates.

"Did you talk to this man?"

She seemed to know what I was asking. She said, "I wasn't scared of him. He smiled a lot." She laughed at something, and we all jumped. "I knew he wanted to talk to me, so I pretended there was a squirrel over by him, and I fed it. He said, Did I like animals and how I could make a lot of money and help the animals of the world."

It wasn't important. A dollar. A thousand. But I had to ask.

"How much money did he tell you?"

"Nine thousand dollars. That's how much I'm going to get, and I'll be able to see it when it's born, and visit it."

She told me how they entered her, how they did it gently while she watched, the instrument clean and bright.

The fertilized egg would affix to the wall of her uterus, they'd told her, and together they would make a placenta. What the fetus needed nutritionally would pass through the placental barrier, and her body wouldn't reject it.

Her eyes looked worried now. She was remembering things—a beating, men in uniforms with guns, a man with a microphone pushed against her belly. *Had her husband hit her there? If so, how many times?* I wondered.

"Will the baby be okay?" she asked, and I realized I'd never seen eyes so colorless, a face so trusting.

"That's what the doctors say," I said, looking up at the side arms, putting it on them.

Nine thousand. More than a man like her husband would ever see stacked in his life, but he'd beaten her anyway, furious that she could get it in her own way when he'd failed again and again, furious that she'd managed to get it with the one thing he thought he owned—her body.

Paranoid somatopaths are that way.

I ought to know. I married one.

I'm thinking of the mess we've made of it, Lissy. I'm thinking of the three hundred thousand grown children of the walking wounded of an old war in Asia who walk the same way.

I'm thinking of the four hundred thousand walljackers, our living dead. I'm thinking of the zoos, the ones we don't have anymore, and what they must have been like, what little girls like Lissy Tomer must have done there on summer days.

I'm thinking of a father who went to war, came back, but was never the same again, of a mother who somehow carried us all, of how cars and smog and cement can make a childhood and leave you thinking you can change it all.

I wasn't sure, but I could guess. The man in the park was a body broker for pharmaceuticals and nonprofits, and behind him somewhere was a species resurrection group that somehow had the money. He'd gotten a hefty three hundred percent, which meant the investment was already thirty-six grand. He'd spent some of his twenty-seven paying off a few W&I people in the biggest counties, gotten a couple dozen names on high-V.R. searches, watched the best bets himself, and finally made his selection.

The group behind him didn't know how such things worked or didn't particularly care; they simply wanted consenting women of childbearing age, good health, no substance abuse, no walljackers, no suicidal inclinations; and the broker's reputation was good, and he did his job.

Somehow he'd missed the husband.

As I found out later, she was one of ten. Surrogates for human babies were a dime a dozen, had been for years. This was something else.

In a nation of two hundred eighty million, Lissy Tomer was one of ten—but in her heart of hearts she was the only one. Because a man who said he loved animals had talked to her in a park once. Because he'd said she would get a lot of money—money that ought to make a husband who was never happy, happy. Because she would get to see it when it was born and get to visit it wherever it was kept.

The odd thing was, I could understand how she felt.

I called Antalou at three A.M., got her mad but at least awake, and got her to agree we should try to get the girl out that same night—out of that room, away from the press, and into a County unit for a complete fetal check. Antalou is the kind of boss you only get in heaven. She tried, but Mendoza stonewalled her under P.C. Twenty-two, the Jorgenson clause—he was getting all the publicity he and his new unit needed with the press screaming downstairs—and we gave up at five, and I went home for a couple hours of sleep before the paperwork began.

I knew that sitting there in the middle of all that glass with two armed medics was almost as bad as the press, but what could I do, Lissy, what could I do?

I should have gone to the hotel room that night, but the apartment was closer. I slept on the sofa. I didn't look at the bedroom door, which is always locked from the outside. The nurse has a key. Some days it's easier not to think about what's in there. Some days it's harder.

I thought about daughters.

We got her checked again, this time at County Medical, and the word came back okay. Echomytic bruises with some placental bleeding, but the fetal signs were fine. I went ahead and asked whether the fetus was a threat to the mother in any case, and they laughed. No more than any human child would be, they said. All you're doing is borrowing the womb, they said. "Sure," this cocky young resident says to me, "it's low-tech all the way." I had a lot of homework to do, I realized.

Security at the hospital reported a visit by a man who was not her husband, and they didn't let him through. The same man called me an hour later. He was all smiles and wore a suit.

I told him we'd have to abort if County, under the Victims' Rights Act, decided it was best or the girl wanted it. He pointed out with a smile that the thing she was carrying was worth a lot of money to the people he represented, and they could make her life more comfortable, and we ought to protect the girl's interests.

I told him what I thought of him, and he laughed. "You've got it all wrong, Doctor."

I let it pass. He knows I'm an MPS-V.R., no Ph.D., no M.D. He probably even knows I got the degree under duress, years late, because Antalou said we needed all the paper we could get if the department was going to survive. I know what he's doing, and he knows I know.

"The people I represent are caring people, Doctor. Their cause is a good one. They're not what you're accustomed to working with, and they've retained me simply as a program consultant, a 'resource locator.' It's all aboveboard, Doctor, completely legal, I assure you. But I really don't need to tell you any of this, do I?"

"No, you don't."

I added that, legal or not, if he tried to see her again I would have him for harassment under the D.A.'s cooperation clause.

He laughed, and I knew then he had a law degree from one of the local universities. The suit was right. I could imagine him in it at the park that day.

"You may be able to pull that with the mopes and 5150's you work with on the street, Doctor, but I know the law. I'll make you a deal. I'll stay away for the next three months, as long as you look after the girl's best interests, how's that?"

I knew there was more, so I waited.

"My people will go on paying for weekly visits up to the eighth month, then daily through to term, the clinic to be designated by them. They want ultrasound, CVS, and amniotic antiabort treatments, and the diet and abstinence programs the girl's already agreed to. All you have to do is get her to her appointments, and we pay for it. Save the county some money."

I waited.

His voice changed as I'd known it would. The way they do in the courtrooms. I'd heard it change like that a hundred times before, years of it, both sides of the aisle.

"If County can't oblige," he said, "we'll just have to try Forty-A, right?"

I told him to take a flying something.

Maybe I didn't know the law, but I knew Forty-A. In certain circles it's known simply as Fucker-Forty. Under it—the state's own legislation—he'd be able to sue the county and this V.R. advocate in particular for loss of livelihood— his and hers—and probably win after appeals.

This was the last thing Antalou or any of us needed.

The guy was still smiling.

"You've kept that face for a reason, Doctor. What do young girls think of it?"

I hung up on him.

With Antalou's help I got her into the Huntington on Normandy, a maternal unit for sedated Ward B types. Some of the other women had seen her on the news two evenings before; some hadn't. *It didn't matter,* I thought. *It was about as good a place for her to hide as possible,* I told myself. I was wrong. Everything's on computer these days, and some information's as cheap as a needle.

I get a call the next morning from the unit saying a man had gotten in and tried to kill her, and she was gone.

I'm thinking of the ones I've lost, Lissy. The tenth-generation maggot casings on the one in Koreatown, the door locked for days. The one named Consejo, the one I went with to the morgue, where they cut up babies, looking for hers. The skinny one I thought I'd saved, the way I was supposed to, but he's lying in a pool of O-positive in a room covered with the beautiful pink dust they used for prints.

Or the ones when I was a kid, East L.A., Fontana, the drugs taking them like some big machine, the snipings that always killed the ones that had nothing to do with it—the chubby ones, the ones who liked to read—the man who took Karenna and wasn't gentle, the uncle who killed his own nephews and blamed it on coyotes, which weren't there anymore, hadn't been for years.

I'm thinking of the ones I've lost, Lissy.

I looked for her all day, glad to be out of the apartment, glad to be away from a phone that might ring with a slick lawyer's face on it.

When I went back to the apartment that night to pick up another change of clothes for the hotel room, she was sitting crosslegged by the door.

"Lissy," I said, wondering how she'd gotten the address.

"I'm sorry," she said.

She had her hand on her belly, holding it not out of pain but as if it were the most comforting thing in the world.

"He wants to kill me. He says that anybody who has an animal growing in her is a devil and's got to die. He fell down the stairs. I didn't push him, I didn't."

She was crying, and the only thing I could think to do was get down and put my arms around her and try not to cry myself.

"I know, I know," I said. The symptoms were like Parkinson's, I remembered. You tripped easily.

I wasn't thinking clearly. I hadn't had more than two or three hours of sleep for three nights running, and all I could think of was getting us both inside, away from the steps, the world.

Maybe it was fatigue. Or maybe something else. I should have gotten her to a hospital. I should have called Mendoza for an escort back to his unit. What I did was get her some clothes from the bedroom, keep my eyes on the rug while

I was in there, and lock the door again when I came out. She didn't ask why neither of us were going to sleep in the bedroom. She didn't ask about the lock. She just held her belly, and smiled like some Madonna.

I took two Dalmanes from the medicine cabinet, thinking they might be enough to get the pictures of what was in that room out of my head.

I don't know whether they did or not. Lissy was beside me, her shoulder pressing against me, as I got the futon and the sofa ready.

Her stomach growled, and we laughed. I said, "Who's growling? Who's growling?" and we laughed again. I asked her if she was hungry and if she could eat sandwiches. She laughed again, and I got her a fresh one from the kitchen.

She took the futon, lying on her side to keep the weight off. I took the sofa because of my long legs.

I felt something beside me in the dark. She kissed me, said "Goodnight," and I heard her nightgown whisper back into the darkness. I held it in for a while and then couldn't anymore. It didn't last long. Dalmane's a knockout.

The next day I took her to the designated clinic and waited for her outside for her. She was happy. The big amnio needle they stuck her with didn't bother her, she said. She liked how much bigger her breasts were, she said, like a mother's should be. She didn't mind being careful about what she ate and drank. She even liked the strange V of hair growing on her abdomen, because—because it was hairy, she said, just like the thing inside her. She liked how she felt, and she wanted to know if I could see it, the glow, the one expectant mothers are supposed to have. I told her I could.

I'm thinking of a ten-year old, the one that used to tag along with me on the median train every Saturday when I went in for caseloads while most mothers had their faces changed, or played, or mothered. We talked a lot back then, and I miss it. She wasn't going to need a lot of work on that face, I knew—maybe the ears, just a little, if she was picky. She'd gotten her father's genes. But she talked like me—like a kid from East L.A.—tough, with a smile, and I thought she was going to end up a D.A. or a showy defense type or at least an exec. That's how stupid we get. In four years she was into molecular opiates and trillazines and whose fault was that? The top brokers roll over two billion a year in this city alone; the local *capi* net a twentieth of that, their street dealers a fourth; and God knows what the guys in the labs bring home to their families.

It's six years later, and I hear her letting herself in one morning. She's fumbling and stumbling at the front door. I get up, dreading it. What I see tells me that the drugs are nothing, nothing at all. She's running with a strange group of kids, a lot of them older. *This new thing's a fad,* I tell myself. It's like not having your face fixed—like not getting the nasal ramification modified, the mandibular thrust attended to—when you could do it easily, anytime, and cheaply, just because you want to make a point, and it's fun to goose the ones who need goosing. *That's all she's really doing,* you tell yourself.

You've seen her a couple of times like this, but you still don't recognize her. She's heavy around the chest and shoulders, which makes her breasts seem a lot smaller. Her face is heavy; her eyes are puffy, almost closed. She walks with a limp because something hurts down low. Her shoulders are bare, and they've got tattoos now, the new metallic kind, glittery and painful. She's wearing expensive pants, but they're dirty.

So you have a daughter now who's not a daughter, or she's both, boy and girl. The operation cost four grand, and you don't want to think how she got the money. Everyone's doing it, you tell yourself. But the operation doesn't take. She gets an infection, and the thing stops being fun, and six months later she's got no neurological response to some of the tissues the doctors have slapped on her, and pain in the others. It costs money to reverse. She doesn't have it. She spends it on other things, she says.

She wants money for the operation, she says, standing in front of you. You owe it to her, she says.

You try to find the ten-year-old in those eyes, and you can't.

Did you ever?

The call came through at six, and I knew it was County.

A full jacket—ward status, medical action, all of it—had been put through. The fetus would be aborted—"for the mother's safety . . . to prevent further exploitation by private interests . . . and physical endangerment by spouse."

Had Antalou been there, she'd have told me how County had already gotten flack from the board of supervisors, state W&I, and the attorney general's office over a V.R. like this slipping through and getting this much press. They wanted it over, done with. If the fetus were aborted, County's position would be clear—to state, the feds, and the religious groups that were starting to scream bloody murder.

It would be an abortion no one would ever complain about.

The husband was down at County holding with a pretty fibercast on his left tibia, but they weren't taking any chances. Word on two interstate conspiracies to kill the ten women had reached the D.A., and they were, they said, taking it seriously. I was, I said, glad to hear it.

Mendoza said he liked sassy women as much as the next guy, but he wanted her back in custody, and the new D.A. was screaming jurisdiction, too. Everyone wanted a piece of the ten o'clock news before the cameras lost interest and rolled on.

Society wasn't ready for it. The atavistic fears were there. You could be on trillazines, you could have an operation to be both a boy and a girl for the thrill of it, you could be a walljacker, but a mother like this, no, not yet.

I should have told someone but didn't. I took her to the zoo instead. We stood in front of the cages watching the holograms of the big cats, the tropical birds, the grass eaters of Africa—the ones that are gone. She wasn't interested in the real ones, she said—the pigeons, sparrows, coyotes, the dull hardy ones that will outlast us all. She never came here as a child, she said, and I believe it. A boyfriend at her one and only job took her once, and later, because she asked her to, so did a woman who wanted the same thing from her.

We watched the lions, the ibex, the white bears. We watched the long-legged wolf, the harp seals, the rheas. We watched the tapes stop and repeat, stop and repeat; and then she said, "Let's go," pulled at my hand, and we moved on to the most important cage of all.

There, the hologram walked back and forth looking out at us, looking through us, its red sagittal crest and furrowed brow so convincing. Alive, its name had been Mark Anthony, the plaque said. It had weighed two hundred kilos. It had lived to be ten. It wasn't one of the two whose child was growing inside her, but she seemed to know this, and it didn't matter.

"They all died the same way," she said to me. "That's what counts, Jo." *Inbred depression,* I remembered reading. *Petechial hemorrhages, cirrhosis, renal failure.*

Somewhere in the nation the remaining fertilized ova were sitting frozen in a lab, as they had for thirty years. A few dozen had been removed, thawed, encouraged to divide to sixteen cells, and finally implanted that day seven months ago. Ten had taken. As they should have, naturally, apes that we are. "Sure, it could've been done back then," the cocky young resident with insubordination written all over him had said. "All you'd have needed was an egg and a little plastic tube. And, of course,"—I didn't like the way he smiled—"a woman who was willing. . . ."

I stopped her. I asked her if she knew what The Arks were, and she said no. I started to tell her about the intensive-care zoos where for twenty years the best and brightest of them, ten thousand species in all, had been kept while two hundred thousand others disappeared—the toxics, the new diseases, the land-use policies of a new world taking them one by one—how The Arks hadn't worked, how two-thirds of the macrokingdom were gone now, and how the thing she carried inside her was one of them and one of the best.

She wasn't listening. She didn't need to hear it, and I knew the man in the suit had gotten his yes without having to say these things. The idea of having it inside her, hers for a little while, had been enough.

She told me what she was going to buy with the money. She asked me whether I thought the baby would end up at this zoo. I told her I didn't know but could check, and hated the lie. She said she might have to move to another city to be near it. I nodded and didn't say a thing.

I couldn't stand it. I sat her down on a bench and told her what the County was going to do to her.

When I was through she looked at me and said she'd known it would happen, it always happened. She didn't cry. I thought maybe she wanted to leave, but she shook her head.

We went through the zoo one more time. We didn't leave until dark.

"Are you out of your mind, Jo?" Antalou said.

"It's not permanent," I said.

"*Of course* it's not permanent. Everyone's been looking everywhere for her. What the hell do you think you're doing?"

I said it didn't matter, did it? The County homes and units weren't safe, and we didn't want her with Mendoza, and who'd think of a soc worker's house—a P.D. safe house maybe, but not a soc worker's because that's against policy, and everyone knows that soc workers are spineless, right?

"Sure," Antalou said. "But you didn't *tell* anybody, Jo."

"I've had some thinking to do."

Suddenly Antalou got gentle, and I knew what she was thinking. I needed downtime, maybe some psychiatric profiling done. She's a friend of mine, but she's a professional, too. The two of us go back all the way to corrections, Antalou and I, and lying isn't easy.

"Get her over to County holding immediately—that's the best we can do for her," she said finally. "And let's have lunch soon, Jo. I want to know what's going on in that head of yours."

It took me the night and the morning. They put her in the nicest hole they had and doubled the security, and when I left she cried for a long time, they told me. I didn't want to leave, but I had to get some thinking done.

When it was done, I called Antalou.

She swore at me when I was through but said she'd give it a try. It was crazy, but what isn't these days?

* * *

The County bit, but with stipulations. Postpartum wipe. New I.D. Fine, but also a fund set up out of *our* money. Antalou groaned. I said, Why not.

Someone at County had a heart, but it was our mention of Statute Forty-A, I found out later, that clinched it. They saw the thing dragging on through the courts, cameras rolling forever, and that was worse than any temporary heat from state or the feds.

So they let her have the baby. I slept in the waiting room of the maternity unit, and it took local troops as well as hospital security to keep the press away. We used a teaching hospital down south—approved by the group that was funding her—but even then the media found out and came by the droves.

We promised full access at a medically approved moment if they cooled it, which they did. The four that didn't were taken bodily from the building under one penal code section or another.

At the beginning of the second stage of labor, the infant abruptly rotates from occiput-posterior to right occiput-anterior position; descent is rapid, and a viable two-thousand-gram female is delivered without episiotomy. Interspecific Apgar scores are nine and ten at one and five minutes, respectively.

The report would sound like all the others I'd read. The only difference would be how the thing looked, and even that wasn't much.

The little head, hairless face, broad nose, black hair sticking up like some old movie comic's. Human eyes, hairless chest, skinny arms. The feet would look like hands, sure, and the skin would be a little gray, but how much was that? To the girl in the bed it wasn't anything at all.

She said she wanted me to be there, and I said sure but didn't know the real reason.

When her water broke, they told me, and I got scrubbed up, put on the green throwaways like they said, and got back to her room quickly. The contractions had started up like a hammer.

It didn't go smoothly. The cord got hung up on the baby's neck inside, and the fetal monitor started screaming. She got scared; I got scared. They put her up on all fours to shift the baby, but it didn't work. They wheeled her to the O.R. for a C-section, which they really didn't want to do; and for two hours it was fetal signs getting better, then worse, doctors preparing for a section, then the signs somehow getting better again. Epidural block, episiotomy, some concerted forceps work, and the little head finally starts to show.

Lissy was exhausted, making little sounds. More deep breaths, a few encouraging shouts from the doctors, more pushing from Lissy, and the head was through, then the body, white as a ghost from the vernix, and someone was saying something to me in a weak voice.

"Will you cut the cord, please?"

It was Lissy.

I couldn't move. She said it again.

The doctor was waiting, the baby slick in his hands. Lissy was white as a sheet, her forehead shiny with the sweat, and she couldn't see it from where she was. "It would be special to me, Jo," she said.

One of the nurses was beside me saying how it's done all the time—by husbands and lovers, sisters and mothers and friends—but that if I was going to do it I needed to do it now, please.

I tried to remember who had cut the cord when Meg was born, and I couldn't. I could remember a doctor, that was all.

I don't remember taking the surgical steel snips, but I did. I remember not wanting to cut it—flesh and blood, the first of its kind in a long, long time—and when I finally did, it was tough, the cutting made a noise, and then it was over, the mother had the baby in her arms, and everyone was smiling.

A woman could have carried a *Gorilla gorilla beringei* to term without a care in the world a hundred, a thousand, a million years ago. The placenta would have known what to do; the blood would never have mixed. The gestation was the same nine months. The only thing stopping anyone that winter day in '97 when Cleo, the last of her kind on the face of this earth, died of renal failure in the National Zoo in DC, was the thought of carrying it.

It had taken three decades, a well-endowed resurrection group, a slick body broker, and a skinny twenty-one-year-old girl who didn't mind the thought of it.

She wants money for the operation, my daughter says to me that day in the doorway, shoulders heavy, face puffy, slurring it, the throat a throat I don't know, the voice deeper. I tell her again I don't have it, that perhaps her friends—the ones she's helped out so often when she had the money and they didn't—could help her. I say it nicely, with no sarcasm, trying not to look at where she hurts, but she knows exactly what I'm saying.

She goes for my eyes, as if she's had practice, and I don't fight back. She gets my cheek and the corner of my eye, screams something about never loving me and me never loving her—which isn't true.

She knows I know how she'll spend the money, and it makes her mad.

I don't remember the ten-year-old ever wanting to get even with anyone, but this one always does. She hurts. She wants to hurt back. If she knew, if she only knew what I'd carry for her.

I'll find her, I know—tonight, tomorrow morning, the next day or two—sitting at a walljack somewhere in the apartment, her body plugged in, the little unit with its Medusa wires sitting in her lap, her heavy shoulders hunched as if she were praying, and I'll unplug her—to show I care.

But she'll have gotten even with me, and that's what counts, and no matter how much I plead with her, promise her anything she wants, she won't try a program, she won't go with me to County—both of us, together—for help.

Her body doesn't hurt at all when she's on the wall. When you're a walljacker you don't care what kind of tissue's hanging off you, you don't care what you look like—what anyone looks like. The universe is inside. The juice is from the wall, the little unit translates, and the right places in your skull—the medulla all the way to the cerebellum, all the right centers—get played like the keys of the most beautiful synthesizer in the world. You see blue skies that make you cry. You see young men and women who make you come in your pants without your even needing to touch them. You see loving mothers. You see fathers that never leave you.

I'll know what to do. I'll flip the circuit breakers and sit in the darkness with a hand light until she comes out of it, cold-turkeying, screaming mad, and I'll say nothing. I'll tell myself once again that it's the drugs, it's the jacking, it's not her. She's dead and gone and hasn't been the little girl on that train with her hair tucked behind her ears for a long time, that this one's a lie but one I've got to keep playing.

So I walk into the bedroom, and she's there, in the chair, like always. She's got clothes off for a change and doesn't smell, and I find myself thinking how neat she looks—chic even. I don't feel a thing.

As I take a step toward the kitchen and the breaker box, I see what she's done.

I see the wires doubling back to the walljack, and I remember hearing about this from someone. It's getting common, a fad.

There are two ways to do it. You can rig it so that anyone who touches you gets ripped with a treble wall dose in a bypass. Or so that anyone who kills the electricity, even touches the wires, kills you.

Both are tamperproof. The M.E. has twenty bodies to prove it, and the guys stuck with the job downtown don't see a breakthrough for months.

She's opted for the second. Because it hurts the most.

She's starving to death in the chair, cells drying out, unless someone I.V.'s her—carefully. Even then the average expectancy is two months, I remember.

I get out. I go to a cheap hotel downtown. I dream about blackouts in big cities and bodies that move but aren't alive and about daughters. The next morning I get a glucose drip into her arm, and I don't need any help with the needle.

That's what's behind the door, Lissy.

We gave them their press conference. The doctors gave her a mild shot of pergisthan to perk her up, since she wouldn't be nursing, and she did it, held the baby in her arms like a pro, smiled though she was pale as a sheet, and the conference lasted two whole hours. Most of the press went away happy, and two of Mendoza's girls roughed up the three that tried to hide out on the floor that night. "Mendoza says hello," they said, grinning.

The floor returned to normal. I went in.

The mother was asleep. The baby was in the incubator. Three nurses were watching over them.

The body broker came with his team two days later and looked happy. Six of his ten babies had made it.

Her name is Mary McLoughlin. I chose it. Her hair is dark, and she wears it short. She lives in Chula Vista, just south of San Diego, and I get down there as often as I can, and we go out.

She doesn't remember a thing, so I was the one who had to suggest it. We go to the zoo, the San Diego Zoo, one of the biggest once. We go to the primates. We stand in front of the new exhibit, and she tells me how the real thing is so much better than the holograms, which she thinks she's seen before but isn't sure.

The baby is a year old now. They've named her Cleo, and they keep her behind glass—two or three vets in gauze masks with her at all times—safe from the air and diseases. But we get to stand there, watching her like the rest, up close, while she looks at us and clowns.

No one recognizes the dark-haired girl I'm with. The other one, the one who'd have good reason to be here, disappeared long ago, the media says. Sometimes the spotlight is just too great, they said.

"I can almost smell her, Jo," she says, remembering a dream, a vague thing, a kitten slept with. "She's not full-grown, you know."

I tell her, yes, I know.

"She's sure funny looking, isn't she."

I nod.

"Hey, I think she knows me!" She says it with a laugh, doesn't know what she's said. "Look at how she's looking at me!"

The creature is looking at her—it's looking at all of us and with eyes that aren't dumb. Looking at us, not through us.

"Can we come back tomorrow, Jo?" she asks when the crowd gets too heavy to see through.

Of course, I say. We'll come a lot, I say.

I've filed for guardianship under Statute Twenty-seven, the old W&I provisions, and if it goes through, Lissy will be moving back to L.A. with me. *I'm hetero, so it won't get kicked for exploitation, and I'm in the right field*, I think. I can't move myself, but we'll go down to the zoo every weekend. It'll be good to get away. Mendoza has asked me out, and who knows, I may say yes.

But I still have to have that lunch with Antalou, and I have no idea what I'm going to tell her.

The Ghost Lemurs of Madagascar

William S. Burroughs

William S. Burroughs has been a major influence on literature in and out of the field of the fantastique for decades. Burroughs burst on the scene with his infamous hallucinogenic novel *Naked Lunch*, and continued with his experimental cut-up *The Ticket That Exploded,* and his more recent (and more accessible) novels *Cities of the Red Night* and *The Western Lands*. He has become a cultural icon, but, more importantly, his work has influenced several generations of writers, some of whom have written fiction for *Omni*. So, thinking it only fitting that *Omni* publish *his* fiction, I commissioned a science fiction story by William Burroughs in 1986, asking only that it not be too sexual (considering his literary reputation). What I received was "The Ghost Lemurs of Madagascar," an inspired literary and science fictional plea to save an endangered species in which Burroughs has taken a special interest. The story was first published in April 1987.

The Ghost Lemurs of Madagascar

William S. Burroughs

The first name of the libertarian pirate Captain Mission, or Mission, is lost to history. All that we know of Mission comes from the book *A General History of the Most Notorious Pirates,* published in London in 1724 and written by one Captain Charles Johnson (although one historian attributes this to Defoe). The memoirs of Mission, handwritten in French, were saved by a member of the crew who survived Mission's last ship; and after passing through several hands they were translated by Johnson and included in his book.

Mission came from a wealthy Provençal family and studied humanity, logic, and mathematics at the University of Angers in the late seventeenth century. His first commission was a French man-o'-war called the *Victoire,* mounting thirty guns and commanded by a distant cousin. They sailed first to Naples, and Mission traveled to Rome, where he met a young priest named Signor Caraccioli. While Mission was making his confession, he was surprised to discover the young priest shared his own disgust for the hypocrisy of earthly power, temporal and spiritual. Caraccioli threw off his frock and signed on to the *Victoire.*

The frigate engaged and defeated two Algerian vessels, Caraccioli receiving a thigh wound. Other engagements were successful. The *Victoire* crossed the Atlantic, and off Martinique in the Caribbean they were set upon by the English *Winchelsea,* commanded by Captain Opium Jones. The first broadside killed the captain, second captain, and three lieutenants, whereupon Mission commanded the men, Caraccioli at his side, and they repulsed the English. Mission was named captain by the whole crew, and for their pirate flag they raised a white ensign with LIBERTY painted on it. After many other adventures on the Guinea coast and West Africa, joined now by a captured English ship and crew, they helped the Queen of Johanna wage war on the neighboring island of Moheli, both islands lying between Mozambique and the great red island, Madagascar. They took a Portuguese ship and decided to settle down permanently on Madagascar. Here, around 1700 A.D., on a remote harbor at the north end of the island, Mission built two great octagonal forts; and with his band of several hundred French and English pirates, renegade seamen, and freed slaves, he established the free colony of Libertatia.

Together with his lieutenant Caraccioli and the converted English pirate captain Thomas Tew, Mission formulated a set of articles by which the settlement might live in peaceful democracy. These articles were remarkably like the ideas of Rousseau and the French and American revolutions of the late eighteenth century—and preceded them by more than sixty years. There would be no capital punishment, no slavery, no imprisonment for debt, and no interference with religion or sexuality. Signor Caraccioli divided the men into groups of ten, called States, and the position of Lord Conservator was established, as well as an annual plenary meeting. This first meeting lasted ten days. Tew was made Admiral, Caraccioli Secretary of State, and Mission became His Supreme Excellence the Lord Conservator.

On a cruise off southern Madagascar, Captain Tew and some English sailors he had recruited were marooned when they drank rum punch too late on the last night as the tide rose and carried the noble *Victoire* out to sea, where she cracked up on the rocks. The crew was lost, and Tew pitched a makeshift camp where he would wait to be rescued.

The word *lemur* means "ghost" in the native language. There were taboos against killing them, and Mission had imposed an article that prohibited the killing of ghosts, on penalty of expulsion from the settlement. If any crime deserved the death penalty, also prohibited under the articles, then this was that crime.

He was seeking a different lemur species, described by a native informant as much bigger . . . like a calf or a little cow.

"Where are the big ghosts?"

The native gestured vaguely inland. "You must be careful of the Evil Lizard that changes its colors. If you fall under its spell, you too will change colors. You too will turn black with anger and green with fear and red with sex."

"Well, what is so wrong about that?"

"In a year you will die. The colors will devour your skin and flesh."

"You were talking about a Big Ghost. Bigger than a goat . . . . Where are they?"

"When you hear Chebahaka, Man-in-the-Trees, then big one not there. Her cannot be where noise is."

"Her?"

"Her He. For Big Ghost is the same."

"So him is where Man-in-the-Trees isn't?"

"No. He is when Man-in-the-Trees is silent." This occurred at dawn and sunset.

Captain Mission strapped on his double-barreled flintlock, which he kept loaded with shot charges, and thrust a short sword through his belt. He picked up his staff and walked out through the settlement, stopping here and there to talk to the settlers.

They had found an excellent red clay for bricks and were constructing two-story dwellings with second-story balconies supported by heavy hardwood pillars. These buildings had been joined to form a tier, with the dining and kitchen areas in the two downstairs rooms and the sleeping and dressing areas upstairs. The balconies were connected and were used for sleeping hammocks and pallets. These structures faced the sea, and steps led down to the bay, where a number of boats were moored. Mission was heading inland, up a steep path that leveled off at five hundred feet above the sea. He stopped, leaning on his staff, and looked back. The steep climb had not touched his breath or brought sweat to his face. He saw the settlement, the freshly molded red bricks and thatch already timeless as houses in fairyland. He could see the shadows under the pier, the lurking fish, the clear blue water of the bay, the rocks and foliage, all floating in a limpid, frameless painting.

Silence descended like a shroud that would crumble to dust when he moved. Now a cat's-paw of wind frisked across the bay and up through the ferns, bringing to his face a breath of panic. Little ghost paws rippled up his spine, stirring the hairs at the nape of his neck, where the death center flares briefly when a mortal dies.

Captain Mission did not fear panic, the sudden, intolerable knowing that everything is alive. He was himself an emissary of panic, of the knowledge that man fears above all else: the truth of his origin. It's so close. Just wipe away the words and look.

He moved through giant ferns and creepers in green shade without need of his cutlass and stopped on the edge of a clearing. A moment of arrested motion, then a bush, a stone, a log moved as a tribe of ring-tailed cat lemurs appeared, parading back and forth around one another, tails quivering above their heads. Then *whisk*—they were gone, drawing the space where they had been away with them. In the distance he could hear the cries of the sifaka lemur the natives called Chebahaka, Man-in-the-Trees. With a quick motion he caught a grasshopper and knelt by a moss-covered log. A tiny face with round eyes and large, trembling ears peered at him nervously. He held out the grasshopper, and the little mouse lemur fell upon it with chirping squeaks of delight, holding it in his tiny paws and nibbling quickly with his tiny needle teeth.

Mission moved toward the sound, which was louder and louder. The Chebahakas saw him and let out a concerted shriek that pierced his eardrums. Suddenly the sound stopped, with an impact that threw him to the ground. He lay for some minutes in a half faint, watching the gray shapes swing away through the trees.

Slowly he rose to his feet, leaning on his staff. Before him stood an ancient stone structure, overgrown with creepers and green with moss. He stepped through an archway, stone slabs under his feet. A large snake, of a glistening bright green, glided down the steps leading to a basement room. Cautiously he descended to an underground room. At the far end an arch opened to admit the afternoon light, and he could see the stone walls and ceiling.

At the end of the room was an animal that looked like a small gorilla or a chimpanzee. This surprised him, since he had been told there were no true monkeys on the island. The creature was motionless and black, as if formed out of darkness. He saw also a large pig creature of a light pink color, lolling on its side against the wall to his right. Then, directly in front of him, he saw an animal that looked at first like a small deer. The animal came to his outstretched hand, and he saw that it had no horns. Its snout was long, and he glimpsed sharp teeth shaped like little scimitars. The long, thin legs ended in cablelike fingers. The ears were large, flaring forward; the eyes, limpid amber in which the pupil floated like a glittering jewel, changing color with shifts of the light: obsidian, emerald, ruby, opal, amethyst, diamond.

Slowly the animal raised one paw and touched his face, stirring memories of the ancient betrayal. Tears streaming down his face, he stroked the animal's head. He knew he must get back to the settlement before dark. There is always something a man must do in time. For the deer ghost there was no time.

Faster and faster downhill, tearing his clothing on rocks and thorny vines, by dusk he was back at the settlement. He knew at once that he was too late, that something was horribly wrong. No one would meet his eye. Then he saw Bradly Martin, standing over a dying lemur.

Mission could see that the lemur had been shot through the body. He felt a concentration of rage, like a hot, red wave, but there was no reciprocal anger in Martin.

"Why?" Mission choked out.

"Stole my mango," Martin muttered indifferently.

Mission's hand flew to the butt of his pistol. Martin laughed. "You would violate your own article, Captain?"

"No. But I will remind you of Article Twenty-three: If two parties have a disagreement that cannot be settled, then the rule of the duel is applicable."

"Aye, but I have the right to refuse your challenge, and I do." Martin was an indifferent swordsman and a poor pistol shot.

"Then you must leave Libertatia, this very night, before the sun shall set. You have no more than an hour."

Without a word, Martin turned away and walked off in the direction of his dwelling. Mission covered the dead lemur with a tarpaulin, intending to take the body into the jungle and bury it the following morning.

In his quarters Mission was suddenly overcome by a paralyzing fatigue. He knew that he should follow Martin and settle the matter, but—as Martin had said—his own articles . . . . He lay down and fell immediately into a deep sleep. He dreamed that there were dead lemurs scattered through the settlement, and woke up at dawn with tears streaming down his face.

Mission dressed and went out to get the dead lemur. The lemur and the tarpaulin were both gone. With blinding clarity he understood why Martin had shot the lemur and what he intended to do: He would go to the natives and say that the settlers were killing the lemurs and that when he objected, they turned on him and he had barely escaped with his life. Lemurs were sacred to the natives in the area, and there was the danger of bloody reprisal.

In a prerecorded and therefore totally predictable universe, the blackest sin is to tamper with the prerecordings, which could result in altering the prerecorded future. Captain Mission was guilty of this sin. He threatened to demonstrate for all to see that three hundred souls can coexist in relative harmony with each other, their human neighbors, and the ecosphere of flora and fauna. Big Ben strikes the hour. In a muted, ghostly room, the custodians of the future convene. Keepers of the Board Books: Mektoub, it is written. And they don't want it changed.

"If three hundred men—then three thousand, thirty thousand. It could spread everywhere. It must be stopped *now*."

"Our man Martin is on target. He is quite reliable."

A woman leans slightly forward. An arresting face of timeless beauty and evil, an evil that stops the breath like a deadly gas. The chairman covers his face with a handkerchief. She speaks in a cold, brittle voice, each word a chip of obsidian: "There is a more significant danger. I refer to Captain Mission's unwholesome concern with *lemurs*." The word slithers out of her mouth writhing with hatred.

    Mission had smoked opium and hashish and had used a drug the Indians of South America called yage. *There must*, he decided, *be a special drug peculiar to this huge island, where there are so many creatures and plants not found anywhere else.* After some inquiries he found that such a drug did exist: It was extracted from a parasitic fungus that grew only on a certain spiny plant found in the arid regions of the south. The drug was called indris, which means *look there* in the native language. With the promise of five gold florins on delivery, he obtained a small supply from a friendly native. The drug was in the form of greenish-yellow crystals. The man, whose name was Babuchi, showed him exactly how much to take and cautioned him against taking any more.
    "Many take indris and see nothing different. Then they take more and see too much different."
    "Is this a day drug or a night drug?"
    "Best at dawn and twilight."
    Mission calculated an hour till sundown—enough time to reach his jungle camp. "How long does it take to work?"
    "Very quick."
    Mission set out walking rapidly. Half an hour later, he took a small amount of the crystals with a sip of water from his goatskin water bag. In a few minutes he experienced a shift of vision, as if his eyes were moving on separate pivots, and for the first time he saw Lizard-Who-Changes-Color. It was quite large, about two feet in length, and difficult to see, not because it took on the colors of its surroundings but because it was absolutely motionless. He moved closer to the lizard, who brought one eye to bear on him and turned black with rage. Evidently Lizard-Who-Changes-Color did not like to be seen. His colors subsided to a neutral orange-yellow, mottled brown. And there was a gurkha lizard on a limb, as if carved from the bark. He winked a golden eye at Mission.
    Despite the need for vigilance, Mission was spending more and more time in the jungle with his lemurs. He had converted the ancient stone structure he had found into a dwelling. It was completely enveloped by the roots of a huge, bulbous tree, as if held in a giant hand. The open arch in the second room was festooned with roots. There was a paved floor. He had covered the entrance with mosquito netting and arranged a pallet on the floor. Brushing the floor, he was surprised to find few insects, certainly no venomous varieties. The stone steps were worn smooth, as if with the passage of many feet, perhaps not human feet.

Who, or what, could have built this structure, and for what purpose?

Since his first encounter he had located a troop of the larger lemurs. These lemurs were too big and heavy to be comfortable in arboreal conditions and lived mostly on the land, in an area of grass and scrub where the forest thinned out, a mile from his campsite. Ideal grazing land, Mission realized with a shudder. The creatures were so trusting and gentle and open to human affection. Mission hurried on. He wanted to reach the ancient stone structure before twilight, and he hoped his special lemur would be there. He often slept with the lemur beside him on his pallet, and had named the lemur Ghost.

As he walked up, Ghost gave a little chittering cry of welcome. Mission took off his boots and hung his outer garments on wooden pegs driven into chinks in the stone wall. The only furniture was a table of rough hewn planks supported on two logs, with an inkpot, quill, pens, and parchment. In one corner was a small keg with a spigot for water, some cooking utensils, an ax, a saw, hammers, a musket. Powder and shot were kept in the footlocker. Mission sat at the table beside his phantom, his Ghost, contemplating the mystery of the stone structure. Who could have built it? *Who?*

He poses the question in hieroglyphs . . . a feather . . . he chooses a quill pen. Water . . . the clear water under the pier. A book . . . an old illustrated book with gilt edges. *The Ghost Lemurs of Madagascar*. Feather . . . a gull diving for garbage . . . the wakes of many ships in many places. A feather of the great bird that lived here once, and the sacred lake two days' walk west, where every year a heifer is sacrificed to a sacred crocodile. Still the *who?* eludes him. He wonders if there are other, similar structures on the island. . . . *Where?*

A loaf of bread . . . water . . . a goose tied to a stake. Looking through the eyes of Lizard-Who-Changes-Color from one end of the island to the other. The appalling answer comes back: nowhere, none. Why appalling? He doesn't know yet, but he knows. *When?*

A reed . . . a loaf of bread . . . a bird wheels in the sky. A woman plucks feathers from a fowl, takes a loaf of bread from an adobe oven. The split between the wild, the timeless, the free, and the tame, the time-bound and binding, the tethered, like the tethered goose of *where?* The tethered who will forever resent their bondage.

The structure was built at the one time it could have been built, before the split widened to an impassable chasm.

The concept of a question is reed and water. The question mark fades into reeds and water. The question does not exist.

Strange creatures are fitting stones together. He can't see them clearly, only their hands, like gray ropes. He senses the immense difficulty of an unaccustomed task. The stones are too heavy for their hands and bodies. Yet for some reason they must build this structure. *Why?*

There is no *why*. Mission is there. *Look there.*

Ghost stirred beside him and belched a sweet scent of tamarind fruit. Despite Babuchi's warning, Captain Mission knew he must learn more.

He lit a candle and poured a very large dose of indris crystals into his hand and downed them with a cup of water. He remembered the dream gorilla in the basement room, the strange pig creature, and then the gentle deer lemur. Mission lay down by his Ghost. He wasn't sure he wanted to see what the indris would show him, knowing that what he saw would be sad beyond his endurance. He looked out through tree roots as night sopped up the remaining light like a vast, black sponge.

He lay there in the gray light, his arm around his lemur. The animal snuggled closer and put a paw up to his face. Tiny mouse lemurs stole out of the roots and niches and holes in the ancient tree and frisked around the room, falling on insects with little squeals. Their tails twitched above their heads; their great flaring ears, thin as paper, quivered to every sound as their wide, limpid eyes swept the walls and floors for insects. They have been doing this for millions of years. The twitching tail, the trembling ears mark the passage of centuries. The little squeak of triumph was heard before the birth of man.

As the light drained into the sponge of night, the room grew ever brighter. He could see for miles in every direction: the coastal rain forests, the mountains and scrub of the interior, the arid southern regions where the lemurs frisk in the tall, spiny cactus. They gambol, leap, and whisk away into a remote past before the arrival of man on this island, before the appearance of man on Earth, before the beginning of time.

An old picture book with gilt-edged lithographs, onion paper over each picture. . . . *The Ghost Lemurs of Madagascar* in gold script. Giant ferns and palms, bulbous tamarind trees, vines, and bushes. In a corner of the picture is a huge bird, ten fat feet high, a plump, dowdy, helpless bird, obviously flightless— never get that off the ground. This bird tells one that here is a time pocket. There can be no predators in this forest, no large cats. In the middle of the picture is a ring-tailed lemur on a branch looking straight out at the viewer. Now more lemurs appear, like a picture puzzle. . . .

The Lemur People are older than *Homo sap*, much older. They date back sixty million years to the time when Madagascar split off from the mainland of Africa. They might be called psychic amphibians—that is, visible only for short periods when they assume a solid form to breathe, but some of them can remain in the invisible state for years at a time. Their way of thinking and feeling is basically different from ours, not oriented toward time and sequence and causality. They find these concepts repugnant and difficult to understand.

One might think that a species that leaves no fossil record is gone forever, but Big Picture, the history of life on Earth, is there for anyone to read. Mountain landmasses and jungles glide past, some slowing, some accelerating, vast rivers of land on the move or stagnating in wide deltas, whirlpools of land like saws splitting off islands, a great fissure, the landmasses rubbing against each other, then splitting, flying apart faster and faster . . . slowing down to the great red island, with its deserts and rain forests, scrub mountains and lakes, its unique animals and plants and the absence of predators or venomous reptiles, a vast sanctuary for the lemurs and for the delicate spirits that breathe through them, the glint in the jeweled eyes of a tree frog.

Above the wild time of Moving Lands, whole continents gliding past each other, gathering silent speed like trains; and any enterprising young man could get a few acres on the move and join up with other folks—going our way? There were accidents aplenty, volcanoes and earthquakes of every magnitude, plugs of molten rock suddenly thrown into the air, and vast, steaming sump holes and boiling lakes.

When attached to Africa, Madagascar was the ultimate landmass, sticking out like a disorderly tumor cut by a rift of future contours, a long rift like a vast indentation, like the cleft that divides the human body. The rift is a mile across in places, and in others narrows down to a few hundred feet. It is an area of explosive change and contrast, swept by violent electrical storms, incredibly fertile and yet barren. The first People of the Rift were a race apart, frenzied entrepreneurs.

"These prices is too good to last, folks!"

An ominous tremor shakes the bargaining table.

The People of the Cleft, formulated by chaos and accelerated time, flash through sixty million years to the split. Which side are you on? Too late to change now. Separated by a curtain of fire. Like a vast, festive ship launched by fireworks, the great red island moved majestically out to sea, leaving a gaping wound in the earth's side, bleeding lava and spurting noxious gases. It has lain moored in enchanted calm for sixty million years.

Time is a human affliction. Not a human invention but a prison. So what is the meaning of sixty million years without time? And what does time mean to foraging lemurs? No predators here, not much to fear. They have opposing thumbs but do not fashion tools: They have no need for tools. They are untouched by the evil that flows in and fills *Homo sap* as he picks up a weapon—now he has the advantage. A terrible gloating feeling comes from knowing you've *got it!*

Lemurs don't need it. Six minutes, sixty million years—no difference. Nothing is happening. A feeling of desolation closes round the human essence at the thought. How long have the lemurs paraded before each other in their sad and perfect beauty? How long have the singing gibbons sung their timeless song, as little gibbons clinging to their backs attempted to sing too?

Beauty is always doomed. "The evil and armed draw near." *Homo sap* with his weapons, his time, his insatiable greed, and ignorance so hideous it can never see its own face."Just let me club down some seal pups, cut an Injun's hands off, burn a Nigra's balls off and watch 'em pop, then we'll all feel a lot better."

These are unsightly tricks.

"Whaddaya think this is, a beauty contest?"

A lemur frisks toward the man, and he slashes it viciously, leaves it bleeding, sobbing, dying. "Try and bite me, will you . . . fucking animals!"

Man was born in time. He lives and dies in time. Wherever he goes, he takes time with him and imposes time.

Captain Mission was drifting out faster and faster, caught in a vast undertow of time. "Out, and under, and out, and out," a voice repeated in his head. . . .

Erase the concept of a question from your mind. The Egyptian glyph is a reed or feather and water. The question dissolves in reed and water as a poet writes on water. Who? The water the feather the book. Wipe it out with the squawking goose of where and the bread of when, fading into a great, extinct, flightless bird in a swampy pool.

Mission knows the stone temple is the entrance to the biological Garden of Lost Chances. Pay and enter. He feels an impact of sadness that stops his breath, a catching, tearing grief. This grief can kill. He is beginning to learn the coinage here.

He remembers the pink pig creature, lost in passive weakness, slumped hopelessly against the wall, and the black simian against the far wall by the entrance, very still and very black, a blackness that glows. And the gentle deer lemur, extinct for two thousand years, the Ghost that shares his pallet. He moves forward through the roots that trail from the ancient stone arch. Somehow the black monkey creature is in front of him, and he looks into his eyes, completely black. He is singing a black song, of a blackness too pure to survive in time. It is only compromise that survives, and that is why *Homo sap* is such a muddled, unsightly creature, precariously and hysterically defending a position that he knows is hopelessly compromised.

Mission moves through a black tunnel, opening on a series of dioramas: The last deer lemur falls to a hunter's arrow. Passenger pigeons rain from the trees to salvos of gunfire and plump down on the plates of fat bankers and politicians with their gold watch chains and gold fillings. They belch out the last passenger pigeon. The last Tasmanian wolf limps through a blue twilight, leg shattered by a hunter's bullet. And the almosts, the might-have-beens, who had one chance in a billion and lost. Seeing the planet as an organism, it is obvious who the enemies of the planet are. Their name is legend. They dominate and populate the planet. "The deceived and the deceivers who are themselves deceived." Did *Homo sap* think other animals were there just for Him to *eat?* Apparently. Bulldozers are destroying the rain forests, the cowering lemurs and the flying foxes, the singing Clos gibbons, who produce the most beautiful and variegated music of any land animal, and the gliding colugo lemurs, who are helpless on the ground. All going, to make way for more and more devalued human stock, with less and less of the wild spark, the priceless ingredient—energy into matter. A vast mud slide of soulless sludge.

Doom and sadness hangs with the gray mist in these damp cages. It's there in every face, and any kid cracks up and starts screaming I CAN'T STAND IT will get slapped by John Wayne. It's Zoo City here. Strange dream animals roam the ghost midways and sideshows. Margaras slinks into the White Cat bar—"Seen any black cats lately?"—"Not lately, Whitey, they all got bleached out like you, got the light inside, you might say, and they lit up with a pure white flame. Wasn't nothing I could do to prevent it."

Margaras turns up the silvery light, the silvery white light, searing moonlight flooding in shredding flesh to silver film flakes—let go and let it happen, let yourself flake on out flake on out like snow it's all raining down behind you all your past life breaking loose and raining down in chunks of malevolence and joy and fear and the pure killing purpose, little scenes like soap bubbles bursting in air. Whose flag was still where? Everything is fading, falling to pieces behind you as you move and now ahead of you as well—where who are you? Who were you why? It has no reality, it leaves nothing behind save the observer. Observe the observer observed.

As indris can give eyes to see another reality, it can also, in the hands of a skilled sorcerer, impose tunnel vision in his native victims: "A man appeared and said they were bad people and had to be killed." While Captain Tew waited at his lonely, distant cove. In the dead of night two huge bands of Malagasy natives swept down upon Libertatia and wiped out the colony. Lieutenant Caraccioli died in this attack, and Mission escaped with only forty-five men and two sloops. In time he found his way to Captain Tew's remote harbor, and the two men decided to retire to America, where they were both unknown. In a great storm off Cape Infantes, Captain Mission's sloop was lost beneath the waves.

Author's note: Now, in 1987, the lemurs of Madagascar are threatened with extinction. When humans first arrived on the island 1,500 years ago, there were some 40 species; now only 22 remain, and all are considered endangered. In some parts of the island the natives hunt the slow lemurs for their meat, although in other places they are protected by a taboo. The human population is growing rapidly and may reach 12 million by the year 2000, and the ongoing forestry and slash-and-burn agriculture have destroyed 90 percent of the forests, the lemurs' habitat. It is projected that the lemurs of Madagascar may be gone in a hundred years—the legacy of 60 million years destroyed in our lifetimes.

In an 8,300-acre forest near Durham, North Carolina, the Duke University Primate Center maintains a colony of more than 600 prosimians, mostly lemurs. This colony was started at Yale in 1958 and moved to Durham in 1968. When a ruffed lemur gave birth in that year, it was the first birth in captivity anywhere in 40 years. More than 300 lemurs have been born at the primate center since then. Director Elwyn L. Simons has established good relations with the Malagasy government and was able to bring nine wild-caught sifakas to the Duke compound last year.

The Duke University Primate Center needs financial support from concerned individuals. Write to DUPC, Duke University, Durham, NC 27706.

Stardust

Harvey Jacobs

Harvey Jacobs is the author of *The Egg of the Glak and Other Stories* and of the novels *Summer on a Mountain of Spices, The Juror,* and most recently, of the futuristic satire *Beautiful Soup.* His stories have appeared in many magazines, including *Omni, Playboy, Esquire, The Magazine of Fantasy and Science Fiction,* and *Paris Review,* and in various anthologies. Jacobs also writes for television.

"Stardust" is a love story and adult fantasy, touched with horror. It was first published in the August 1987 issue.

Stardust

Harvey Jacobs

Herman Horman lived the schizophrenic life of an artist in America and found a kind of contentment. Compromise was his cocoon. For ten months of the year Herman illustrated annual reports, catalogs, advertisements, slides for industrial shows. He created covers for paperback romances. This allowed him to live modestly in a small Brooklyn brownstone and hoard a few dollars. Then, for two months, he could do what he wanted to do.

What he wanted to do was to paint skyscapes. In late August he began to pack paints, pads, charcoal sticks, and canvas. He carefully oiled the bearings and cleaned the delicate lens of his Heidelman telescope. It was a beautiful instrument, a wand on a pedestal. The pedestal plugged into standard house current and turned the Heidelman with the precise rhythm of the stars. The scope magnified to four hundred times. That was enough vision for Herman. Flecks of light turned to peas and pearls.

The first day of September he drove a rented car to a rented beach house on Shell Island, Long Island—a dot of protected land near the Hamptons where the North Shore and the South Shore split and form a crotch. Shell Island rests in the crotch, shaped more like a fig leaf than a genital.

After Labor Day the island was all but deserted and a splendid nature observatory. Crisp, thin autumn air did wonders for light. The sun made changing trees glow. The moon was a polished silver disc. Most important, all of the three thousand stars visible to the human eye sparkled in a vast dome of black sky. Ancient light fell on Shell Island, uninhibited by city mists and miasmas.

It was the stars' abstraction that Herman enjoyed. The fact that the heavens moved to a rigid code bothered him a little, but there was mystery enough even in that. Stars, planets, moons, comets weren't a bunch of Germans going to work on time. They were celestial bodies, things hanging in space, moving like mobiles. Precision is not always the enemy of romance. As a boy, Herman himself had fallen in love with a particular Rockette in the line at Radio City Music Hall. She went with the rest, but her movements were surrounded by silence. If the stars were making pictures, Herman was determined to see them first and paint them with his own brush. His starscapes were not for sale. He showed them only to intimate friends and the one cousin he could call family. There was no need to turn his paintings to rent, food, or utilities. He had no need for fame. He made clear choices. They involved time. His own time. Free time. Pure time. Soul time. Bought and paid for.

Certainly he yearned for more of those sweet hours. The older he got, the more he dreamed of a bonanza that would liberate him from the muck. He bought his lottery ticket like the rest of the tribe. But essentially, Herman accepted his situation.

In young September, when he first came to Shell Island, two fat months stretched before him like a plain. On his first days he walked leisurely along beaches, thought about meals, bent to examine shells. He set up the Heidelman on his deck and looked for his favorite stars. His early sketches and paintings were only rehearsals. Those drawings would end in the fireplace. The paintings would be painted over. He was in training. It was a necessary use of precious hours. There had to be some break between his life in the city and life out where the sky was a living organ instead of a sewer. By September seventh he was comfortably changed. And it was September eighth, at exactly 3:17 A.M., that the Feinbacher Galaxy came into view.

The Feinbacher Galaxy was Herman's special terrain. He didn't know why. Maybe it was because the Feinbacher appeared in months when the prices dropped on Shell Island and the weather was still reasonable. If Herman were a painter of women, the Feinbacher would have been his favorite model, with a flood of hair, avocado breasts, and a behind like joined honeydews.

For this painter of stars, the Feinbacher released passion.

Herman had first read about the Feinbacher Galaxy in a magazine for amateur astronomers called *Harvest Star*. It was not even given a full page. The Feinbacher was not part of any important star system. It was just another face in the glittering crowd. But when Herman searched it out and found it in the eastern sky, he knew immediately that it was his own. Feinbacher orbs twinkled at him, signaled to him. There was a hot connection over a million light-years. He did his best paintings. At September's end Herman always felt like he was rolling down a mountain. The luxury of two months became the rush of one. Soft plains of available time suddenly sprouted bent trees of anxiety, mushrooms of doubt. October days and nights flared, burned, and flew in the wind like the ashes from newspaper.

Herman was vulnerable when October came. He turned sad and defensive, feeling his own leaves turn. He envied insects and animals already drowsy with winter sleep. Fortunately, it was in October that the Feinbacher was most magnificent, most visible, most present. When Herman put his head to the Heidelman's eyepiece, he became witness to wonders. Always he saw something new. The Feinbacher was full of gifts. On chilly mornings he gulped orange juice and instant coffee and began to paint with eyes that still whirled images in urgent color. Ten years of painting the Feinbacher had yielded more than a hundred oils and thousands of sketches. They ranged from dots of white on black squares to birthing shapes that could be faces or bodies or anything. Old, traveled light came through the Heidelman's tunnel and poured into Herman's brain. There it pooled with mystery. His hand held a brush that moved like the pointer on a Ouija board. He sensed some perfect fusion, deliciously elusive. He would capture it someday or die trying. Time, time, time. Two months a year was not enough to chase the kind of glory he suspected.

Once Herman saw a movie about settlers in the West who went through terrible indignities in search of a promised land. They stopped, collapsed only a hill away from a splendid valley filled with fruit, lakes, and lush soil to encourage the most reluctant seeds. One of their children saw the valley, but nobody would believe his story. The movie ended with a high camera showing the beaten pilgrims building houses of logs and mud on arid acres just inches from Eden. Herman cried and heaved while the film rolled the final credits. The usher brought him water. The pathos he felt was unbearable. It was not made up of self-pity or even of pity for all those who stopped too soon. It was the recognition of the worst of all possible jokes. He might be a whisper from the ultimate Feinbacher truth, whatever that was, forced to his knees and defeated by a cuckoo clock.

Meanwhile Herman persisted. Alone in his rented cottage he ate lettuce and sardines, slept as little as possible, forgot to smoke, hummed songs, watched the calendar melt, cursed the system, challenged the skies. He did the best he could.

In October's center, Shell Island weather turned foul. The place turned the color of a Brillo pad. Crusts of black cloud hung like barrage balloons. It stayed that way for three days and nights. Herman tried to work from memory, but that was no good. So he took to taking long walks down black-tar roads under dripping trees. He shuffled through spongy leaves and dead twigs. He roamed beaches with the look of damp cardboard. He collected bags of shells, then threw them away. Not a bird flew. There were no signs of clearing.

One sullen, rainy morning, Herman wandered to the rich part of Shell Island, called Crescent Harbor. There great mansions hid in wooded hills overlooking the water. He went along thinking about the cost of such houses. Any one of them represented a lifetime of paid bills, including incidentals. He thought about the people who owned property like that. They owned time. They didn't buy lottery tickets. And they saved more money by not buying lottery tickets. It boggled the mind.

By October those temples were deserted. Small, red signs, the eyes of rabid animals, warned trespassers away. PATROLLED. PROTECTED. WARNING.

The jewel of Crescent Harbor was Castle Avnolet, an authentic castle brought to Shell Island stone by stone, window by window, door by door from someplace on the Rhine. It even had a moat. The castle rested like a lump on the highest rise of land with a view of everything.

Herman went along a soggy beach stepping on horseshoe crabs that cracked under his sneakers. He looked up to the castle's towers. A curl of smoke twisted away from one chimney. Someone was in residence, but surely not the king or queen. They would be in Palm Springs or Palm Beach listening to the stock market rise and fall in lulling waves. The resident would be a caretaker. On a whim, Herman walked up toward Castle Avnolet. Ominous billboards warned him against proceeding, but he went anyway. And what if somebody shot him for a prowler or mistook him for a deer? He would lay dying in the drizzle, thinking of the Feinbacher Galaxy until his own lights dimmed. Who would miss him?

He made himself an obvious target, walking briskly, as if circles and a bulls-eye were painted on his chest. But there was no evidence of the castle guard No matched Dobermans salivated, waiting to pounce.

The castle was a magnificent conceit. Herman knew it had been bought and shipped by a family of manipulators who dated back a century before the Revolution. Eons of wheeling and dealing added up to a stupendous fortune. Their land on Shell Island was bought cheap after a horrendous storm that left the island desolate. When the puddles dried, the land soared in value. The castle itself had once housed a minor German conqueror, a modest despot who beheaded himself lamenting a lost war. *The Shell Island Reporter* carried articles about the castle's exotic history at least once a year. At the castle's iron gate, Herman looked through ornate bars to the sludgy moat. A lone duck swam there, probably a forgotten pet. More sensible ducks had left weeks ago. Beyond the moat was a drawbridge pulled up like a Murphy bed.

How nice it would be to have a moat with a duck and a door that gave the same protection as a turtle shell.

When the door began to lower with a grand creaking and moaning—a terminal grinding of gear teeth, a shudder Herman could feel through his feet—he had the impulse to run. It was a peasant reaction, and he fought it. After Labor Day Shell Island reverted to the elements. Property rights were suspended. Despite all the signs, he had as much right to be where he was as the wind. Those thoughts gave Herman a flush of courage, enough to hold his ground. The rain came harder. There was a growl of thunder from over the water.

Now the moat was bridged by a gangplank of wood and metal. At its root there appeared an arch like the mouth of a shrieking cartoon character. The Castle Avnolet was sticking out its tongue at Herman Horman. He was being insulted by the pile of transplanted rocks. For a brief moment his detente with the fates came unhinged. He stuck his tongue back like a boy wagging at a playmate. Herman stood there amazed at how close his species was to the grandfather apes.

Just as he was about to turn and go on his way, a woman appeared at the castle's entrance. He saw immediately that she was a good fit—the right height, the right width, the right age. He always measured women first by the way they might jigsaw in embrace. She wore brown leather pants and a russet wool jacket with a large collar that cradled a face set with huge eyes and topped by a mop of brown, frizzy hair. As she came closer he heard her high boots crack on the wooden ramp. Her movements echoed breeding. Herman saluted with a casual wave. She waved back. When they came face to face, she said. "Hello, strange man with the Heidelman."

"You know about my telescope?"

"You aren't the only trespasser on Shell Island. I see you on your deck at night browsing the stars. Are you some kind of astronomer, then?"

"No astronomer. I am an artist named Herman Horman. No, don't say,'That name sounds familiar,' because you've never seen it on a painting. I sign my commercial work with made-up names, and my own masterpieces have never been exhibited."

"Herman Horman? That name doesn't sound familiar. I'm Madeline Avnolet."

"Avnolet? Then you're not the caretaker."

"The castle is mine, Mr. Horman. By accident of birth."

"Happy accident."

"My grandfather bought it and mailed it over here. My father added a few touches of distinction, like the television room and me. My mother ran away with a Sioux Indian activist named Fat Otter who she met while doing good works. So when Daddy died in a helicopter crash, everything came to me. Please don't hold it against me, Herman Horman."

"I'll certainly try. I never met a castle owner before."

"The first time is hard. I don't envy you."

"Should I bow and scrape?"

"That's the least you can do. And you can come in out of the rain for a drink. It is dismal out here."

"Three days of dismal."

Herman followed Madeline Avnolet along the wooden tongue to the entrance arch, feeling like a tourist on parade. He looked at her straight back and round rump. She was a bit stringy but nicely turned. Her legs impressed him most, long as highways.

She led him through a barn of a hall, then up fifty granite steps to a balcony They turned off the balcony and went down another hall lined with marble. Then up more steps, around two turns, down a short staircase, through a greenhouse filled with flowering plants, past a large swimming pool, and into a room paneled in rosewood, where a fire crackled at logs thick as thighs. The room was filled with soft chairs and deep sofas.

"A nice place you've got here."

"It is cozy. What's your pleasure?"

"Better weather. Short of that, maybe a glass of wine."

Madeline went to a cabinet filled with bottles resting on their sides. She picked one, slid it out of its crib, and opened it with a giant corkscrew crowned with the head of a panther. Herman got his wine in a heavy goblet initialed with a curly A. While he sniffed the bouquet, she poured herself Chartreuse. Her pony glass was of delicate crystal, with a stem no thicker than a reed. Its A was etched inside a tiny shield.

"To fair and warmer," she said.

They toasted fair and warmer. His elephant glass and her insect glass clinked a pure note. They drank. Herman sipped. Madeline gulped her Chartreuse. That surprised Herman, who knew the green sap should be savored, not swallowed like an oyster. Then Madeline hurled her glass into the fireplace, where it disintegrated to splinters. "Luck," she said.

"You wasted a perfectly good glass," he said before he could stop himself. That glass would be thirty dollars at Steuben.

"Now you waste a glass," Madeline said. "Go on."

"Me? No. I couldn't."

Madeline smiled. Herman downed his wine, then stood and faced the fireplace as if it were a catcher giving signals. He pumped, shook his head no, shook his head yes, raised his left leg, reared back, and threw the goblet. It missed the fireplace but hit the mantle like a bomb.

"I never saw anyone miss an entire fireplace. A very large fireplace."

"I'm out of practice," Herman said.

"We'll keep trying until you get it right."

Madeline brought him another goblet of wine. This time she drank Grand Marnier from the bottle. She led him to one of the sofas. It must have been made of cashmere. It was like sitting on a chubby baby.

"So," Herman said. "Comfortable. Very nice. The queen's chamber. I could get used to this."

"Could you? There's responsibility being lord of the manor."

"I knew there had to be a catch. Tell me, Madeline, do you live here alone? I mean, except for the cleaning lady."

"I'm not a person who needs people very much. I love being on Shell Island this time of the year."

"The same with me. The same. I come back year after year. My friends tell me, 'Herman, go other places; see other things.' But I come here. I'm still a renter, though. I should have bought years ago when it was possible. But now? Forget it. You're lucky your people knew real estate. Is that the kind of thing you say to a lady who owns a castle?"

"What do you paint, Mr. Horman?"

"Herman. What does Herman paint? That's a hard question to answer. For a living I paint things that sell products. Girls with dimples who twirl batons. Homos in cowboy suits. Boxes, bottles, appliances, you name it. For salvation I paint the Feinbacher Galaxy. That's . . ."

"Discovered in 1525 by Zoltan Feinbacher?"

"No, not that one. Of course that one. How in hell do you know about the Feinbacher Galaxy?"

"Come with me," Madeline said.

"You mind if I carry my drink?"

"As you wish."

Herman went through more corridors, rooms, foyers. He went up so many steps he lost his breath. At the end of the journey he found himself in the most beautiful room he had ever seen.

"This is how I know about the Feinbacher. Grandfather believed in his horoscope. He kept astrologers."

The room was a circle with a glass roof. Through an opening in the glass a polished brass tube protruded up into a closed dome. The tube rested on spider legs set in a heavy base. Star charts had been carved into the room's walnut walls, then filled with silver Zodiac signs in gold against blue enamel decorated the curve where those walls met the transparent ceiling. A huge bookcase held a library of ancient volumes that could have been bound with the pelts of dead geniuses. A globe of the heavens split like an egg held a desk fashioned into some kind of mythical beast. A chair covered in dark green leather faced the desk.

"You have your own observatory," Herman said, his awe evident.

"A house is not a home without an observatory. The dome up there parts. If the sky clears up tonight, I'll show you."

Tonight? Herman did not miss the significance of her tonight. He was being invited to stay, or was it assumed?

"Madeline, I certainly would like to see that. But not on the first date. I might begin salivating or foaming at the mouth."

"It's just a great big wonderful toy. A toy is a toy, Herman."

"A toy? That scope probably brings Feinbacher right into a person's lap. No toy. A blessing. I can't believe what I see."

"Well, you can play with it anytime you want. The barometer over there is rising, and the wind is blowing from the west. The mess will probably clear out in a few hours. Meanwhile I thought we might have ourselves a light supper."

"I accept. I'm hungry as a horse. Thank you, your majesty."

"Potluck, though."

"You are talking to a man who thaws his food. Anything would be fine."

"Then why don't you stay up here and enjoy yourself while I go down to the kitchen? I'll call you when I'm ready. There's an intercom on the desk."

"No. I'll never find you again. This house is a maze. I have no idea where we are."

"Trust me."

Herman sat in the green leather chair, absorbing emanations from the Avnolet observatory Her grandfather kept astrologers? He believed in his horoscope? No wonder. That telescope made the Heidelman into nothing. Focusing on the Feinbacher with such magnification would be the difference between having a model sitting in the studio instead of glimpsing a nostril, a breast, a toe, a lip through a smoky tunnel.

A few nights of such inspired observation could catapult over years and trigger luminous insight, maybe even revelation. Herman felt himself sweating.

There were dangers. Madeline Avnolet might allow him a peek under the skirt of the universe, then lose interest and withdraw her magic. What then? After that, working with the feeble Heidelman would be impossible. Everything would change. Terminal discontent would be the only inheritance. It would be wiser to say thanks but no thanks to the lady who threw crystal into the fire. He might be next, smashed against stone while flames fed on his entrails.

His urge was to get out and go home, to follow the instinct of flight he'd felt when the moat first groaned. Herman Horman had no business in that room.

The intercom buzzed like an arrogant bug. He let it buzz three times before he picked up the receiver.

"Ready when you are, Herman. I hope you like simple."

"Simple is a gift."

"Then come and dine."

"You come get me. Or send a Saint Bernard. I have a terrible sense of direction."

"Just go out into the hall, and all will be perfectly clear."

"Ah, rich, rich, rich," Herman said when he followed her instructions. In the corridor outside the observatory a trail of tiny lights flashed along the wall. The whole castle was mapped by light. Madeline guided him by programming his course.

Herman felt giddy as he went along, up and down and around, until he heard music. He thought to himself, "Not bad for a rainy afternoon." The lights stopped at a door. The music came from behind the door. What would the dining room be like? Herman envisioned a forest of chandeliers and utensils of heavy silver. He conjured masses of flowers and silk napkins embroidered with curly A's. Near the door he smelled delicious odors. Potluck?

He turned a knob with a lion's head and swung open the door inlaid with mandalas. Herman found himself in a bathroom large enough to hold whole families. Madeline thought of everything. She knew instinctively it was his ritual to pee and wash up before taking food. She knew he would never ask where the toilet was, under such circumstances. She had provided.

Herman noticed that the tempting smells were not from cooking but from perfumes. The bathroom was filled with a fine mist that rose from a steaming tub set on an onyx throne. White Turkish towels hung over a warmer. An emperor's bathrobe was also kept warm. Maybe Madeline was a cannibal. He could cook in the tub, basted by herbal perfumes, and nobody would ever know. His bones could be discarded in the sea. He found the toilet behind a Chinese screen. Then he washed his hands in a sink shaped like a swan.

Another door opened. Madeline stood holding a martini. "I thought you might want a hot bath to wash away the mildew. Here, I made this for you."

"A bath? Before supper?" He always bathed after dinner or took a quick shower in the morning.

Madeline left him alone to decide. He tasted the icy gin. Then he undressed quickly and looked around for hidden cameras. Maybe a whole group of castle dwellers was waiting in tuxedos for the chance to laugh at his white, skimpy body. When he got into the tub, small waves moved the water. His weight switched on some automatic tide. He watched the waves roll along and break against porcelain shores. After his bath Herman put on the velour robe with a large A on the breast pocket. A for Avnolet, for immense effort in the pursuit of happiness. Smelling like a garden, Herman went through the door where Madeline had appeared.

He was not in a dining room. He was in a bedroom. He saw a bed for giants covered by a canopy of frills and tufts. Near the bed was a bidet trimmed with fleur-de-lis. In the space between the bidet and an armoire covered with pictures of songbirds was an elegant golden table draped with a paper cloth printed with comic book images. Herman recognized Bugs Bunny, Batman, Superman, and The Human Torch. The table was set with plastic party plates, knives, forks, and spoons. There were Wonder Woman wax cups. Then there was a centerpiece, a black iron candelabra hammered clean of sin—monastic, stark, and strong. It held seven white candles in tulip-shaped cups. The candles burned with flames that waved like swamp grass.

Another door opened into the room. Herman's eyes fastened on a rolling cart that held the potluck. He saw steamed lobsters, a dish of pink crabmeat, plates holding clams and mussels resting on platforms of chipped ice. There was a glass salad bowl, with the engraved A, filled with endive, romaine, tomatoes the size of marbles, and mounds of mushrooms. At the cart's base, on a small shelf, two silver buckets held magnums of Dom Perignon.

"Are you pleased, artist?" said Madeline.

"So this is your light supper. What do you eat for breakfast? Unicorn?"

"Herman, please take your eyes off the food for a second."

"I can't. This is the kind of thing I taste on bicentennials. Should I eat it or frame it? And the decorative mix. I mean, the pop art contrasted with the baroque and medieval. Red Grooms meets Vivaldi. And there's the bed. Oh, yes. the bed. And the bidet. What a nice luncheonette."

"Don't be hostile."

"Hostile? Me? No, just edgy. Edgy. I love surprises."

"You haven't looked at me."

Herman peeled his eyes from the delectables and saw that Madeline Avnolet was naked except for a black band around her waist. From the band hung a spoon of translucent blue.

"I know. You're nude. Except for the spoon."

"I am glad you noticed."

"Madeline, don't make me feel like an asshole. Since I came here it's been one thing after another. I'm resilient. But first meeting you on a damn drawbridge, then the observatory, then the bath, and now the food, and you standing naked dangling a spoon. Everything is anticlimactic at this particular moment. Is the Vienna Boys' Choir next?"

"My timing is bad. Should I slip into something less comfortable? Would that relax you?"

"I don't know. Let's drink some champagne and talk. I was expecting a quiet, rainy day. And yes, if you're wondering, I like your body. It's a beautiful body. Just the kind of body I enjoy. There's a softness disciplined by form. The curves and angles clash. The candles make you shimmer. Of course I like your body."

Madeline sat on a velvet-covered chair. Herman sat across from her, opening a Road Runner napkin, trying to focus on her face.

"So talk, Herman. Tell me why you artists clip off your ears."

"The better to see with. Now, do you mind if I go ahead? I never saw so many lobsters in one place. A cluster. A surfeit of lobster. None of this is happening. I'm home, asleep."

"Try the salad. And the little bowl is cucumber soup."

"Cucumber soup? Why not?"

Herman filled a plastic plate. Madeline watched him eat. He stopped eating.

"I'm sorry," she said. "It's just that you're so hungry."

"What about you? Aren't you hungry? Supper was your idea."

"I eat very little. But I will nibble."

She reached under the table and somehow detached the sapphire spoon. Herman watched her take a few flakes of crabmeat and touch it to her lips.

"Did you eat cucumber soup as a child, or did they spring it on you later?"

"We ate cucumber soup from July fifteenth until the first of November."

"I'm not criticizing, Madeline. And I will try some if you don't tell me the ingredients. I don't want to know about ingredients. There's always something that starts with a y or a z that makes me want to throw up. Yogurt. Zucchini. Barf."

"There are no ingredients."

"Good news. But you're not taking in much nourishment. Are you anorexic? No, I can see you're not. And you have your own special spoon, and I get plastic. You get . . . what is that?"

"Sapphire. My grandpa gave it to me when I was born."

"A jewel for a baby spoon. Sweet. So use it. Keep me company. I feel like a hog eating alone."

"Don't push at me, Herman."

Herman shrugged and dipped a shrimp the size of a comma on a billboard into tangy red sauce. A drop of sauce spilled on the white robe. He dipped his napkin into cold water and dabbed at the dot.

"Forget it. Please."

"I am such a slob. I always dribble. I should sit in a high chair."

"Here, let me help."

"I suppose you have a laundry in the basement staffed by Oriental philosophers. Or is the robe disposable?"

Madeline got up and came around the table. She took the wet napkin from Herman's hand and began to rub gently at the spot, which was near his navel. He chewed a mouthful of clam while she worked. He swallowed the clam down with champagne, blotted his lips with another napkin, Woody Woodpecker this time, and felt a flush of heat between his legs. It had been spring since he last touched a woman and years since his navel was massaged. His erection surprised him as much as it must have surprised Adam. He jumped from the chair, trying to conceal the bulge.

"So what's your game? Pick up a stranger, fill him with phosphorus, give him a little rub, and zap him into the sack? Is that it? It's no accident that you're stark naked, is it? Or am I leaping to conclusions?"

"Come back here."

"Miss Avnolet, I am no slut. And neither are you. Look at the advantages you've had. The best schools, the genes of conquerors, your own castle. And see how you behave. We might have had a real relationship. That's the pity."

"Shut up, star man. Cease and desist. Just stop it now and leave my castle out of this. We are having a relationship. But it's already half through October, and your time is running out. We have no time for the usual preliminaries. And yes, I am rushing things. And I have been lonely. I am lonely, Herman. I like you. I want to lie with you and be touched by you. I want my nipples to turn to pebbles and feel you at my breasts. I want you to come inside me and gush. That's what I'm hungry for. Now, should I get dressed and wait around for you to undress me, or should we go to bed? Which?"

"When you put it that way, I suppose we can wait for coffee and dessert."

Later, still in his robe, Herman followed lights back up to the observatory. Madeline was asleep. He kissed her cheek before he left the room. She had switched on the trail of light and told him which buttons to press to make the telescope work.

The sky had cleared. When he manipulated the right controls, the shell guarding the scope parted with a whoosh. The scope rose on hydraulic legs and turned toward the Feinbacher. Before taking his first look he hesitated, remembering earlier qualms. First he put his eye to the eyepiece, keeping it shut tight. Then he opened it quickly.

There was the Feinbacher, the peas and pearls turned to grapefruits. Melons. Herman gasped. Instantly he saw things he'd never seen before. Moons, rings, flares, colors, shapes, shadows, nooks, dents. He always heard music when he looked through his Heidelman. Now the music boomed. He walked through the Feinbacher like a street kid carrying a radio. His right hand curled around a nonexistent paintbrush. He was in a creative spasm. Through the pain he knew he had never been so happy.

Then Herman saw that a star was missing. In the left quadrant of the fourth grid there was an empty space that broke the visual harmony. It was as if Garbo smiled with a missing tooth or a word had been deleted from familiar poetry. *To be or to be.* Herman blinked and pressed more buttons. The Feinbacher came into sharper focus, but the space was still there. He laughed. For all its majesty, the castle's telescope was defective. The problem could be as simple as a stray raindrop or bird droppings on the lens. But the little Heidelman never deleted what might be a world. The Heidelman's lens could be wiped with optical paper or even Kleenex. To clean the monstrous Avnolet eye would take a mop. Space or no space, the rest of the picture was astonishment. Herman stayed up there until dawn's early light.

He went back down and got into bed. Madeline was a perfect temperature. He felt himself warming like a frog on a lily pad. They made gentle morning love. Then Madeline brought Herman personally squeezed orange juice, thick black coffee, a croissant, and cherry jam.

"Only in America," he said. "Lying here with an Avnolet. If you are an Avnolet. I didn't ask to see your birth certificate. If my mother could only see me, she should rest in peace. And your grandfather, may he corner every market in heaven. What would the old man say?"

"Buy soybeans; that's what he would say. He said it once during a seance. A spirit medium contacted his shade, and that's what he told my father."

"Soybeans went up, correct?"

"They rocketed."

"I knew it. Madeline, this has been the optimum night of my life. As the kiddies say, awesome."

"Do you mean that?"

"I do. And yes, I'll call you in the city If you want me to. Do you want me to?"

Madeline cuddled closer. Stained glass windows turned her breasts rosy pink. Herman nearly fainted from a surge of love as he reached out to her.

"Tonight you'll come over to my place. I'll retaliate with stuffed eggplant, my specialty. My dish."

"Don't tell me the ingredients."

"Be there at seven. We have better sunsets than you have here at the castle. We'll have drinks, carrots, and celery chunks at Villa Horman. For dessert we'll lick rainbows. And don't bring anything but yourself. This one is on me. I'll pull out all the stops. Money is no object."

"I'll be there, darling."

"I know, darling. I know."

"Are you excited about us, Herman?"

"Very excited about us. We have real potential, even if you do come from the wrong side of the tracks. I'm a democrat. I can look the other way."

"I would hate a mere castle to come between us."

"I wish I could write," Herman said. "We are a major motion picture."

"Seven," Madeline said while the moat was bridged, and Herman pranced out of Castle Avnolet like a carriage horse.

Walking down toward the curve of beach, Herman Horman had a strange sensation. He imagined a long, thick rubber band fused to his flesh and stretching around the castle's highest tower. He'd had that feeling once before. He was nine, leaving New York for the first time for a week in the country. The Fresh Air Fund sent him to look at a cow. As his bus moved across George Washington Bridge toward New Jersey, he sensed an elastic that linked him to the Empire State Building. A week later he snapped back to the city. Here was the feeling again, this time mixed with an emotion Herman had to recognize as joy.

He shouted greetings to a heron. He was making a *joyful noise*. Herman was not a man who made many joyful noises. The whole idea of joy made him edgy. Joy was a poison apple. Horror was always taking on the guise of happiness. For Herman the worst thing would be to die laughing. When intimates accused him of being depressive, he told them he was a pessimistic optimist, and it was true. He drew the freckled faces of impossible Hallmark children for a living. His work sold products. Something in him still longed for a cookie jar. The best idea was to be very careful, to expect quicksand but to seek messages from the stars. His usual joyful noise was a suspicious growl. Here he was, greeting indifferent birds, and so he had to consider the possibility that he truly was *in love*.

Herman began to jog along the damp sand. He had not been in love since adolescence. He had fallen for a serious girl named Margy, who gave her virginity to his best friend. While Herman read manuals about erogenous zones, his best friend jumped in. Since then he had *liked*, felt *gratitude, warmth, compassion, lust, sensuality, longing,* but never love. Now the image of Madeline Avnolet throbbed inside him. He felt as if he had swallowed her along with her lobsters, clams, shrimps, cucumber soup, and wine. He tried to separate her from the castle, the telescope, stained glass windows. But she was those things. Herman fought his first impulse to get home to his pads and canvas. The fingers of his right hand still curled and twitched to record what he had seen of the Feinbacher. But instead he stopped at the Shell Island Market and bought his eggplants, chopped chuck, an onion, a green pepper, rice, and spices. He chose a package of frozen broccoli, two seeded rolls, and a packaged apple pie. With his last coins he bought a red candle.

When he got back to his house he felt rabbits, foxes, deer, squirrels judge his return. Even trees watched. He had been gone all night. He disrupted the October environment. If he could, he would have told the witnesses what happened, but they wouldn't have believed him. A clerk from the market, maybe. But Madeline Avnolet?

First he put the food away, then began sketching. He drew the Feinbacher's stars in majestic proportions. In the left quadrant of the fourth grid he added the missing star.

Out on the deck, he fondled his Heidelman. The scope seemed pathetic, like coming home to a friend hopelessly outgrown, like visiting a room best left to memory. "What I have seen, Heidelman. What I have seen. Not that I feel any less affection for you, wonderful instrument. But there are entire realms you can never share. A man must cross horizons to discover new horizons. Don't worry. I won't sell you. But you may go into storage. You may become nostalgia.

"She has deep feelings for me, Heidelman. A man can interpret the language of moans and groans. She comes packaged with millions. And an equipped observatory. Do you understand what that could mean to me? A slow walk around the universe. No interruptions, Heidelman. Endless hours. Not to mention family connections to the best galleries and museums. My father used to say, 'Herm, what's wrong with falling for a rich lady?' I winced when he said it. Because he was telling me not to fall for poor. But this is different. The woman is nice. A pleasure to look at and a comfort to lay with. She warms me, Heidelman. Give me your blessing, premature as it may be. Who knows, we may never go back to the city. To that place of blank skies. Don't laugh, Heidelman. It could happen."

By the time Madeline came, Herman had the fire going and his table set. He poured glasses of wine. His eggplants were bubbling in the oven. His radio played Mozart. When he heard the bell from her bicycle, he lit the red candle. This was the package he came in, take it or leave it. "If she walks in here and vomits," he said to the air, "then we'll be good friends."

At the door Madeline handed Herman some wildflowers. They kissed. He put the flowers in a jar, then took her out to see the orange-gold sky. They made love on the grass while the eggplants baked.

"You know what we remind me of?" Madeline said. "Bread in an oven."

"The rolls. I've got to warm the rolls."

"My object was not to remind you to remember to warm the rolls."

"I forgot salad."

"Not yet."

"Madeline, we are being watched by animals. They've never seen this side of me. I've got to live with these creatures. Please show some restraint."

"Herman?"

"What?"

"Nothing."

At the table Herman served his hot meal. He lifted his wineglass, which was the same as his water glass.

"To us," he said.

"To us," Madeline said. While she drank she reached into a leather purse and took out her blue spoon.

"I have spoons," Herman said.

"And I have a few quirks."

"How come your grandpa didn't give you a complete matched set? At least a fork."

Herman ate with his usual gusto. He watched Madeline touch her spoon to the rice and find a few grains.

"I slaved over this dinner. This is no potluck. Don't do this to me."

"I'm a puffball. Herman. I've got to diet. Be supportive."

"What puffball? You have a perfect figure. These eggplants come from a genuine garden. The chopped meat is chuck. I thawed the broccoli. Come on. this is a celebration. A party. It's our anniversary."

"I can't explain it, but all I can think of is holding you. You're my nourishment. Let it be."

"If I am preferable to a baked, stuffed eggplant, then I accept that graciously. You're crazy, you know that? Let's go to bed."

Madeline told no lies. She bit at Herman's ears, chewed his mouth, took his honey, found vitamins he didn't know he had to give. Herman and Madeline flowed in and out of one another like breaking waves. After, Herman had coffee and apple pie. Madeline had tea, no sugar. He took her out to see the Heidelman.

"My observatory. Have a look."

"That's very effective. It has more power than I would have guessed."

"Don't patronize me. If you feel contempt, show it."

"I love your Heidelman," Madeline said.

Herman took a peek at the Feinbacher. No more melons. The stars were the familiar grapes. He squinted. In the south quadrant of the seventh grid another star was missing. He slapped the telescope as if it were a bad puppy. The scope vibrated the picture. He looked again. Two stars were gone.

"Is something wrong?" Madeline asked.

"With my head. I'm seeing things. Or I'm not seeing things I should see. Stars are vanishing from the Feinbacher."

Madeline laughed. Herman scowled at her, then began to giggle himself. They laughed together for five minutes.

"I know you're a night worker. Are you planning to work tonight?"

"Yes, definitely. I missed four nights already, what with you and the rain."

"Suppose I sulk."

"The meter is running, Madeline. As you so frankly pointed out, October is half over. I have less than two weeks left."

"Not so."

"Meaning?"

"Meaning what you already know. That you'll stay on Shell Island. Meaning that when we aren't conjugating the best verb, you can spy on your Feinbacher and make as many pretty pictures as you want. Meaning that you have a patron."

"So fast, Madeline. Are you sure?"

"I am sure. Herman. And you? Are you sure?"

"I think I was sure when I first saw you clomp across your moat. Nobody told me I would go for a girl with a moat."

"Will you marry me on a beach?"

"I hate being married on beaches. But I'll make an exception for an Avnolet. Marry me on a beach, the beach of your choice. Where will we live? Here or at the castle? If you insist, the castle. I hate breaking the news to my landlord, but if I must, I must."

"You bastard. You want me for my material possessions. You don't love me."

"I do. I'll prove it. Tonight I won't work vertically. I'll work horizontally Come, or I'll start without you."

"Kiss me a lot."

"A lot. Come, Madeline, be my valentine. I never had a valentine, and I always wanted one. Like I always wanted to pull a hamstring or have arthroscopic surgery like the jocks. Now at least I have a valentine."

"I love you."

"I love you."

"I love us."

Herman woke near four o'clock. He moved his arm toward Madeline and felt empty blankets. He got up, put on a pair of shorts, and went searching for her. She wasn't in the house. He went out into the waning night. She wasn't on the deck or near the walk. But her bike was still in place.

Herman was not concerned. A woman like Madeline would go down to the beach on impulse. She probably needed to cool. So much pleasure delivered so quickly required time to absorb, like water after a downpour. If Madeline had to be alone, so be it. He decided not to go after her. If she wanted a taste of loneliness to measure their closeness, then she deserved her solitude. It was holy.

So instead of pursuing, Herman went to look up through the Heidelman's short tube. And there was the dependable Feinbacher, fainter with the oncoming dawn but still very visible. The two disappeared stars were still absent. Could there have been a vast explosion eons ago to pock the Feinbacher's enormous cheek with black holes? The rest of the stars seemed intact. Or were they? Herman zeroed in on one fleck at the galaxy's center. It flickered like his red candle, sputtering at life. He knew it was dying. He was watching a star die. Standing in his shorts, Herman saw the final battle. He shuddered. The star was fighting like an insect in a web. But it grew dimmer. This had to be studied. This was for the other telescope.

"Madeline?"

Herman ran down the driveway and onto the road. He cut through brush and headed for the beach. He knew she would be someplace down there. And he was right. Past a large dune he could see her silhouette against a bright moon. The wind scattered sound when he called her name. So he ran toward her. When he got close enough he saw that she held her hand up toward the sky. Her hand held the little blue spoon. She brought it to her lips. Then Herman saw a shimmer of light ripple through her body. He knew she was eating a star.

"Madeline?"

She turned and put her hand over her mouth like a child caught with candy.

"Herman? I thought you were sound asleep."

"What are you doing?"

"If you must know, having a snack."

"Having a snack? Madeline, I have the most insane feeling that your snack is the Feinbacher Galaxy."

"If we're going to be married, this is no time for coy secrets. Don't question your sanity, Herman. You're quite correct."

"Madeline. A star?"

"I know it seems awful to you. And I am sorry it has to be your Feinbacher. You're going to yell at me, and because of something some ancestor did light-years ago. My little nibble won't even show up for centuries."

"Your family has been nibbling at the Feinbacher for centuries?"

"Don't upset yourself. There are zillions of stars. You'll find another galaxy far off the menu."

"The menu?"

"Herman, the Avnolets are a very wealthy family, and we have been for rather a long while. Face it, we're not franks and beans. In fact, we gave up ordinary food when it got, well, boring."

"Boring? So you learned to eat stars?"

"Yes, exactly. It's not very complicated, is it? In fact, it's quite logical, even predictable. We've eaten stars for as long as anyone close can remember, and we're not the only ones. What was I to do, Herman? Change our eating habits? And admit that stars do make a plentiful food supply."

"I admit that."

"And we're not talking about a cheap meal. Stars are for the taking. But when they just... go... that requires some heavy explaining. The Avnolets have paid out a fortune to the best scientists to come up with a theory that took the focus off our silly little nibbling. Of course, they did. Novas, black holes, all sorts of charming ideas. The sad part for you is that the menu was planned far back. And each of us, in turn, promises to follow it. Once I took a star at random just because I was famished, and I never heard the end of it. I hate that the Feinbacher came up, especially at such an inopportune time. But even with two meals a day, the Feinbacher will last for millennia."

"Only two meals a day, Madeline?"

"I knew you would be upset."

"Upset. Yes, I am a bit upset."

"It's a small thing, really. Herman, once you learn the technique you'll adore the change. Stars are quite tasty. And no dishes to wash. No tables to clear. That means more time, and time is what you want. Time to work, time for us to be together, time for the children."

"Little star eaters. The whole bunch of us."

"They just slide down, darling. No cholesterol. Our family lives forever. Herman, instead of picking at the universe, now you can feast."

"Low calories?"

"That, too. The perfect food."

"And what about special occasions? Birthdays, Christmas, Thanksgiving?"

"Nebulae. Comets. There is some variety on the menu."

"Do I get my own spoon?"

"Daddy's amethyst."

Madeline came to Herman and held him. He held her as hard as he could. Love. Time. And what if the Feinbacher would vanish in a few thousand years, so long as there was an explanation? His children—bright, strong boys and wise, soft girls—would sit with their parents and suckle at the cosmos. Herman slid his hands up Madeline's body and stopped at her neck. His thumb could feel a wild pulse. He kissed her glittering mouth and could taste diamonds on her tongue. Then he tried to squeeze light out of her, but no light exploded from between her teeth. When she was dead he dragged her corpse to the surf and watched the tide float her out. There was some phosphorescence, but it faded quickly.

Madeline, who had swallowed stars, was now harvested by the sea. Herman felt a rush of sorrow, then strange peace. The night turned absolutely still. In the silence, Herman could hear time. Then an owl moaned and broke the crystal quiet.

Her blue spoon lay on the beach near a broken conch. Herman left the spoon but picked up the shell and traced its spirals. He wondered if such sea things had the urge to dream. Then he held the shell to his eye and peered through a crevice that broke its armor. He scanned the sky, looked past a moon webbed with clouds, to a nourishment of stars.

This story is for Adam Jacobs on the occasion of his twenty-first birthday.

Unidentified Objects

James P. Blaylock

James P. Blaylock is the author of the novels *The Digging Leviathan, Homunculus, Land of Dreams, The Last Coin, The Paper Grail*, and *Lord Kelvin's Machine*. Blaylock won the Philip K. Dick Award for *Homunculus* in 1986. He has also won the World Fantasy Award for his story "Paper Dragons."

"Unidentified Objects," another of Blaylock's rare short stories, was honored by being chosen for inclusion in the prestigious *The O. Henry Awards: Prize Stories* anthology. It was first published in *Omni*, July 1989. It's a fresh and charming variation on the theme of missed chances.

Unidentified Objects

James P. Blaylock

In 1956 the downtown square mile of the city of Orange was a collection of old houses: craftsman bungalows and tile-roofed Spanish, and here and there an Old Queen Anne or a gingerbread Victorian with geminate windows and steep gables, and sometimes a carriage house alongside, too small by half to house the lumbering automobiles that the second fifty years of the century had produced. There were Studebakers at the curbs and the Hudsons and Buicks with balloon tires like the illustrations of moon-aimed rockets on the covers of the pulp magazines.

Times were changing. Science was still a professor with wild hair and a lab coat and with bubbling apparatus in a cellar; but in a few short years he would walk on the moon—one last ivory and silver hurrah—and then, as if in an instant, he would grow faceless and featureless and unpronounceable. There would come the sudden knowledge that Moon Valley wasn't so very far away after all, and neither was extinction; that the nation that controlled magnetism, as Diet Smith would have it, controlled almost nothing at all; and that a score of throbbing bulldozers could reduce the jungle wilds around Opar and El Dorado to desert sand in a few short, sad years. The modern automobile suddenly was slick and strange, stretched out and low and with enormous fins that swept back at the rear above banks of superfluous taillights. They seemed otherworldly at the time and were alien reminders, it seems to me now, of how provincial we had been, balanced on the back edge of an age.

The pace of things seemed to be accelerating, and already I could too easily anticipate stepping out onto my tilted front porch some signifying morning, the wind out of the east, and seeing stretched out before me not a shaded avenue of overarching trees and root-cracked sidewalks but the sleek, desert-like technology of a new age, a new suburbia, with robots in vinyl trousers sweeping fallen leaves into their own open mouths.

There is a plaza in the center of town, with a fountain, and in the autumn—the season when all of this came to my attention—red-brown leaves from flowering pear trees drift down onto the sluggish, gurgling water and float there like a centerpiece for a Thanksgiving table. On a starry evening, one November late in the Seventies, I was out walking in the plaza, thinking, I remember, that it had already become an artifact, with its quaint benches and granite curbs and rose garden. Then, shattering the mood of late night nostalgia, there shone in the sky an immense shooting star, followed by the appearance of a glowing object, which hovered and darted, sailing earthward until I could make out its shadow against the edge of the moon and then disappearing in a blink. I shouted and pointed, mostly out of surprise. Strange lights in the sky were nothing particularly novel; I had been seeing them for almost twenty years. But nothing that happens at night among the stars can ever become commonplace. At that late hour, though, there was almost certainly no one around to hear me; or so I thought.

So when she stood up, dropping papers and pencils and a wooden drawing board onto the concrete walk, I nearly shouted again. She had been sitting in the dim lamplight, hidden to me beyond the fountain. Dark hair fell across her shoulders in a rush of curl and hid her right eye, and with a practiced sweep of her hand she pulled it back in a shock and tucked it behind her ear, where it stayed obediently for about three quarters of a second and then fell seductively into her face again. Now, years later, for reasons I can't at all define, the sight of a dark-haired woman brushing wayward hair out of her eyes recalls without fail that warm autumn night by the fountain.

She had that natural, arty, blue-jeans-and-floppy-sweater look of a college girl majoring in fine arts: embroidered handbag, rhinestone-emerald costume brooch, and translucent plastic shoes the color of root beer. I remember thinking right off that she had languorous eyes, and the sight of them reflecting the soft lamplight of the fountain jolted me. But the startled look on her face implied that she hadn't admired my shouting like that, not at eleven o'clock at night in the otherwise deserted plaza.

There was the dark, pouting beauty in her eyes and lips of a woman in a Pre-Raphaelite painting, a painting that I had stumbled into in my clodlike way, grinning, I thought, like a half-wit. I too hastily explained the shooting star to her, gesturing too widely at the sky and mumbling that it hadn't been an ordinary shooting star. But there was nothing in the sky now besides the low-hanging moon and a ragtag cloud, and she said offhandedly, not taking any notice of my discomfort, just what I had been thinking, that there was never anything ordinary about a shooting star.

I learned that her name was Jane and that she had sketched that fountain a dozen times during the day, with the blooming flowers behind it and the changing backdrop of people and cars and weather. I almost asked her whether she hadn't ever been able to get it quite right, but then, I could see that that wasn't the point.

Now she had been sketching it at night, its blue and green and pink lights illuminating the umbrella of falling water against night-shaded rosebushes and camphor trees and boxwood hedges.

It was perfect—straight out of a romantic old film. The hero stumbles out of the rain into an almost deserted library, and at the desk, with her hair up and spectacles on her nose, is the librarian who doesn't know that if she'd just take the glasses off for a moment . . .

I scrabbled around to pick up fallen pencils while she protested that she could just as easily do it herself. It was surely only the magic of that shooting star that prevented her from gathering up her papers and going home. As it was, she stayed for a moment to talk, assuming, although she never said so, that there was something safe and maybe interesting in a fancier of shooting stars. I felt the same about her and her drawings and her root beer shoes.

She was distracted, never really looking at me. Maybe the image of the fountain was still sketched across the back of her eyes and she couldn't see me clearly. It was just a little irritating, and I would discover later that it was a habit of hers, being distracted was, but on that night there was something in the air and it didn't matter. Any number of things don't matter at first. We talked, conversation dying and starting and with my mind mostly on going somewhere—my place, her place—for a drink, for what? There was something, an atmosphere that surrounded her, a musky sort of sweater and lilacs scent. But she was distant; her work had been interrupted and she was still half lost in the dream of it. She dragged her hand in the water of the fountain, her face half in shadow. She was tired out, she said. She didn't need to be walked home. She could find her way alone.

But I've got ahead of myself. It's important that I keep it all straight—all the details; without the details it amounts to nothing. I grew up on Olive Street, southwest of the plaza, and when I was six, and wearing my Davy Crockett hat and Red Rider shirt, and it was nearly dusk in late October, I heard the ding-alinging of an ice cream truck from some distant reach of the neighborhood. The grass was covered with leaves, I remember, that had been rained on and were limp and heavy. I was digging for earthworms and dropping them one by one into a corral built of upright sticks and twigs that was the wall of the native village on Kong Island. The sky was cloudy, the street empty. There was smoke from a chimney across the way and the cloud-muted hum of a distant airplane lost to view. Light through the living room window shone out across the dusky lawn.

The jangling of the ice cream bell drew near, and the truck rounded the distant corner, the bell cutting off and the truck accelerating as if the driver, anticipating dinner, had given up for the day and was steering a course for home. It slowed, though, when he saw me, and angled in toward the curb where I stood holding a handful of gutter-washed earthworms. Clearly he thought I'd signaled him. There were pictures of frozen concoctions painted on the gloss-white sides of the panel truck: coconut-covered Neapolitan bars and grape Popsicles, nut and chocolate drumsticks, and strawberry-swirled vanilla in paper cups with flat paper lids. He laboriously climbed out of the cab, came around the street side to the back, and confronted me there on the curb. He smiled and winked and wore a silver foil hat with an astonishing bill, and when he yanked open the hinged, chrome door there was such a whirling of steam off the dry ice inside that he utterly vanished behind it, and I caught a quick glimpse of cardboard bins farther back in the cold fog, stacked one on top of another and dusted with ice crystals.

I didn't have a dime and wouldn't be allowed to eat ice cream so close to dinner time anyway, and I said so, apologizing for having made him stop for nothing. He studied my earthworms and said that out in space there were planets where earthworms spoke and wore silk shirts and that I could fly to those planets in the right sort of ship.

Then he bent into the freezer and after a lot of scraping and peering into boxes found a paper-wrapped ice cream bar—a FLYING SAUCER BAR, the wrapper said. It was as big around as a coffee cup saucer and was domed on top and fat with vanilla ice cream coated in chocolate. He tipped his hat, slammed his door, and drove off. I ate the thing guiltily while sitting beneath camellia bushes at the side of the house and lobbing sodden pink blooms out onto the front yard, laying siege to the earthworm fortress and watching the lamps blink on one by one along the street.

There are those incidents from our past that years later seem to us to be the stuff of dreams: the wash of shooting stars seen through the rear window of the family car at night in the Utah desert; the mottled, multilegged sun star, as big as a cartwheel, inching across the sand in the shallows of a northern California bay; the whale's eyeball floating in alcohol and encased in a glass fishing float in a junk store near the waterfront; the remembered but unrecoverable hollow sensation of new love. The stars vanish in an instant; the starfish slips away into deep water and is gone; the shop with its fishing float is a misty dream, torn down in some unnumbered year to make room for a hotel built of steel and smoked glass. Love evaporates into the passing years like dry ice; you don't know where it's gone. The mistake is to think that the details don't signify—the flying saucer bars and camellia blooms, rainy autumn streets and lamplight through evening windows and colored lights playing across the waters of a fountain on a warm November evening.

All the collected pieces of our imagistic memory seem sometimes to be trivial knickknacks when seen against the roaring of passing time. But without those little water-paint sketches, awash in remembered color and detail, none of us, despite our airy dreams, amount to more than an impatient ghost wandering through the revolving years and into an increasingly strange and alien future.

I came to know the driver of the ice cream truck. We became acquaintances. He no longer sold ice cream; there was no living to be made at it. He had got a penny a Popsicle, he said, and he produced a slip of paper covered with numbers—elaborate calculations of the millions of Popsicles he'd have to sell over the years just to stay solvent. Taken altogether like that it was impossible. He had been new to the area then and hadn't got established yet. All talk of money aside, he had grown tired of it, of the very idea of driving an ice cream truck—something that wouldn't have seemed possible to me on the rainy evening of the flying saucer bar, but which I understand well enough now.

He had appeared on our front porch, I remember, when I was ten or eleven, selling wonderful tin toys door-to-door. My mother bought a rocket propelled by compressed air. It was painted with bright, circus colors, complete with flames swirling around the cylindrical base of the thing. Looking competent and serious and very much like my ice cream man was a helmeted pilot painted into a bubblelike vehicle on the top of the rocket, which would pop off, like a second stage, when the rocket attained the stupendous height of thirty or forty feet. I immediately lost the bubble craft with its painted astronaut. It shot off, just like it was supposed to, and never came down. I have to suppose that it's rusting in the branches of a tree somewhere, but I have a hazy memory of it simply shooting into the air and disappearing in a blink, hurtling up through the thin atmosphere toward deep space. Wasted money, my mother said.

Our third meeting was at the Palm Street Market, where I went to buy penny candy that was a nickel by then. I was thirteen, I suppose, or something near it, which would have made it early in the Sixties. The clerk being busy, I had strayed over to the magazine shelves and found a copy of *Fate*, which I read for the saucer stories, and which, on that afternoon, was the excuse for my being close enough to the "men's" magazines to thumb through a couple while the clerk had his back turned. I had the *Fate* open to the account of Captain Hooton's discovery of an airship near Texarkana, and a copy of something called *Slick* or *Trick* or *Flick* propped open on the rack behind. I read the saucer article out of apologetic shame in between thumbing through the pages of photographs, as if my reading it would balance out the rest, but remembering nothing of what I read until, with a shock of horror that I can still recall as clearly as anything else in my life, I became aware that the ice cream man, the tin toy salesman, was standing behind me, reading over my shoulder.

What I read, very slowly and carefully as three fourths of my blood rose into my head, was Captain Hooton's contempt for airship design: "There was no bell or bell rope about the ship that I could discover, like I should think every well-regulated air locomotive should have." At the precise moment of my reading that sentence, the clerk's voice whacked out of the silence: "Hey, kid!" was what he said. I'd heard it before. It was a weirdly effective phrase and had such a freezing effect on me that Captain Hooton's bit of mechanical outrage has come along through the years with me uninvited, pegged into my memory by the manufactured shame of that single moment.

Both of us bought a copy of *Fate*. I *had* to, of course, although it cost me forty cents that I couldn't afford. I remember the ice cream man winking broadly at me there on the sidewalk, and me being deadly certain that I had become as transparent as a ghost fish. Everyone on Earth had been on to my little game with the magazine. I couldn't set foot in that market without a disguise for a solid five years. And then, blessedly, he was gone, off down the street, and me in the opposite direction. I stayed clear of the market for a couple of months and then discovered, passing on the sidewalk, that the witnessing clerk was gone, and that went a long way toward putting things right, although Captain Hooton, as I said, has stayed with me. In fact, I began from that day to think of the ice cream man as Captain Hooton, since I had no idea what his name was, and years later the name would prove strangely appropriate.

It was in the autumn, then, that I first met Jane on that November night in the plaza, and weeks later when I introduced her to him, to Captain Hooton. She said in her artistic way that he had a "good face," although she didn't mean to make any sort of moral judgment, and truthfully his face was almost inhumanly long and angular. She said this after the three of us had chatted for a moment and he had gone on his way. It was as if there were nothing much more she could say about him that made any difference at all, as if she were distracted.

I remember that it irritated me, although why it should have I don't know, except that he had already begun to mean something, to signify, as if our chance meetings over the years, if I could pluck them out of time and arrange them just so, would make a pattern.

"He dresses pretty awful, doesn't he?" That's what she said after he'd gone along and she could think of nothing more to say about his face.

I hadn't noticed, and I said so, being friendly about it.

"He's smelly. What was that, do you think?"

"Tobacco, I guess. I don't know. Pipe tobacco." She wasn't keen on tobacco, or liquor either. So I didn't put too fine a point on it because I didn't want to set her off, to have to defend his smoking a pipe. It was true that his coat could have used a cleaning, but that hadn't occurred to me, actually, until she mentioned it, wrinkling up her nose in that rabbit way of hers.

"I keep thinking that he's got a fish in his pocket."

I smiled at her, suddenly feeling as if I were betraying a friend.

"Well . . ." I said, trying to affect a dropping-the-subject tone.

She shuddered. "People get like that, especially old people. They forget to take baths and wash their hair."

I shrugged, pretending to think that she was merely trying to be amusing.

"He's not that old," I said. But she immediately agreed. That was the problem, wasn't it? You wouldn't think . . . She looked at my own hair very briefly and then set out down the sidewalk with me following and studying my shadow in the afternoon sun and keeping my hands away from my hair. It looked neat enough there in the shadow on the sidewalk, but I knew that shadows couldn't be trusted, and I was another five minutes worrying about it before something else happened, it doesn't matter what, and I forgot about my hair and my vanity.

Her own hair had a sort of flyaway look to it, but perfect, if you understand me, and it shone as if she'd given it the standard hundred strokes that morning. A dark-red ribbon held a random clutch of it behind her ear, and there was something in the ribbon and in the way she put her hand on my arm to call my attention to some house or other that made me think of anything but houses. She had a way of touching you, almost as if accidentally, like a cat sliding past your leg, rubbing against you, and arching just a little and then continuing on, having abandoned any interest in you. She stood too close, maybe, for comfort— although *comfort* is the wrong word because the sensation was almost ultimately comfortable—and all the while that we were standing there talking about the lines of the roof, I was conscious only of the static charge of her presence, her shoulder just grazing my arm, her hip brushing against my thigh, the heavy presence of her sex suddenly washing away whatever was on the surface of my mind and settling there musky and soft. There hasn't been another man in history more indifferent to the lines of a roof.

In the downtown circular plaza each Christmas, there was an enormous Santa Claus built from wire and twisted paper, lit from within by a spiral of pin lights, and at Halloween, beneath overcast skies and pending rain, there were parades of schoolchildren dressed as witches and clowns and bed-sheet ghosts. Then in spring there was a May festival, with city dignitaries riding in convertible Edsels and waving to people sitting in lawn chairs along the boulevard. One year the parade was led by a tame ape followed by fezzed Shriners in Mr. Toad cars.

Twice during the two years that Jane studied art, while the town shrank for her and grew cramped, we watched the parade from a sidewalk table in front of Felix's Cafe, laughing at the ape and smiling at the solemn drumming of the marching bands. The second year one of the little cars caught fire and the parade fizzled out and waited while a half-dozen capering Shriners beat the fire out with their jackets. It was easy to laugh then, at the ape and the Edsels and the tiny cars, except that even then I suspected that her laughter was half cynical. Mine wasn't, and this difference between us troubled me.

In the summer there was a street fair, and the smoky aroma of sausages and beer and the sticky-sweet smell of cotton candy. We pushed through the milling crowds and sat for hours under an ancient tree in the plaza, watching the world revolve around us.

It seems now that I was always wary then that the world in its spinning might tumble me off, and there was something about the exposed roots of that tree that made you want to touch them, to sit among them just to see how immovable they were. But the world couldn't spin half fast enough for her. You'd have thought that if she could get a dozen paintings out of that fountain, then there would be enough, even in a provincial little town like this one, to amuse her forever.

Captain Hooton always seemed to be turning up. One year he put on a Santa costume and wandered through the shops startling children. The following year at Halloween he appeared out of the doorway of a disused shop, wearing a fright wig and carrying an enormous flashlight like a lighthouse beacon, on the lens of which was glued a witch cut out of black construction paper. He climbed into a sycamore tree in front of Watson's Drugs and shined the witch for a half hour onto the white stone facade of the bank, and then, refusing to come down unless he was made to, was finally led away by the police. Jane ought to have admired the trick with the flashlight, but she had by then developed a permanent dislike for him because, I think, he didn't seem to take her seriously, her or her paintings, and she took both of those things very seriously indeed, while pretending to care for almost nothing at all.

He ate pretty regularly for a time at Rudy's counter, at the drugstore. It was a place where milk shakes were still served in enormous metal cylinders and where shopkeepers sat on red Naugahyde and ate hot turkey sandwiches and mashed potatoes and talked platitudes and weather and sports, squinting and nodding. Captain Hooton wasn't much on conversation. He sat alone usually, smoking and wearing one of those caps that sports car enthusiasts wear, looking as if he were pondering something, breaking into silent laughter now and then as he watched the autumn rain fall and the red-brown sycamore leaves scattering along the street in the gusting breeze.

There was something awful about his skin—an odd color, perhaps, too pink and blue and never any hint of a beard, even in the afternoon.

A balding man from Fergy's television repair referred to him jokingly as Doctor Loomis, apparently the name of an alien visitor in a cheap, old science-fiction thriller. I chatted with him three or four times when Jane wasn't along, coming to think of him finally as a product of "the old school," which, as Dickens said, is no school that ever existed on Earth.

There were more sightings of things in the sky—almost always at night, and almost always they were described in slightly ludicrous terms by astonished citizens, as if each of them had mugged up those old issues of *Fate*. The things were egg-shaped, wingless, smooth silver; they beamed people up through spiraling doors and motored them around the galaxy and then dropped them off again, in a vacant lot or behind an apartment complex or bowling alley and with an inexplicable lapse of memory. The *City News* was full of it.

Once, at the height of the sightings, men in uniforms came from the East and the sightings mysteriously stopped. Something landed in the upper reaches of my avocado tree one night and glowed there. Next morning I found a cardboard milk carton smelling of chemicals, the inside stained the green of a sunlit ocean, lying in the leaves and humus below. It had little wings fastened with silver duct tape. The bottom of it had been cut out and replaced with a carved square of pumice, a bored-out carburetor jet glued into the center of it.

It happened that Captain Hooton lived on Pine Street by that time, and so did I. I rented half of a little bungalow and took walks in the evening when I wasn't with Jane. His house was deceptively large. From the street it seemed to be a narrow, gabled Victorian with a three-story turret in the right front corner, and with maybe a living room, parlor, and kitchen downstairs. Upstairs there might have been room for a pair of large bedrooms and a library midway up in the turret. There was a lot of split clinker brick mortared onto the front in an attempt to make the house look indefinably European, and shutters with shooting stars cut into them that had been added along the way. Old newspapers piled up regularly on the front porch and walk as if he were letting them ripen, and the brush-choked flowerbeds were so overgrown that none of the downstairs windows could have admitted any sunlight.

Jane seemed to see it as being a shame—the mess of weeds and brush, the cobbled-together house, the yellowing papers. Somehow I held out hope that it would strike her as—what?—original. Eccentric, maybe. At first I thought that they were too much alike in their eccentricities. I considered her root beer shoes and her costume jewelry and her very fashionable and practiced disregard for fashion and her perfectly disarranged hair, and it occurred to me that she was art, so to speak—artifice, theater. And although she talked about spontaneity, she was a marvel of regimentation and control, and never more so than when she was being spontaneous. The two of them couldn't have been more unalike.

He was vaguely alarming, though. You couldn't tell what he was thinking; his past and his future were misty and dim, giving you the sort of feeling you get on cheap haunted-house thrill rides at carnivals, where you're never quite sure what colorful, grimacing thing will leap out at you from behind a plywood partition.

I could see the rear of his house from my backyard, and from there it appeared far larger. It ran back across the deep lot and was a wonder of dormers, gables, and lean-to closets, all of it overshadowed by walnut trees and trumpet flower vines on sagging trellises and arbors. Underneath was a sprawling basement which at night glowed with lamplight through above ground transom windows. The muted ring of small hammers and the hum of lathes sounded from the cellar at unwholesomely late hours.

The double doors of his garage were fastened with a rusted iron lock as big as a man's hand, and he must have had a means by which to enter and leave the garage—and perhaps the house itself—without using any of the visible doors. I rarely saw him out and about. When I did, he sometimes seemed hardly to know me, as if distracted, his mind on mysteries.

Once, while I was out walking, I came across him spading up a strip of earth beneath his kitchen window, breaking the clods apart and pulling iron filings out of them with an enormous magnet. I recalled our distant meeting behind the ice cream truck, but by now he seemed to remember it only vaguely. I took him to be the sort of eccentric genius too caught up in his own meanderings to pay any attention to the mundane world.

He'd started a winter garden there along the side of his house, and a dozen loose heads of red-leaf lettuce grew in the half-shade of the eaves. We chatted amiably enough, about the weather, about gardens. He gave me a sidewise squint and asked if I'd seen any of the alleged "saucers" reported in the newspaper, and I said that I had, or at least that I had seen some saucer or another months ago. He nodded and frowned as if he'd rather hoped I hadn't, as if the two of us might have sneered at the notion of it together.

A spotted butterfly hovered over the lettuce, alighting now and then and finally settling in "to eat the lettuce alive," as he put it. He wouldn't stand for it, he said, and very quietly he plucked up a wiremesh flyswatter that hung from a nail on the side porch, and he flailed away at the butterfly until the head of lettuce it had rested on was shredded. He seemed to think it was funny, particularly so because the butterfly itself had got entirely away, had fluttered off at the first sign of trouble. It was a joke, an irony, a metaphor of something that I didn't quite catch.

He gave me a paper sack full of black-eyed peas and disappeared into the house, asking after the "young lady" but not waiting for an answer, and then shoving back out through the door to tell me to return the sack when I was through with it, and then laughing and winking and closing the door, and winking again through the kitchen window so that it was impossible to say what, entirely, he meant by the display.

There wasn't much I could have told him about the "young lady." Much of what I might have said would already be a reminiscence. The thing that mattered, I suppose, was that she made me weak in the knees, but I couldn't say so. And she was entirely without that clinging, dependent nature that feeds a man's vanity at first but soon grows tiresome. Jane always talked as if she had places to go to, people to meet. There was something in the tone of her voice that made such talk sound like a warning, as if I weren't invited along, or weren't up to it, or were a momentary amusement, like the May parade, perhaps, and would have to suffice while she was stuck there in that little farflung corner of the globe.

She wanted to travel to the Orient, to Paris. I wanted to travel, too. It turned out that her plans didn't exclude me. I would go along—quit work and go, just like that, spontaneously, wearing a beret and a knapsack. And that's just what I did, finally, although without the beret; I'm not the sort of a man who can wear a hat. I'm too likely to affect the carefree attitude and then regret the hat, or whatever it is I'm wearing, and then whatever it is I'm not wearing but should have. It's a world of regrets, isn't it? Jane didn't think so. She hadn't any regrets, and said so, and for a while I was foolish enough to admire her saying so. I don't believe that Captain Hooton would have understood her saying such a thing, let alone have admired it.

I brought around his paper sack, right enough, two days later, and he took it from me solemnly, nodding and frowning. At once he blew it up like a balloon—inflated it until it was almost spherical—and then, waving a finger in order to show me, I suppose, that I hadn't seen anything yet, he pulled a slip of silver ribbon out of his vest pocket, looped it around the bunched paper at the bottom, and tied it off. He lit a kitchen match with his fingernail and held it to the tails of the ribbon. Immediately the inflated sack began to glow and rocketed away through the curb trees like a blowfish, the ribbons trailing streams of blue sparks. It angled skyward in a rush and vanished.

I must have looked astonished, thinking of the milk carton beneath my tree. He pretended to smoke his pipe with his ear. Then he sighted along the stem as if it were a periscope, and made whirring and clicking sorts of submarine noises with his tongue. Then waggling his shoulders as if generally loosening his joints, he blew softly across the reeking pipe bowl, dispersing the smoke and making a sound uncannily like Peruvian panpipes. He was full of tricks. He suddenly looked very old—certainly above seventy. His hair, which must have been a transplant, grew in patterns like hedgerows, and in the sunlight that shone between the racing clouds, his skin was almost translucent, as if he were a laminated see-through illustration in a modern encyclopedia.

And so one evening late I knocked on the cellar window next to his kitchen door, then stood back on the dewy lawn and waited for him. He was working down there, tinkering with something; I could see his head wagging over the bench.

In a moment he opened the door, having come upstairs. He didn't seem at all surprised to see me skulking in the yard like that but waved me in impatiently as if he had been waiting for my arrival, maybe for years, and now I'd finally come and there was no time to waste.

The cellar was impossibly vast, stretching away room after room, a sort of labyrinth of low-ceilinged, concrete-floored rooms. I couldn't be certain of my bearings any longer, but it seemed that the rooms must have been dug beneath the driveway alongside his house as well as under the house itself—maybe under the house next door; and once I allowed for such a thing, it occurred to me that his cellars might as easily stretch beneath my own house. I remembered nights when I had been awakened by noises, by strange creaks and clanks and rattles of the sort that startle you awake, and you listen, your heart going like sixty, while you tell yourself that it's the house "settling," but you don't believe it. And all this time it might have been him, muffled beneath the floor and perhaps a few feet of earth, tapping away at a workbench like a dwarf in his mine.

All of this filled my head when I stood on the edge of his stairs, breathing the musty cellar air. It was late, after all, and a couple of closets with lights casting the shadows of doorways and shelves might have accounted for the illusion of vast size. We wandered away through the clutter, with me in my astonishment only half-listening to him, and despite all the magical debris, what I remember most, like an inessential but vivid element in a dream, was his head ducking and ducking under low, rough-sawn ceiling joists that were almost black with age.

I have a confused recollection of partly built contrivances, some of them moving due to hidden, clockwork mechanisms, some of them sighing and gurgling, hooked up to water pipes curling out of the walls or to steam pipes running in copper arteries toward a boiler that I can't remember seeing but could hear sighing and wheezing somewhere nearby. There were pendulums and delicate hydraulic gizmos, and on the corner of one bench a gyroscope spun in a little depression, motivated, apparently, by nothing at all. The walls were strewn with charts and drawings and shelves of books, and once, when we bent through a doorway and into a room inhabited by the hovering, slowly rotating hologram of a space vehicle, we surprised a family of mice at work on the remains of a stale sandwich. What did they make, I wonder, of the ghost of the spacecraft? Had they tried to inhabit it, to build a nest in it? Would it have mattered to them that they were inhabiting a dream?

What did I make of it? *Here's Captain Hooton's airship*, I remember thinking. *Where's the bell rope?* But it wasn't his airship, not exactly; the ship itself was in an adjacent room.

The whole thing was a certainty in an instant—the lights in the sky, the odd debris beneath the avocado tree, even the weird pallor of his see-through skin. It had all been his doing all these years. That's no surprise, I suppose, when it's taken altogether like this. When all the details are compressed, the patterns are clear.

He had come from somewhere and was going back again. With the lumber of mechanical trash spread interminably across bench tops, and the cluttered walls and the mice, and him with his pipe and hat, he seemed so settled in, so permanent. And yet the continual tinkering and the lights on at all hours made it clear that he was on the edge of leaving—maybe in a week, maybe in the morning, maybe right now; that's what I thought as I stood there looking at the ship.

UNIDENTIFIED OBJECTS

It was nearly spherical, with four curved appendages that were a hybrid of wings and legs and that held the craft up off the concrete floor. Circular hatches ringed the ship, each covered with lapped plates that looked as if they'd spiral open to expose a door or a glassed-over window. The metal of the thing was polished to the silver shine of a perfect mirror that stretched our reflections like taffy as I stood listening to him tell me how we were directly under the backyard, and how he would detonate a charge, and one foggy night the ship would sail up out of the ground in a rush of smoke and dirt and be gone, affording the city newspapers their last legitimate saucer story.

I didn't tell Jane about it. There were a lot of things I couldn't or wouldn't tell her. I wanted some little world of my own, which was removed from the world we had together, but which, of course, could be implied now and then for effect, but never revealed lest it seem to her to be amusing. One day soon the papers would be full of it anyway—the noise in the night, the scattered sightings of the heaven bound craft, the backyard crater. There would be something then in being the only one who knew.

And he no doubt wasn't anxious that the spaceship became general knowledge. There was no law against it, strictly speaking, but if they'd jailed him for the trick with the flashlight and the paper witch, or rather for refusing to come down out of a tree, then who could say what they might do if they got wind of a flying saucer buried in a cellar?

Then there was the chance that I might be aboard. He was willing to take me along. We talked about it all that night, about the places I'd see and the people I'd meet—a completely different sort of crowd than Jane and I would run into in our European travels.

It was then, about two years after I'd met Jane, that I gave up the house on Pine Street and moved in with her. She was free of school at last and was in an expansive, generous mood, which I'll admit I took advantage of shamelessly, and when, in early July, she received money from home and bought a one-way ticket to Rome, I bought one, too, only mine was a round-trip ticket with a negotiable return date. That should have bothered her, my having doubts, but it didn't. She didn't remark on it at all. From the start it had been my business—another aspect of her modern attitude toward things, an attitude I could neither share nor condemn out loud.

The rest is inevitable. I returned and she didn't. Captain Hooton was gone, and there was a crater with scorched grass around the perimeter of it in the backyard of his empty house. I might have gone along with him. But I didn't, and what I get to keep is the memory of it all—the hologram, so to speak, of the ship and of faded desire, having given up the one for the already fading dream of the other.

There's the image in my mind of a card house built of picture postcards pulled from a rusting wire rack of memories—the sort of thing that even a mouse wouldn't live in, preferring something more permanent and substantial. But then, nothing is quite as solid as we'd like it to be, and the map of our lives, sketched out across our memory, is of a provincial little neighborhood, crisscrossed with regret and circumscribed by a couple of impassable roads and by splashes of bright color that have begun to fade even before we have them fixed in our memory.

The Gates of Babel

J. R. Dunn

J. R. Dunn has published short fiction in *The Writers of the Future* anthology, *Isaac Asimov's Science Fiction Magazine*, and *Amazing*, in addition to having had two stories in *Omni*. "The Gates of Babel" (May 1989) was his second published story and was chosen by David S. Garnett for *The Orbit Science Fiction Yearbook #3*. Dunn's first novel, *This Side of Judgment*, will be published by Harcourt, Brace and Company in spring 1994.

The Gates of Babel

J.R. Dunn

The thing appeared a few minutes after they left the highway for the coast road: a huge, gray-white blockhouse peering over the hills outside of Lompoc, distorted by distance and the afternoon heat. McCune stared at it for a few seconds before turning to Parkinson. "That's it? That's Vandenberg?" "That's it," Parkinson said, shifting in the seat. "It won't be too far now." McCune studied him before turning back to the road, wondering for the dozenth time what was on his mind. He looked normal enough, considering his story. He was well dressed, in an academic sort of way—tweed jacket, corduroys, loafers—but that didn't mean much. They didn't have to wear medallions or flowing robes. McCune had seen them all since he had started at the *Journal*: Atlanteans, witches, flat-earthers. California bred 'em like oranges and the first place they headed was a newspaper. He'd had his fill early and had hoped he'd see the end of them somewhere along the line, but no such luck. The nuts are always with us.

    He had to admit that Parkinson was different. It wasn't the usual line, and a surprising amount of his information had checked out. There had been someone named Vandenberg, an Air Force general back in the Forties, and a base had been named after him on the coast north of Santa Barbara. It was a test center of some sort, though there was no mention of it being abandoned as Parkinson had said. And there was that other item, too, the booklet marked SECRET, TRANSPOLAR SHUTTLE PROBLEMS, or something.

    "What was the name of that handbook you gave me again?"

    Parkinson rubbed his forehead and sighed. "*STS Polar Launch Parameters.*" He put his hand out the window and began to tap the side of the car. "Did you read it?"

McCune shook his head. "I tried, but I couldn't follow any of it. I meant to bring it along so that I could ask you about a few things, but like I said, I lost it."

"You didn't lose it."

He glared at Parkinson for a moment, then turned his eyes back to the road. "You know, you'd do a lot more for your case if you thought twice about remarks like that. Your story is wild enough as it is without implying that I threw your evidence away, much less trying to tell me what I wrote three years ago."

"You didn't bother to check your files?"

"Why the hell should I? You think I wouldn't remember?"

"How about a three-part series on cost overruns at Slick-6?"

McCune answered with a snort of disgust. Parkinson, for his part, smiled sourly before turning his head back to the road. He sat up suddenly and pointed. "There you go," he said. "Gantries."

They had topped the last hill overlooking the coastal plain. Scattered across it was a collection of large metal structures, openwork towers painted orange and white. They were big, over a hundred feet high, and McCune had never seen anything like them.

"And what are they?"

"Missile launching platforms."

McCune shrugged. "Right."

As they drove down the hill, he inspected the rest of the base. There was little that he recognized: no runway, no control tower, no aircraft of any kind, just roads, a few buildings, the huge concrete blockhouse surrounded by smaller structures of the same type, and the enigmatic towers running up the coast against the blue of the Pacific. A long paved track meandered from the big blockhouse south to the hills near the shore, and for a moment he thought that might be a runway, but no, it wasn't wide enough and it made a number of hairpin turns, avoiding the hummocks and gullies of the plain for level ground.

The road went past a chain-link fence topped with barbed wire before leading to a gate. It was wide open; the guardhouse next to it was wrecked, with only small shards of glass in the windows. Despite this, McCune stopped the car. He sat clutching the steering wheel for a moment before turning to Parkinson. "Maybe we should check in with somebody."

"Nobody to check in with," Parkinson said. "We passed administration five minutes ago, past Lompoc. You saw it was empty."

McCune thought back. It hadn't struck him at the time, but the last stretch of buildings they had passed had seemed deserted, with no one in sight and no cars on the streets. He looked out again at the guardhouse. There had been a sign beneath the front window, but all that remained now were twisted bolts and discolored brick. "How could they leave a military base open like this?"

"They didn't, the first few months. They kept up a guard for a while, but that petered out just like everything else."

"But this damage..."

"Kids," Parkinson said, nearly spitting the word. "They ride their minibikes on the tow route. You can't keep 'em out."

Nodding, McCune put the car in gear and drove through the gate. The road took them past other buildings, most of them brick but a few made of prefab metal. None were in any better shape than the guardhouse, and a few were much worse: doors kicked down, smoke stains showing around the windows, with desks and wrecked office equipment scattered across the parched lawns.

After a few blocks Parkinson told him to take the next left, and they drove out into the base itself, toward the towers that rose above the sand.

For about a mile they paralleled the curved path he had noticed from the top of the hill, heading for the blockhouse at the center of the base. He was unable to take his eyes off it as they drew nearer and it began to dominate the landscape. He didn't hear Parkinson telling him to turn until they were well past the spur, and he had to back up fifty yards to get to the right road.

A few minutes later they pulled up in front of a building that was in much better shape than those they had passed near the gate. The windows were intact, the door undamaged, and though the chaparral was making a valiant effort to reclaim the small hill it stood on, the area in front had been kept clear. A four-wheel-drive Blazer was parked next to it, and as they pulled up, a man not much smaller than the truck stepped out to meet them.

"Running a little late," he bellowed cheerfully as Parkinson got out. He was dressed casually in slacks, a *guayabera* shirt that flapped over his ample belly, and a baseball cap with an odd acronym in front: NASA with the bars of the A's removed so that they looked like arrow-heads. Like McCune he was bearded, but in proportion to the rest of his frame; it took up most of his face and spilled down to meet his shirt, giving him the air of a prospector or robber baron.

"Sorry about that," said Parkinson. "He kept me sitting in the waiting room all morning." He took a step toward the building, then looked questioningly at the big man. "Where's everybody else?"

"Sherry saw one of those spheres floating around the assembly building about noon," the big man said, waving an arm to the south. "I sent everybody home after she told me."

McCune was halfway out of the car, arm draped over the open door.

Spheres, floating spheres—that brought back something. Hadn't there been some kind of flying ghosts people were seeing a few years back? Ofos or something? He was trying to catch the thought when the big man stepped around the front of the car. He closed the door and held out his hand. "Robert McCune, *LA Journal.*"

"Ben Everly, avionics engineer," the big man boomed back. "Welcome to North Vandenberg." He released McCune's hand and glanced at Parkinson with a crooked smile. Parkinson scowled and turned away.

McCune eyed them for a moment, then looked at the blockhouse, grown overwhelming at this distance. From where he stood he could see an American flag painted on the side. Everly followed his gaze. "Impressive in a miserable sort of way. Makes you wonder what Baikonur looks like these days." He saw McCune frown and said, "Baikonur, the Russian . . . well, forget it, it's not important."

Tearing his eyes away, McCune turned back to him. "These spheres you just mentioned. What are they like? Glowing? Making noises?"

Crossing his arms, Everly leaned back against the car, which settled alarmingly under his weight. "No, sir, nothing like that. Black. Blacker than anything you've ever heard of. No lights, no sound, no emissions at all, as far as we can tell. There's supposed to be a shimmer directly underneath from close up, but I've never seen it. They show up once a month, sometimes more often. We think they're unmanned." He smiled through his beard. "Or whatever."

"Who's 'we'?"

"Bunch of people trying to salvage what they can. People who remember."

McCune was about to ask him what it was they remembered when Parkinson spoke. "Look, we haven't got much daylight left, and there's a lot to look at. We ought to get started."

Everly nodded and pushed himself away from the truck. "Don's right. There's too much to see here in one day and we haven't even got that." He hitched up his pants and walked over to Parkinson. "Well, what do you think? Where do we hit first?"

Parkinson pointed to the concrete structure. "Slick-6."

The big man ran his fingers through his beard. "That's a hell of a lot to take in at once. Let's build up to it, show him the Titan first."

"Fine by me," said Parkinson. "Just as long as he gets a look at the orbiter."

"Oh, he will," Everly said. He walked with bulky grace toward the Blazer. "I'll take the truck and you follow me."

They drove about five miles north, through the shadow of the blockhouse that stretched for hundreds of yards across the sands. Again McCune was unable to tear his eyes away and kept staring at the thing as they drove past. The size of the towers, now that he was down among them, was bad enough, but this, this thing was something else. He could not imagine what it was for. The other side of it was hollow, and a tower similar to the others but much larger stood a short distance away, attached to it by a sort of track. Inside he caught a glimpse of a white shape before the glare of the sun forced him to turn his eyes back to the road. Ahead was one of the towers, standing near the low hills that ringed the base. Even from this distance he could see that it differed from the others. A long, low object lay behind it, bending upward so that one end rested on the platform below the tower. He looked away, taking in the rest of the base, nearly shivering as he did so. Incomprehensible as most of it was, the place had an air of bleakness, of total desolation that he could barely stand. He glanced at Parkinson, wondering if he felt the same. "What's this Titan he was talking about?"

Parkinson nodded at the tower ahead. "Titan 34D7. Standard military lifter."

McCune turned back to the road. "Uh-huh. Standard military lifter. I should have known."

Parkinson stared blankly out the windshield, resting his chin on his hand. "You'll see."

Neither of them spoke again before reaching the tower. Everly had pulled up near the metal object behind it and was surveying the thing, his hands on his hips. He turned as they approached. "Well, here we are. A Titan, or most of one, anyway." He and Parkinson walked up to it, McCune following reluctantly.

It was in three parts, sheet-metal tubes about ten feet in diameter and ninety feet long, each attached on one side to another. The ends of the two on the outside were rounded off to blunt cones, while the one in the middle was flat and open. They had broken a little more than halfway down, and the other ends, hidden from McCune, leaned against the platform and jutted toward the sky. The tubes were badly damaged, with sheets of metal cracked, torn, and curling from the sides. McCune could see that it had fallen from the platform, where it had rested with the cones pointing upward. Looking at the tower he could see where it, too, had suffered, with struts and beams bent and left hanging by the fall of the thing.

Everly had stopped at the side of it and was patting the metal affectionately when McCune reached him. There was writing on the metal: numbers, symbols, and strange words. "What is it?"

"It's a rocket," said Everly, taking a few steps back. "Two-stage, two solid boosters, nearly three million pounds thrust at liftoff." He pushed back the

THE GATES OF BABEL

baseball cap. "Came down in that big storm spring of last year. We thought it was secure enough, but we were wrong." There was a windblown piece of chaparral stuck in a curled sheet of metal, and Everly kicked it away. "Wasn't fueled, of course, except for the boosters. If it had been, people would have noticed. I was here in '86 when that one blew at Slick-4. That was something to write home about."

McCune looked back at the pointed ends. "They look like fuel tanks to me."

Parkinson, who had been watching him intently, snickered and turned away. "Fuel tanks, my God . . ."

"Wait a second, Don," said Everly. "He's not wrong. They are fuel tanks, except for the engines." He began to walk the length of the tubes toward the tower. "We may as well take a look at those now."

Parkinson glared at McCune and followed, muttering. After a few seconds McCune set out after them, keeping well away from the side of the tubes.

They had already climbed the metal stairs to the platform when he reached the base of—what had Parkinson called it—the gantry. He hesitated, staring up at them before mounting the steps himself. When he reached the top, a brisk wind was coming in off the Pacific, bringing with it the salt smell of the sea. He had left his jacket in the car, and he shivered in the cool breeze. The two of them stood near the center of the platform, gesturing at the tubes twenty feet overhead. McCune looked up and studied them. Like the center tube at the far end, they were flat but set with flaring nozzles that gaped at the sky. The middle nozzle was relatively small, only a few feet in diameter, but the outlying two were enormous: He could have walked into them without bending over. He shivered again and looked down at the two men standing underneath them. Everly had noticed him standing at the railing and he led Parkinson over. "Well," he said as they drew nearer, "I guess they're not fuel tanks."

"Yep," Everly said as he rested his bulk against the railing. "It's true they are not."

"They look like jet engines."

"Close," said Everly, "real close. They operate roughly the same as jets." He gestured at the tubes, buckled and torn by the edge of the platform. "Fuel and oxidizer flow from the tanks into a chamber just behind the nozzles and they ignite and the exhaust pushes this sucker"—he thrust his palm into the air—"straight up."

McCune bit his lip, looking again at the nozzles, then back at Everly. "Okay, granted. Obviously a lot of hard work went into these things and that may be what they're for. But why would anybody want to do such a thing?"

"You took a course in physics in college, am I right?" McCune nodded, wondering how he knew. "Well, remember your Newton. You push an object hard enough and fast enough, it doesn't come down. It goes into a circular path around the planet, an orbit."

McCune thought for a minute before speaking. "But . . . that'd be fifteen or twenty thousand miles an hour."

"Sure," Everly said. He pointed at the nozzles above them. "You think those couldn't do it?"

He looked up and tried to picture flames shooting out of the tubes but felt a shiver of unease and dropped his eyes. "But what good would that do? Something floating around out there?"

It seemed Parkinson had been awaiting his moment. He leaned forward eagerly. "Satellites. From orbit you can see anything. Reconnaissance, meteorology, communications, astronomy . . ." His voice fell. "Space stations . . ." He took a step back, his mouth twisted. "This doesn't mean a damn thing to you, does it? Just words." He looked desperately at Everly. "We're not getting through to him." Everly remained silent, and Parkinson, shaking his head, pushed past him to the stairs. McCune leaned over the railing and watched Parkinson descend. "What the hell is his problem?"

The big man leaned back on the railing with his arms crossed and his lips pursed. A few seconds passed before he answered. "Don," he said slowly, "is going through something the rest of us have left far behind. He's an astrophysicist from back East with no direct connection to the program, although he was working on a project for the space telescope—but that's Greek to you anyway. He's only been out here for two months and still has to get his feet on the ground."

"All well and good; I did him a favor coming out here."

"I know," Everly said, stepping away from the railing. "I appreciate it. Believe me, most people wouldn't have gotten this far." He turned and looked out over the base. "This beginning to mean anything to you?" he asked, sweeping an arm across the vista.

"I can't really say. I don't know if it means anything concrete, but I'm getting a weird feeling from it all."

Everly nodded. "As if you've forgotten a word, and it seems ready to pop out of your mind, but you can't quite grasp it."

"Right. But a lot stranger than that."

"How so?"

McCune looked the big man in the eyes. "I'm scared," he said. "Really scared."

He pointed at the tubes looming up against the sky. "I tried to picture that thing working, and I couldn't make myself do it. And the rest of the place." He gripped the top of a railing. "The towers, that block over there." He shivered in a gust of wind. "It frightens me, and I don't know why."

Everly nodded and walked to the top of the stairs. "I think I understand." After a moment McCune let go of the railing and followed. The two of them silently descended the metal steps and walked over to the cars. Parkinson was leaning on the front of the truck, looking out to sea, ignoring their approach. When they were a few yards away, McCune stopped and Everly turned to him, his eyebrows raised. "Those satellites he was talking about, those are real?"

"Sure. There's one of them not five minutes from here."

"Here? Now?"

Everly laughed. "Yeah. Want to see it?"

"Well . . ." McCune thought for a minute. "Why not?"

"Okay. It's in a hangar a couple miles down the road."

Parkinson didn't ride with him this time, instead getting into the truck with Everly. The wind had grown colder, and McCune put his jacket on before starting the engine. Out to sea, the sun nearly touched the horizon as he followed the truck down the long, bare road to the white hangar near the shore.

Everly stopped in front of it but stayed inside talking to Parkinson while McCune waited. This close to the water the smell of the sea was overwhelming, the salt odor overlaid with the iodine of rotting kelp and the smell of dead things.

The gulls wheeled across the sky, calling to each other, silhouetted by the setting sun. Finally Everly emerged from the Blazer, flashlight in hand, followed by Parkinson. "We'll need this," he said, waving the flash, a big utility model, at McCune. "They cut the damn power off and it'll be dark in there." They walked to the sliding door of the hangar, which had been left open a few feet.

Everly flicked on the flashlight as they entered, pointing it at an object resting on a wheeled pallet at the center of the concrete floor. It was the same diameter as the tubes—the rocket—that they had just seen but was much shorter, about forty feet overall. The shape was different as well, lacking the smooth aerodynamic simplicity of the Titan. The bulk of it was an irregular polygon, set with circular hatches flush against the surface. From the rear end protruded a rectangle with a number of metal plates, antennas, and boxes poking from it. The other end was covered, umbrella-like, by a folded panel of shiny metal. There was nothing startling or extraordinary about it—it looked like any machine—but McCune felt the same sense of discomfort, of foreboding, that had touched him back at the gantry.

"KH-14," said Everly. "*KH* stands for *Keyhole*. It's a long-duration recon satellite, a modification of the KH-12 that went up on the shuttle. Never was a 13. We figured we'd had enough bad luck." He walked toward the machine, the circle of the flashlight beam shrinking against the side of it. "It was supposed to go up on that bird we just saw, on the twentieth." He paused for a moment, staring at the thing. "Mice and men."

Oppressed by the place's darkness, McCune whispered, "What does it do?"

Apparently this was Parkinson's forte. He walked to the machine and began rattling off a string of terms that made no sense: *pixels, multispectral scanners, digital filters*. Everly must have seen him shaking his head. "Cameras," he said quietly. "Fancy cameras." McCune made no response. His gaze was drawn to the shadows dancing around the hangar as the flashlight beam followed Parkinson. He kept seeing that block of concrete and steel in the growing darkness outside, the tomb of a devil or a god. The smell of the sea had penetrated the hangar, underlining the sense of bleakness while the cries of the gulls mocked it all. After a few minutes he said, "I've heard enough," and walked stiffly outside. Behind him he heard Parkinson's voice raised in anger but could make out no words.

The sun had vanished, leaving the western sky awash with red and yellow that faded as he watched. He sat down on the hood of the car, breathing deeply, trying to understand what he felt. The wind from the sea was much colder than it had any right to be. Everly and Parkinson walked out of the hangar, the big man shutting off the flashlight as he neared the car. He sat down next to McCune. "A little too much, eh?"

McCune nodded. He looked out at the dark shapes of the base, beginning to fall into night. A glow from the eastern hills backlit the gantries strangely. He shook his head. "I don't know," he said. "This place must have cost millions . . . ."

"Billions," said Everly.

"Billions, then, and nobody knows about it. It's abandoned." He looked back at the Titan pad. "That thing, that rocket, you'd see it fifty miles off when it went up, but nobody ever has." He turned to Everly. "How many of them have been . . ."

"Launched? Hundreds, worldwide."

McCune stared at the sand in front of the car. "I guess you'd better tell me how this happened."

Parkinson held his hands out, as if speaking to a child. "On August eighteenth, two years ago..." he began, but Everly cut him off. "Hold on, Don, one thing at a time." He got up and brushed off his pants. "We'll drive over to Lompoc, get a drink maybe, something to eat. It's too dark...."

"No, sir. He sees the orbiter."

"Don..."

"God damn it, Ben, that's why I brought him out here in the first place. He sees the STS. If that doesn't shake him up, nothing will."

"He's already shook up quite a bit, Don." Nonetheless, he looked questioningly at McCune, who rose from the hood of the car and said, "Okay, I'll look at your orbiter, whatever the hell that is. But first, I want you to tell me everything."

Everly shrugged. "No problem. I can do it on the way over, if you don't mind riding with me."

"Not at all," McCune said. He turned to Parkinson. "I suppose that I can trust you to drive?"

"I've driven a car," Parkinson said, and walked around to the door.

McCune got into the Blazer and sat back looking at the glow in the eastern sky. "By the way, where is this thing?"

Everly started the truck, then pointed to the blockhouse that brooded in darkness two miles away. "Slick-6."

"Well," McCune said after they had driven a few hundred yards from the hangar. Everly didn't answer and sat steering the truck with one hand, a thoughtful look on his face. "I'd like you to clear this up before we get over there," he went on. "And one other thing: I'll look at this orbiter from outside, but I'm not going in that building."

"You won't have to."

McCune relaxed and sank back into the seat. "All right, but tell me the rest of it. I'd sooner believe you than what's-his-name there." He gestured toward the lights of the car ahead of them.

"Yeah, you would at that," Everly said. "We got along pretty well last time we met, even though you were here to give me a hard time."

McCune turned and stared. "What?"

Without a word, Everly leaned over and opened the glove compartment. He took out a small cassette recorder and handed it to McCune. "Listen to it," he said.

McCune took the recorder and turned it on. Everly's voice boomed out. "...have it, Bob. You can't make polar launches from the Cape, not with Miami and the Caribbean islands in the way. Here you've got a clear shot down the

Pacific, straight to the South Pole."

There was a short pause, then another voice continued. "But isn't it true that a lot of congressmen have been criticizing the shuttle complex here since the *Challenger* disaster?"

He gasped, and his grip on the recorder tightened convulsively. He fumbled with it, punching several buttons until it shut off.

It was his voice.

He hit the eject button and the tape popped out, nearly falling to the floor of the truck. He held it close to his face to see what was written on the label, but the trembling of his hand made it impossible. He took a deep breath and looked again. *Bob McCune—Journal* and a date three years ago. He dropped it all, recorder and tape, into his lap and was shaking uncontrollably when he felt the big man's hand on his shoulder. "Easy, son."

Still shaking, McCune looked up at him. "What is this?"

The truck was stopped, sitting in the middle of the road. Ahead the lights of his car disappeared in the direction of the blockhouse. Everly bent forward, his elbows resting on the dash, his arms enveloping the steering wheel. He stared out of the windshield a moment before speaking. "You came here to do a hatchet job three years back. Your target was Slick-6. As I recall, you supported the space program but didn't like military launches. You wanted to see a working engineer, so PR sent you to me. We toured the base, same as we did today. I recorded the interview, just as I always . . . did, to avoid, ah . . . honest errors."

He looked at McCune and smiled. "You were pretty amused."

"I don't remember any of it."

The big man's eyes dulled, and he looked back at the road. "Nobody does. Two years ago, on August seventeenth, they remembered it all. *Sputnik*, Apollo, the shuttle. Glenn, Gagarin, Armstrong. They went to bed that night—at least in this country—and when they got up the next day, it was gone." He sat back, and his arms dropped to his sides. He looked very old. "I came here that morning—Christ, I'll remember it on my deathbed—it was like a dead city. Weber was in hysterics. Couldn't reach the base commander, couldn't reach the Pentagon. There were about twenty of us here that knew. Some of the others had shown up for work but were just wandering around, not knowing what they were here for." He closed his eyes as if in pain. "Some of the best men I've ever known, lobotomized. Their whole lives taken from them." He shook his head. "It took us days to get a handle on it, weeks to believe it. Some of us never have."

He sat silently for a moment before continuing. "After a couple of months we set up a network, and started getting data from the observatories—the ones that were still operating, anyway. Strange things going on in the rest of the system. Gravitational waves of incredible magnitude, point sources of laser and ionizing radiation, disturbances in the atmosphere of Jupiter . . . then, after a while, you could see them." He looked out the side window at the eastern hills, then turned back, his mouth a thin line. "We don't know where they came from, what they look like, what they're doing.

"We don't know how they did it either, a tailored virus, a field, something we can't even understand, but they wiped the idea of space travel from the mind of the race."

He put the truck in gear and started the engine. "Not all of us, of course, or I wouldn't be here. Some remember. One, two percent, tops. A hundred million worldwide, maybe. We're trying to keep it alive. Fargas at Transorbit remembers, thank God. He's got money and a launch site in Peru we can use to put up essential stuff, communications, weather. Otherwise when whatever is in orbit now runs down, the whole planet goes down the tubes." He raised a hand and waved it out the window at the base. "And we stay here. Me, Don, a few others, salvaging what we can. Scavenging. Don thought that bringing you up here would waken the dormant memories, that you'd write something about it, start an investigation. The rest of us know better." He put the truck in gear and started it rolling. "Well, how do you like that story?"

McCune realized that he was gaping at the man and turned to the windshield. His thoughts would not come together. There were images floating through his mind: something like the rocket he had seen back there leaping into the sky on a pillar of smoke and flame; a group of smiling men dressed in outlandish silvery suits holding glass-visored helmets; another suited man, wearing the helmet now, saluting the flag in a dark, barren landscape. Something that Everly had said—Apollo?—he kept seeing the moon. He searched the sky for it, but it was nowhere in sight. Of course not. It was—a new moon.

Was there such a thing? "No," he said finally. "No, that's insane. There isn't anything like that. People would know. The government. There'd be more evidence . . . ." He was beginning to babble, and he cut himself off.

Not taking his eyes off the road, Everly nodded. "Oh, there is. You can check unemployment figures for science professors, aerospace—sorry, aeronautics—engineers, and research scientists. Look at the companies, hundreds of them, that have gone out of business in the last few years, particularly down your way, and check what they were involved with. And some of it is worse. The Indian Ocean weather satellite broke down a year back, just before the monsoon. A typhoon hit Bangladesh the week after and killed two million people. Their UN ambassador, Basra, was one of us. He couldn't take it. He shot himself."

"I heard about that." McCune said. "He had a breakdown. He made a crazy speech in the Assembly. They were going to send him home."

"Yeah," said Everly, smiling bitterly. "A crazy speech. All about weather satellites and what had happened to his country."

McCune shook his head. "I don't care, it's still insane. There aren't any things up there. If you think . . ."

Chuckling, Everly raised his hand. "Okay, okay, I've heard it before." They were now driving through the mass of smaller buildings that surrounded the blockhouse. Turning the last corner, he saw his car a few hundred yards away with Parkinson standing next to it. He took a step toward the truck as they pulled up, but Everly shook his head, and he turned away abruptly. McCune opened the door before they stopped moving and was getting out when the cassette clattered to the floor. He picked it up and was about to hand it to Everly when the big man spoke. "As long as you're here why not take a look? I'll light it up for you." McCune gazed up at the blockhouse and the white shape inside, barely visible with the glow of the sky behind it. He wanted to get away from there as soon as possible, but he turned back to Everly. "All right, but then I'm leaving."

Everly nodded. "Sure. No hard feelings." He shut the door and drove toward the blockhouse. McCune took a step in the direction of his car, but Parkinson was standing there, and he turned away, in the direction of the sea.

They were both nuts. They couldn't possibly believe that story. God alone knew what they were actually doing here. He'd thought Everly was normal, but no, he was just as bad. How had Parkinson ever talked him into this, anyway? Wouldn't he ever learn to say no?

He looked past the dunes at the gray ocean. The wind seemed to have increased and grown colder, and the odor it brought made him want to gag. He knew he would never again come upon the smell of the sea without feeling an echo of the fear that he felt now. He wished he had never left Los Angeles. He clasped his jacket closed and shivered. The cassette was still in his hand, so he shoved it in the jacket pocket. Then Parkinson spoke, he turned to look, and he knew.

It stood in sharp relief, lit by the spotlight on Everly's truck. It was gigantic, gleaming white in the harsh glare, the stubby wings, the wide body, the single fin rising from the tail. A picture rose in his mind of this thing roaring into the night in a burst of fire that lit up the sky, a vision of power and glory, fearsome beyond dreams. Moaning, he drove the image away and stumbled toward the car. Parkinson stood in front of it, blocking his way. McCune stopped and stared at him. "It's an airplane," he said through clenched teeth. Parkinson frowned.

"It's an airplane," McCune shouted. "You brought me here to see an airplane!" He tried to push past, but Parkinson grabbed his arm and held him there, smiling fixedly. "So it's an airplane. What about the rest?"

"Do you think I'm crazy?" He flung an arm toward the sky. "Something coming down from those lights up there?"

Parkinson yanked McCune closer, nearly pulling him off his feet. "Those lights up there."

Chin trembling, McCune looked away. "The stars," he said, his voice a croak.

"Right," said Parkinson, shaking him. "But what are they?"

McCune looked up at them, the cold dots in the sky, nearly washed out by the glare from behind the blockhouse. His eyes returned to Parkinson's grinning face. "They're lights up there."

Parkinson gave a wordless cry of disgust and pulled him to the car, shoving him inside and across the passenger seat. He sat behind the wheel and started the engine. The gears screamed in protest as he swung around and drove off to the shore. McCune huddled against the door, staring at him. In a moment they were out of the shadow of the buildings, into the full glare of the light from the east. Parkinson drove to the top of a small hill, stopped the car, and got out. McCune nearly fell to the ground when the door was yanked open but was caught and dragged out past the front of the car. Parkinson let him go and pointed to the eastern sky. "What about that?" he shouted. "Is that just a light up there?"

McCune had no words for what was rising above the horizon. It was two hand spans wide and half that high, and bright enough to make him squint. It seemed shapeless at first glance, with bright wings of shining matter reaching out in all directions, but there were hints of an inner structure impossible to make out past the sharp, actinic flashes that came every few seconds from its center. The white edges changed as he watched, turning to deep crimson and then to purple that spread out and faded into darkness. Around it points of light moved in elaborate patterns, sometimes disappearing into the thing itself while others emerged to join in the dance. "It's been growing out there for a year and a half," Parkinson bellowed. "The asteroids are gone, along with most of Jupiter. It doesn't rotate, doesn't revolve, doesn't move at all. I've seen Mars rise in front of it and it's just a spot, a particle. Do you know what that means?"

McCune whimpered, shook his head, and turned back to the car. He struck out blindly when Parkinson tried to stop him, hitting him in the face. The door was open when he reached it, and he collapsed inside. He shut it and pushed down the lock, then realized the window was open and fumbled with the switch, but nothing happened. He sat back in the seat shaking, than looked up to see Parkinson approaching the front of the car, his face wet, his teeth clenched in fury. He nearly screamed when a bright light touched Parkinson's face before he became aware of the truck pulling up next to him.

It stopped a few feet away, and the big man leaned out the side window. "Now you know, Donny," he said in a quiet voice. "You can't get through to them. Sometimes it's panic, sometimes contempt, sometimes confusion, but it always ends the same way. They've lost it, and they can't get it back."

He looked over at McCune and seemed about to go on but instead just dropped his eyes and looked away.

McCune waited no longer. He reached for the keys and tried to start the car, but the engine died, and for a moment he was convinced that they had done something to it to keep him there. He thought of running, anything to get away from that place, and was about to bolt out the door when the engine caught and the car shot forward, nearly hitting Parkinson. He did not look back.

Breathing heavily, Parkinson watched the taillights recede. He looked up at the eastern sky, his expression unreadable, then turned to Everly. "It's over," he said.

The big man shook his head. "No, it's not over, not yet anyway." He fell silent, looking out over the dark sea as if there were something out there that he wanted but did not quite know how to obtain. "There's still us, few as we are. It'll be a hard road, no question, but I promise you this: Someday we'll go out there and ask them who the hell they think they are."

Parkinson rubbed his face, nodded, then walked head down back to the truck. "I guess I've made a fool of myself," he said as he got in.

"No, you didn't," the big man replied. "It's something we all go through." He looked back at the base, the towers and buildings nearly lost against the black of the sea. "Rite of passage," he said softly, then swung around and started the truck toward the gate.

As they went up the ramp to 101 they passed McCune parked at the side of the road. He was looking at a cassette he had found in his pocket, wondering how it had gotten there, and he failed to see them. But it didn't matter. They had nothing more to say to him, and after all, he didn't know them anymore.

Hoover's Men

Howard Waldrop

Howard Waldrop is the author of numerous short stories collected in *Howard Who?*, *All About Strange Monsters of the Recent Past*, and *Night of the Cooters*. He has also authored three novels, one—*The Texas-Israeli War*—a collaboration with Jake Saunders, and two solo: *Them Bones* and *A Dozen Tough Jobs*. He has won both the Nebula Award and the World Fantasy Award.

Waldrop is *the* expert on alternate histories as far as I'm concerned and has been published in *Omni* regularly since 1982. "Hoover's Men" was commissioned by me for a group of fantasy short-shorts I ran in the October 1988 issue. It is a clever look at the early days of radio broadcasting in the United States.

Hoover's Men

Howard Waldrop

On March 30, 1929, three weeks after Al Smith's presidential inauguration, four gunmetal-gray Fords were parked on a New Jersey road. On the tonneau top of each was a large silver loop antenna.

There were fifteen men in all—some inside the cars in their shirtsleeves, earphones on their heads, the others sitting on the running boards or standing in stylish poses. All those outside wore dark blue or gray suits, hats, and dark ties with small checks on them. Each had a bulge under one of his armpits.

It was dusk. On the horizon two giant aerials stood two hundred feet high, with a long wire connecting them. They were in silhouette, and here and there they blotted out one of the early stars. Back to the east lay the airglow of Greater Manhattan. Men in the cars switched on their work lights. Outside the first car Carmody uncrossed his arms, opened his pocket watch, noted the time on his clipboard. "Six fifty-two. Start your logs," he said. Word passed down the line.

He reached in through the window, picked up the extra set of headphones next to Dalmas, and listened in: "This is station MAPA coming to you from Greater New Jersey with fifty thousand mighty watts of power. Now, to continue with The Darkies' Hour for all our listeners over in Harlem is Oran 'Hot Lips' Page with his rendition of 'Blooey!' featuring Floyd 'Horsecollar' Williams on the alto saxophone...."

"Jesus," said Dalmas, looking at his dials, "the station's all over the band, blocking out everything from seven fifty to twelve forty-five. Nothin' else is getting through nowhere this side of Virginia!"

Carmody made a note on his clipboard pages.

* * *

"The engineer—that's Ma—said sorry we were off the air this afternoon for a few minutes, but we blew out one of our heptodes, and you know how danged particular they can be. She says we'll get the kinks out of our new transmitter real soon.

"Don't forget—at 7:05 tonight Madame Sosostris will be in to give the horoscopes and read the cards for all you listeners who've written her, enclosing your twenty-five-cent handling fee, in the past week. . . ."

"Start up the wire recorders," said Carmody.

"Remember to turn off your radio sets for five minutes just before seven P.M. That's four minutes from now. First, we're going up to what, Ma?—two hundred ninety thousand watts—in our continuin' effort to contact the planet Mars, then we'll be down to about three quarters of a watt with our antenna as a receiver in our brand-new effort to make friends with the souls of the departed.

"Here to end our Negro music broadcast for this evening are Louis 'Satchmo' Armstrong and Dwight 'Ike' Eisenhower with their instrumental 'Do You Know What It Means to Miss New Orleans?' Hang on; this one will really heat up your ballast tubes. . . ."

Some of the sweetest horn and clarinet music Dalmas had ever heard came out of the earphones. He swayed in time to the music. Carmody looked at him. "Jeez. You don't have to enjoy this stuff so much. We have a job to do." He checked his pocket watch again.

He turned to Mallory. "I want precise readings on everything. I want recordings from all four machines. Mr. Hoover doesn't want a judge throwing anything out on a technicality like with the KXR2Y thing. Understood?"

"Yeah, boss," said Mallory from the third car.

"Let's go, then," said Carmody.

Just then the sky lit up blue and green in a crackling halo that flickered back and forth between the aerials on the horizon.

"Yikes!" yelled Dalmas, throwing the earphones off. The sound coming out of them could be heard fifty feet away: "EARTH CALLING MARS! EARTH CALLING MARS! THIS IS STATION MAPA, MA AND PA, CALLING MARS. HOWDY TO ALL OUR MARTIAN LISTENERS. COME AND SEE US! EARTH CALLING MARS. . . ."

They burst through the locked station door. Small reception room, desk piled high with torn envelopes and stacks of quarters, a glass wall for viewing into the studio, locked power room to one side. A clock on the wall that said 7:07. There was a small speaker box and intercom on the viewer window.

An old woman was sitting at a table at a big star-webbed carbon mike with a shawl wrapped around her shoulders and a crystal ball in front of her. An old man stood nearby holding a sheaf of papers in his hand.

". . . and a listener writes, Dear Madame Sosostris—"

Carmody went to the intercom and pushed down the button. He held up his badge. "United States Government, Federal Radio Agency, Radio Police!"

They both looked up.

"Cheese it, Pa! The Feds!" said the woman, throwing off her shawl. She ran to the racks of glowing and humming pentodes on the far wall, throwing her arms wide as if to hide them from sight.

"Go arrest some bootleggers, G-man!" yelled Pa.

"Not my jurisdiction. And Prohibition ends May first. You'd know that if you were fulfilling your responsibilities to keep the public informed," said Carmody.

"See, ladies and gentlemen in radio land," yelled Pa into the microphone, "this is what happens to private enterprise in a totalitarian state! The airwaves belong to anybody! My great-uncle invented radio—he did!—Marconi stole it from him in a swindle. Government interference! Orville Wright doesn't have a pilot's license! He invented flying. My family invented radio. . . ."

". . . you are further charged with violation of nineteen sections of the Radio Act of 1929," said Carmody, continuing to read from the warrant. "First charge, operating an unlicensed station broadcasting on the AM band, a public resource. Second, interfering with the broadcasts of licensed operations—"

"See, Mr. and Mrs. Radio Listener, what putting one man in charge of broadcasting does! Ma! Crank it back up all the way!" Ma twisted some knobs.

The sky outside the radio station turned blue and green again. Carmody's hair stood up, pushing his hat off his head. His arms tingled.

"SOS!" yelled Pa. "SOS! Help! This is station MAPA. Get your guns! Meet us at the station! Show these fascists we won't put up with—"

"We'll add sending a false distress call over the airwaves, incitement to riot, and breach of the peace," said Carmody, penciling in his notes. "Having astrologers, clairvoyants, and mediums in contravention of the Radio Act of 1929. . ."

The first of the axes went through the studio door.

". . . use of the airwaves for a lottery." Carmody looked up. "Give yourselves up," he said. He watched while Ma and Pa ran around inside the control room, piling the meager furniture against the battered door. "Very well. Resisting arrest by duly authorized federal agents. Unlawful variation in broadcast power—"

"Squeak! Squeak! Help!" said Pa. Dalmas had bludgeoned his way into the shrieking power room and threw all the breaker switches.

Ma and Pa turned into frantic blurs as all the needles dropped to zero. The sky outside went New Jersey dark, and Carmody's hair lay back down.

"Good," he said, still reading into the intercom. "Advertising prohibited articles and products over the public airwaves. Broadcast of obscene and suggestive material. Use of . . ."

The door gave up.

"Book em, Dalmas," he said.

"Two minutes, Mr. Hoover," said the floor manager. He waved his arms. In a soundproof room an engineer put his foot on a generator motor and yanked on the starter cord. Then he adjusted some knobs and gave an okay signal with a circled thumb and finger.

Hoover sat down at the bank of microphones in front of him. A four- by eight-foot panel of photosensitive cells lowered into place in front of him. In a cutout portion in its center was a disc punched with holes. As the panel came down, the disc began to spin faster and faster. The studio lights came up to blinding intensity. Hoover blinked, shielded his eyes.

Carmody and Mallory stood in the control room behind the engineers, the director, and the station manager. Before them on the bank of knobs and lights was a two- by three-inch flickering screen filled with lines in which Mallory could barely make out Mr. Hoover. Carmody and the other chiefs had turned in their reports to Hoover an hour before.

"I never thought he'd take this job," said an engineer.

"Aw, Hoover's a public servant," said the director.

The STAND BY sign went off. Hoover arranged his papers.

ON THE AIR blazed in big red letters over the control booth. The announcer at his mikes at the side table said, "Good evening, ladies and gentlemen. This is Station WRNY, and it's eleven P.M. in New York City. Tonight, live via coast-to-coast hookup on all radio networks, the Canadian Broadcasting System, and through the television facilities of WIXA2 New York and W2JA4 Washington, DC, we present a broadcast from the head of the new Federal Radio Agency concerning the future of the airwaves. Ladies and gentlemen of the United States and Canada, Mr. Hoover."

The graying, curly-haired gentleman looked into the whirling Nipkow disc with the new Sanabria interlaced pattern and pushed one of the microphones a little farther from him.

"I come to you tonight as the new head of the Federal Radio Agency. After the recent elections, in which I lost the presidency to Mr. Alfred Smith, I assumed that after eight years as your secretary of commerce under the last two administrations I would be asked to leave government service.

"Imagine my delight and surprise when Mr. Smith asked me to stay on, but in the new position of head of the Federal Radio Agency. If I may quote the President, 'Who knows more about *raddio* than you do, Herbert? It's all in a *turrible* mess, and I'd like you to straighten it out, once and for all.'"

"Well, tonight, I'm taking your President's words to heart. As chief enforcement officer under the new and valuable Radio Act of 1929, I'm announcing the following: Today my agents closed down fourteen radio stations. Nine were violating the total letter of the law; five were, after repeated warnings, still violating its spirit. Tomorrow, six more will be closed down. This will end the most flagrant of our current airwave problems.

"As to the future"—Hoover pushed back a gray wisp of hair that had fallen over his forehead—"tomorrow I will begin meetings with representatives of the Republic of Mexico and see what can be done about establishing frequencies for their use. They were summarily ignored when Canada and the United States divided the airwaves in 1924."

The station manager leaned forward intently.

"If this means another division and realignment of the frequencies of existing stations, so be it," said Hoover.

The station manager slapped his hand against his forehead and shook his head from side to side.

"Furthermore," said Hoover, "under powers given to me, I am ready to issue commercial radiovision/radio movie/television licenses to any applicant who will conform to the seventy-line, thirty-frame format for monochrome . . . ."

"He's gone meshuga!" said the engineer. "*Nobody* uses that format!"

"Quiet," said Carmody. "Mr. Hoover's talking."

". . . or the one-hundred-forty-line, sixty-frame format for color transmission and reception, with the visual portion on the shortwaves and the audio portion on the newly opened frequency-modulated bandwidths."

"Aaiiii!!" yelled the station manager, running out of the booth toward the desk phone in the next office.

"He's *crazy!* Everybody's got a different system!" said the director.

"No doubt Mr. Hoover's in for some heat," said Mallory.

"To those who say radio-television is too primitive and experimental to allow regular commercial broadcasting, I say, *you're* the ones holding up progress. The time for review is *after* new and better methods are developed, not before. This or that rival concern have been for years trying to persuade the government to adopt *their* particular formats and methods." He looked into the whirling lights, put down his papers. "I will say to the people of those concerns: Here is your format, like it or lump it."

Then he smiled. "For a wholesome and progressive future in America, dedicated to better broadcasting for the public good, this is the head of your nation's Federal Radio Agency, Herbert Hoover, saying goodnight. Goodnight."

The STAND BY sign came back on. The blinding light went down, and the disc slowed and stopped, then the whole assembly was pulled back into the ceiling.

In the outer office the station manager was crying.

Mr. Hoover was still shaking hands when Carmody and Mallory left.

Early tomorrow they had to take off for upstate New York. There was a radio station there with an experimental-only license that was doing regular commercial broadcasts. It would be a quiet shutdown, not at all like this evening's.

As they walked to the radio car, two cabs and a limo swerved up to the curbing, missing them and each other by inches. Doors swung open, David Sarnoff jumped out of the NBC Studebaker limo. He was in evening clothes. The head of CBS was white as a sheet as he piled out of the cab, throwing money behind him. One of the vice presidents of the Mutual System got to the door before they did. There was almost a fistfight.

There was a sound in the air like that of a small fan on a nice spring day. Overhead the airship *Ticonderoga* was getting a late start on its three-day journey to Los Angeles.

Mallory pulled away from the curb, heading back to the hotel where Dalmas and the other agents were already asleep. He reached forward to the dashboard, twisted a knob. A glowing yellow light came on.

"Jeez, I'm beat," said Carmody. "See if you can't get something decent on that thing, okay?"

Nine years later, after his second heart attack and retirement, Carmody was in his apartment. He was watching his favorite program, *The Clark Gable-Carole Lombard Show* on his brand-new Philco console color television set with the big nine- by twelve-inch screen.

He punched open the top of a Rheingold with a church key, foam running over onto his favorite chair.

"Damn!" he said, holding the beer up and sucking away the froth. He leaned back. He now weighed two hundred seventy pounds.

Gable was unshaven; he'd apologized at the show's opening; he'd come over from the set where they were filming Margaret Mitchell's *Mules in Horse's Harnesses* to do the live show. They'd just started a sketch with Lombard carrying a bunch of boxes marked ANACONDA HAT COMPANY, asking Gable for directions to some street.

Then the screen went blank. "Shit!" said Carmody, draining his beer.

"Ladies and gentlemen," said an announcer, "we interrupt our regularly scheduled program to bring you a news bulletin via transatlantic cable. Please stand by."

A card with the message NEWS BULLITIN. ONE MOMENT PLEASE. came up onscreen. Then there was a hum, and a voice said "Okay!"

A face came on-screen, a reporter in a trench coat stepped back from the camera holding a big mike in one hand.

"This morning, three A.M. Berlin time, the prime minister of Great Britain and the chancellor of Germany seemed to have reached an accord on the present crisis involving Germany's demands in Austria." Past his shoulder there was movement, flashbulbs went off like lightning. "Here they come," said the newsman, turning. The camera followed him, picking up other television crews with their big new RCA/UFA all-electronic cameras the size of doghouses trundling in for the same shot.

On-screen SA and SS men in their shiny coats and uniforms pushed the reporters back and took up positions, machine guns at the ready, around the chancellery steps.

Atop the steps the prime minister and the führer, followed by generals, aides, and diplomats of both countries, stepped up to a massed bank of microphones.

"Tonight," said the prime minister of Great Britain, "I have been reassured, again and again, by the chancellor that the document we have signed"—he held up a white piece of paper for the cameras, and more flashbulbs went off, causing him to blink—"will be the last territorial demand of the German nation. This paper assures us of peace in our time."

Applause broke out from the massed NSDAP crowds with their banners, standards, and pikes. The camera slowly focused into a closeup view—while the crowd chanted *Sieg heil! Sieg heil!*—of Herr Hitler's beaming face.

"Bastid!" yelled Carmody and sent the empty beer can ricocheting off the console cabinet.

A few minutes later, after the network assured viewers it would cover live any further late-breaking news from Berlin, they went back to the show.

There were lots of wrecked hats on the street set, and Gable was jumping up and down on one.

Lombard broke up about something, turned away from him, laughing. Then she turned back, eyes bright, back in character.

"Jeez, that Gable . . ." said Carmody. "What a lucky bastid!"

Phase Change

Joyce Carol Oates

In addition to being a respected novelist, short-story writer, playwright, poet, and essayist, Joyce Carol Oates is the Roger S. Berlind Distinguished Professor in the Humanities at Princeton University. She is the author of more than 20 novels, one of which won the National Book Award. Her most recent novel is *Foxfire: Confessions of a Girl Gang* (Dutton), and her newest collection, *Haunted: Tales of the Grotesque* (Dutton) will be published in early 1994. While Oates is best known for her work in the literary mainstream, at least two of her collections, *Night-Side* and the aforementioned upcoming one (which reprints several stories first published in *Omni*), are firmly entrenched in the fantastique and the grotesque.

"Thanksgiving," just published in *Omni*'s November 1993 issue, takes place in a strangely altered America. "Phase Change" takes place in a more immediately recognizable world, but most definitely crosses over into the realm of science-fictional dreams and nightmares as its troubled protagonist manipulates her own reality and that of those around her.

Phase Change

Joyce Carol Oates

Who is it? Did he follow me in here, or was he waiting just inside the door? Julia Matterling sensed rather than saw the man watching her. She had not yet looked at him, had not confronted him. He stood motionless to her extreme left (against a wall?), at the very periphery of her vision; it seemed that he exerted a palpable gravitational tug. Julia was alert rather than alarmed, or even apprehensive, for, in this public place, she was certainly in no danger—in the County Clerk's office in the basement of the Broome County Courthouse, on a busy weekday afternoon. She had come to get her and her husband's updated passports and was now about to leave, having given a check to the woman behind the counter and having slipped the passports and the receipt into her handbag. Turning, with a studied casualness, Julia glanced at the man she believed had been watching her—seeing, to her surprise, that he was in uniform!—he was one of the numerous sheriff's deputies stationed at intervals in the courthouse. And, with an unsettling bluntness, he *was* watching her.

Do I know him?—impossible. Does he know me?

A swarthy-skinned man in his mid-thirties, with deep-set derisive eyes, lank graying-brown hair, an ironic mouth. He had a coarse, country-boy attractiveness, but had grown thick-bodied, beefy. His gunmetal-gray uniform with blue trim fitted him snugly at the torso; Julia could see, or believed she could see, the bulge of his shiny black leather holster and the grip of his revolver, above his left thigh. He was a stranger, and could not possibly know Julia Matterling or her husband Norman, yet, rudely, he continued to stare at her as if they were acquainted.

No. Stop. I don't know you.

Their eyes met, and held for several seconds. Then confused, blushing,

Julia looked pointedly away, and walked quickly out of the Clerk's office. She wondered at the womanly instinct to feel guilt for arousing male interest—as if there would be any reasonable grounds for *her* complicity.

What a dreary place, the Broome County Courthouse. Julia was eager to be gone, but hesitated between taking the stairs back up to the first floor, or the elevator. She had taken the stairs down, but the stairway was grimy and dim lit, not very pleasant. (She had recently learned that a friend from college, a woman executive at CBS, had been raped and badly beaten in a stairwell in some presumably safe building in New York City. What horror!) The elevator was a safer prospect, Julia thought, so she punched the *up* button, and waited.

Is he watching?—following me?—no.

She glanced covertly over her shoulder, but saw only an elderly black woman and a boy entering the County Clerk's office. The sheriff's deputy was nowhere in sight. *My imagination! Ridiculous.* For Julia Matterling was not a young woman—she was thirty-seven years old. Even as a girl, in the prime of her small-boned, dark-eyed prettiness, she had not been one to feel eyes drawn irresistibly to her as she entered a room or walked down a street; nor had she wanted such attention. For what in fact does such abstract male interest mean, does it hold a promise, or a threat?

The elevator was maddeningly slow. Like the courthouse generally, it was old, even antiquated. Julia pressed the *up* button again and waited, trying to forestall nervousness. How eager she was, like a silly, frightened child, to be gone.

The Matterlings, Julia and Norman, lived in the suburban village of Queenston, twenty miles away; like most Queenston residents, they rarely visited the grimy industrial city that was the county seat, except on unavoidable official business. Julia had not been here for years; Norman, perhaps, had never been here. He held the title of Distinguished Research Fellow at the Center for Advanced Study in the Sciences at Queenston, and when, grudgingly, he agreed to travel at all, it was usually thousands of miles, to scientific conferences in distant parts of the globe. So absorbed in his work! So preoccupied, like an overgrown child! Even when, during dinner, Norman frowned at his plate, chewing slower and slower, the man was busy, he was *working,* and Julia had learned not to interrupt.

She had a job as an assistant curator at a privately endowed art museum in Queenston, but she attended to all of the household chores and local errands, like getting her and Norman's passports updated. (Norman was scheduled to give an important paper on phase changes in the early universe, in Tokyo, next month; Julia hoped to accompany him.) She did not mind being responsible for the practical, domestic side of their lives; she had never minded. She had no children to care for, and no dependents (except Norman).

A contract between the practical and the celestial?—between the ordinary and the extraordinary?

At last the elevator arrived: the door opened, and Julia automatically stepped inside.

Seeing, too late, even as the door slid shut behind her, that there was a single other passenger in the car: *the sheriff's deputy.*

Julia stared at him, too surprised at first to be frightened. It *was* him! But how had he slipped past her, to get to another floor of the building? He was smiling at her, baring his uneven, yellowed teeth in a sniggering grimace. He shook his head, brusque as a dog, flicking a strand of greasy hair out of his eyes.

Julia whispered, "What are you—? Who are—?"

Even as he moved toward her. At her. As Julia gave a little scream and pushed at him with her handbag, the deputy took hold of her by both shoulders, shoved her back against the wall of the elevator so that she cried out in pain; pressed himself against her in a lewd, grinding manner. "No! Stop! Help!"— Julia's words were cut off as her assailant jammed the palm of his hand against her mouth.

Seen so closely, the man's skin was roughly textured, as if pitted; his eyes were damp, cruel, derisive; an oily sheen covered his face. Julia could no longer cry aloud, her protests were silent, interior, *Don't! Don't hurt me! Who are you!* as the elevator rose in drunken lurches—past the first floor—past the second— past the third—and now her assailant, laughing, panting, had pulled the skirt of Julia's beige linen suit up past her hips, crudely he'd unzipped his trousers, with no mind for how he was hurting her, slamming her back against the wall, he thrust his penis at her, between her legs, and then into her, *or was he thrusting the barrel of his revolver into her,* Julia screamed behind his hand, *No! Not me!* as a sensation of scalding water splashed over her, centered in her loins, coursing rapidly through her body, and—

Julia woke, terrified, panting. Desperate to free herself from something twisted between her legs. Bedclothes? Was she in bed?

Dazed, she groped beside her to feel a presence in the bed: dark, warm, heavy, inert: her husband, asleep. Her brutal assailant vanished.

"Thank God! Oh, thank God!" Julia whispered aloud.

What an ugly dream! how vivid, lifelike! and what shame to it!

But Norman had not been disturbed. He lay on his back, a damp hoarse rattle in his throat. Oblivious of Julia's anguish.

It must have been about four o'clock in the morning. Julia lay shivering in her sweat-soaked nightgown, stiffly, on her side of the bed, drifting in and out of a troubled sleep for the remainder of the night. She was grateful for Norman's uninterrupted sleep, which was like that of a great infant: Norman sometimes worked through the night, and slept fitfully during the day; but when he slept at night, it was this enviable sleep of oblivion, as if the very particles of his being were in dissolution, like that of the early universe which was his life's work. *He will never know.*

By the time the room lightened with dawn, Julia had forgotten most of her dream. When, examining her face in the bathroom mirror, next morning, she noticed a plum-like bruise on her throat, she had no idea what might have caused it—she'd forgotten even the struggle of her dream, her abrupt wrenching into consciousness.

Next morning, after Norman left for the Center, Julia drove to the Broome County Courthouse, as she'd planned. How odd, how uncanny... as she parked her car, approached the building, began climbing the stairs, she began to feel a curious sensation of apprehension and excitement. How familiar the old courthouse was, outside and in, how familiar its very odor, as if she'd been there only recently!—when, in fact, she had not been there for years. Julia took the elevator to the basement, hurried to the County Clerk's office, picked up her and Norman's passports, paid the fee, without incident. Yet, to her embarrassment, her hands shook visibly as she made out a check. She looked around the room—seeing only strangers, clerks behind the counter, a sheriff's deputy stationed beside the door; no one taking the slightest notice of Julia Matterling.

She knew herself as an attractive woman past the bloom of her youth; but not strikingly attractive. Norman had once believed her beautiful—telling her, shyly, clumsily, as if it were a modest truth that might be refuted with uneasy laughter on Julia's part. (It had not been. Deeply moved, willing to believe that, in Norman's inexperienced eyes, she *was* beautiful, Julia had remained silent.) This morning, wearing her tailored beige linen suit and tasteful shoes with a modest heel, pearl button-earrings in her ears, Julia would surely not have expected, nor indeed welcomed, any attention from strangers; and it seemed quite fitting that, passing through the Broome County Courthouse on her perfunctory errand, she drew no one's attention at all—as if she were invisible.

Like one of Norman's quarks. Or—is it leptons? hadrons? gluons? squarks? passing invisibly, by magic through a vacuum?

Julia noticed several sheriff's deputies in their smart gray uniforms with blue trim stationed at intervals around the building. There seemed little need for them, at the present time; but Julia supposed that, when a trial was in session, there might be the threat of sudden violence. How bored some of them looked, like museum guards! She wondered idly, a curious thought for her, whether, in their enforced lethargy, they dreamt with their eyes open.

When Julia left by the front door of the courthouse, one of the deputies, politely pushed the door open for her, murmuring, "Exit here, ma'am!"—but even he scarcely glanced at her.

Yet—how good Julia Matterling felt, her morning's errand completed, and her quick return to Queenston, and the solace of her weekday schedule before her! The sensation of dread and excitement was already beginning to lift.

What is happening to me, what change is coming over me? And why at this time?

The visit to the courthouse was on a Tuesday. Three days later, slipping into a seat at the rear of a crowded amphitheater at the Center for Advanced Study at Queenston, where a symposium on the structure of the universe was in session, Julia felt again that uncanny sensation: a dread so extreme as to be almost nausea, overlaid with a childlike excitement and yearning.

She had hurried to the Center from the art museum in which she worked, not wanting to be late for the four-thirty session; or, if late, which was seemingly unavoidable, hoping not to be conspicuous in her lateness. Norman would surely not notice—Norman was not a man to notice such trivial matters—but others, his colleagues and their wives, would see, and disapprove. Julia entered the room breathless, sat quickly, tried to collect her thoughts. *Why is my heart beating so fast? Am I going to faint?* For the fourteen years of her marriage to Norman Matterling, Julia had been attending professional sessions to hear her distinguished husband speak; surely she had no reason to feel, this afternoon, a wife's anxiety?

On a raised platform at the front of the room, a panel of five male scientists, prominent among them Norman Matterling with his silvery-blond wispy hair and his thick-lensed glasses, was discussing a problem of some urgency. Julia strained to hear: such terms as "radius of curvature," "supersymmetry," "phase change," "horizon problem," were being uttered. These were teasingly familiar to Julia: had not her husband tried to explain them to her, many times?—for we are living in a revolutionary epoch, Norman Matterling believed, and it is a pity, if not a tragedy, for anyone to be left behind.

Julia saw with pride how everyone in the amphitheater, rows and rows of men and women, leaned forward intently as the panelists debated the significance of recent laboratory experiments in which, astonishingly, the conditions of the early universe—*the universe as it was when it was a mere one ten-billionth of a second old*—had been simulated, by way of machines that accelerated two beams of protons to nearly the speed of light, then let them collide head-on; in these collisions, temperatures were raised to the probable levels of that point in time when the weak and the electromagnetic forces in the universe unified. "Therefore," Norman Matterling said in a quavering voice, "—it is possible to theorize—"

Julia winced to see that Norman was wearing the bulky, frayed, hunter-green corduroy jacket she was certain she had thrown out years ago; and that his wispy hair rose from his scalp as if charged with static electricity. Why didn't he wet it down! When Norman was in earnest, as he was now, rising clumsily from his seat to hurry to the blackboard, to scrawl a lengthy, illegible equation, he began to stammer; spittle flew from his lips; he had the look of a bear on its hind legs, gaze turned inward with the effort of keeping its balance. Yet—with what respect the other panelists turned to him! With what hushed interest the entire audience listened! Norman was promulgating a theory about an early phase change of the universe, which occurred at a time so immediately after the Big Bang as to defy comprehension by any means other than mathematical: 10^{-35} seconds. (Which was represented by a decimal point, thirty-four zeros, and then a one.) Prior to this, apparently, "quarks had frozen into hadrons."

Julia smiled uneasily. Had she known that?

A phase change was a change from one state to another, as when gas changes to liquid, liquid to solid, solid to gas, the seemingly whole into the infinitely fragmented. A phase change was not deducible but only to be experienced. A phase change was/was not irrevocable.

Norman Matterling was speaking of supersymmetrical particles forming a mirror image of the observed world; from this, one could deduce an entire shadow universe, a mirror of the universe we inhabit—"Interacting with ours," Norman said excitedly, "only through the force of gravity. So—" At this, another panelist, an astrophysicist from Caltech, rudely interrupted, and strode to the blackboard to scribble an unintelligible equation of his own.

Julia was deeply absorbed in the exchange, even as, heart pounding as if she were approaching a crisis of which she had no conscious awareness, she slipped quietly out of her seat, needing to find a lavatory.

How many times had she attended meetings and social gatherings at the Center, yet, to her frustration, she invariably had difficulty locating a women's room. (Perhaps, in this monastic place so primarily male, there were in fact few facilities for women?) And the maze of corridors, flights of stairs, glass cul-de-sacs overlooking empty Japanese gardens—what did it remind her of but the phenomenon of the rapidly expanding universe? *Faintness means farness. And madness.*

But Julia was not thinking of such things. Gripping her handbag so tightly her knuckles turned white, she was thinking only of the weakness in her bowels.

And then—what relief! She found a women's lavatory just around a corner from the Center's kitchen facilities.

She used a toilet; then stood at a sink splashing cold water onto her face. At an adjacent sink stood a plump, plain-faced woman with gray hair wrapped in braids around her head, washing her hands vigorously. Julia said, with forced vivacity, wiping her face, "I wish I could understand them, don't you? I know they hold the secrets to the universe—the *real* universe, not *ours*. Actually, I got A's in high school physics and calculus, I'm not an ignorant person, but I can't remember anything I've ever learned, and it's getting worse. Dozens of times I've been told what a 'quark' is, what a 'black hole' is, what 'omega' means— but I never remember, I never *know*. Sometimes I just wish it would all go away! Just—*vanish!*" Julia laughed, expecting the woman to join in; but the woman merely stared at her coldly, wiped her hands on a towel, and left the room. Julia realized belatedly, to her extreme embarrassment, that the woman was none other than Elsa Heisenberg, a relative of the great Werner Heisenberg, and a renowned astronomer at Palomar Observatory.

Julia caught her own blurry gaze in the mirror above the sink. "Aren't you a fool, mistaking *her* for *you!*"

She did not want to miss any more of the symposium, but, in her haste to return to the amphitheater, apparently she took a wrong turn, and lost her way. She found herself wandering in an airless, overheated corridor smelling of cooking odors; turned a corner, and found herself at the rear of the Center's kitchen area, where several workers, husky young black men in white uniforms, were lounging around a table, smoking cigarettes. (Marijuana? Hashish? Julia's nostrils pinched at the sweet, acrid, piercing odor.) As soon as the black men saw Julia their eyes opened wide, and their postures stiffened perceptibly.

Shyly Julia said, "Excuse me, but I—I seem to be lost. How do I get back to the amphitheater?"

The men continued to stare at her, as if they had never seen anyone quite like her. They were now standing, as if at attention. The youngest, a lanky brown-skinned youth with a bizarre flattop haircut and woolly hair shaved and sculpted around the base of his head, giggled shrilly and hid his cigarette behind his back. Another, squat and thick-necked, with a broad, brutal, purplish-black-skinned face and lips that looked swollen, grinned at Julia suggestively.

Do they know me? Do I know them?

Were they waiting for me, at this juncture of time and space and contingency?

PHASE CHANGE

There were four black men, in dazzling-white waiter's uniforms. White teeth, white smiles. Gold fillings glittering amid those smiles. Several gold earrings in the left ear of the youngest... if these constituted a code, what did the code mean? Julia saw that the men were exchanging glances; easing slyly forward. One, surely no less than six feet seven inches tall, with a glaring ebony-black skin, had sidestepped adroitly to the right, blocking Julia's path should she try to flee.

Julia gripped her handbag tight in both hands. She stood tall and with as much authority as she could summon. Very frightened, faintness washing over her, but she tried to speak calmly, reasonably. "I—I seem to have taken a wrong turn. Can you help me, please? Which way is—" she paused, wondering if these uncouth men would know what the word "amphitheater" meant, "—the foyer? The front of the building?" The men's eyes widened yet further, and glittered with mirth. Their lips twitched. "I'm attending the symposium on the structure of the universe, in fact my husband is one of the participants, so I don't want to miss a word. The secrets of the universe are being revealed! Mankind's conception of the heavens is being revolutionized totally! So, if you could help me, please—" Julia was backing away, even as the black men were advancing upon her; springy and lithe on their feet as great supple black predator cats.

Suddenly panicked, Julia turned to run; turned her ankle, and nearly fell; her handbag went flying. The youngest black man caught her, his fingers strong as steel, long enough to encircle her rib cage. "No! Please! Let me go! Oh, please!" she begged. "I've never been a prejudiced woman, I swear! I know that Queenston is a—a white enclave—but I don't share in the—prejudices of my neighbors! I am the wife of—" The young black man squealed with laughter, shoving Julia roughly at one of his friends, who caught her by the upper arm, and shut his fist in her hair, and gave her head a cruel shake. Julia drew breath to scream, but could not. She was groveling, panting, whispering, "*I am the wife of*—"

But her mind had gone blank. She could not remember her husband's name, nor even her own.

I am not here, then, am I? Or, if here—who?

Julia Matterling struggled courageously with her assailants, even as, cruelly outnumbered and overpowered as she was, so petite and terrified a woman, she must have known it was hopeless to resist. She could not scream except inwardly, silently—*No! no! please! Don't you know who I am?* Disgusting rude lips mashed against hers, a slap to the side of her head made her ears ring. The men towered over her, laughing shrilly, exuding a smell of primal male sweat—horrible! Julia was being shoved this way, and that; passed from man to another as if this were a game, and she a living basketball or football—no matter how she wept, thrashed from side to side, pleaded, *No! don't! have mercy!*

But the black men in their dazzling-white waiters' uniforms had no mercy for Julia Matterling.

In the very building in which her distinguished husband was speaking on the subject of the structure of the universe, its probable origin and its probable end, Julia Matterling was being dragged into the steamy interior of a kitchen; her wrists gripped tight, as by steel manacles; the nape of her neck gripped, too; she was flung like a carcass over a table, as, with prudent dexterity, black hands quickly shoved aside trays of fruit cup and dinner salads (for a banquet for the two hundred participants of the symposium was shortly to begin); now nearly hysterical crying, *Help! no! please!* as the skirt of her navy-blue serge suit was yanked up, her panties dragged down, fingers poked her private parts and Julia blinked dazed at the floor seeing blood dripping from her nose onto the linoleum tile, and had one of her teeth come loose?—*No! no! have mercy! oh, please!* but there was no mercy for Julia Matterling, their hands on her now-naked squirming body pinning her fast to the table, one of them straddling her, hot and harsh and pitiless as a jackhammer.

Now Julia Matterling did draw breath to scream, and screamed and screamed.

And woke, another time, in her bed, in the dark, amid tangled sweat-smelling bedclothes.

I am not here, then, am I? Or, if here—who?

How shameful. Unspeakable.

Julia was revulsed by the dream—so vivid, *had* it been a dream?—and did her best to forget. Yet, the following day, and the following, even as details rapidly faded, the horror stayed with her—as if, somehow, it continued to exist in some other dimension of the universe.

Of course Julia was determined to hide her agitation from Norman, who would have been confused and upset, if he knew. *Can one inhabit madness, yet not be mad?* Julia wondered if madness might pass through a human being, like those subatomic particles whose name she could never quite recall, neurons? neutrinos?—passing through solid matter, bearing chaos, yet causing not so much as a ripple on the surface of the observed would.

He will never know. Will he?

PHASE CHANGE

* * *

Julia could not remember the details, nor the very outline, of her dream (except to know. that it had taken place at the Center, of all unlikely settings for a nightmare); but she understood guiltily, with a sense of womanly shame that, another time, she had had a lethal effect upon a man. Or men.

Touching her, a man, or men, *vanished*.

She smiled. No, she was not smiling—she was concerned. Disturbed.

Am I a "fatal" woman, then? Without my knowing?

She knew it was all absurd; sheerly fantasy; yet, days passed, and nights, and she dreaded sleep, dreaded its power over her. Norman noticed nothing—fortunately! Julia was fiercely protective of him, the way a mother might be with a gifted child obscurely handicapped, disabled. *He will never know. Must never.* When Julia kissed him, in greeting, or as he was about to leave the house, he frequently smiled at her startled and pleased, and hugged her, indeed like a child: "Dear Julia. I love you," he would murmur.

Julia was equally determined to keep *whatever the horror was, of which she must not think* separate from her work at the Queenston Art Museum. For she was a professional woman, after all wasn't she?

Yet it happened, to Julia's dismay, that she began to feel, even in the museum, that sense of anticipation and dread she'd felt elsewhere; even in the sanctuary of her office. *What is happening to me? What is this change coming upon me?* Suddenly one morning, a few days after the Symposium on the Structure of the Universe, hosted by the Center for Advanced Study at Queenston (for indeed there had been a symposium), Julia realized, at her desk, that her pulse was unnaturally fast; and that she was startled by the most innocuous of things—her ringing telephone, the sound of voices in the corridor, the museum's curator summoning her into his office. (The curator, a man of self-consciously vigorous middle age, was subtly, yet unmistakably, gay; with absolutely no erotic interest in Julia Matterling, or in any other woman.)

Passing by the museum guards, as she'd done countless times, Julia felt strangely dizzy; did not dare glance up at them, still less smile and greet them by name as she normally did. *No. Don't look. It's better not to know.* The thought haunted her, since that last, incompletely recalled nightmare (the kitchen of the Center? but why the *kitchen*?—and had there been more than one assailant?), that, without her wish, she had the curious power to destroy: for, when men advanced upon her, when actually they dared touch her, they were punished severely, by imploding: *vanishing*.

Which was what they deserved. Animals.

Yes, but Julia did not want that sort of thing, that violence, to occur, certainly she did not want it to occur. She was not a vindictive woman. She was not a hysterical woman.

That morning, the curator had arranged for Julia to meet with a Hawaiian-born sculptor whose work the museum was considering for an exhibit. As Julia nervously examined slides of the man's sculptures through a viewer, and asked questions of him meant to be friendly, polite, she became acutely aware of him staring at her: frowning at her; sitting at the edge of his chair, head thrust forward in a way that could only be belligerent. (Or was the man shy? awkward? socially disadvantaged?) Julia blinked at the massive, ugly, teasingly obscene hulks of scrap metal that constituted the sculptor's "art" and had no idea what to think, or to say. Her mind was going blank. Evaporating. Waves of panic stirred in her belly. She moved her arm, and the sculptor moved his, as in a mirror. Mocking? His features were Oriental, yet Caucasian, his skin dark, as if tanned; his eyes hooded. *Who are you? Do I know you? Do you know me?*

Julia had asked the sculptor about his background, and he had answered gruffly, in monosyllables; then fell silent, staring at her. On Julia's desk was a brass lamp, small but heavy; covertly, her fear increasing, she measured the distance between the lamp and her right hand. *If you dare. Threaten me.* Now her pulse was racing erratically and she understood that the sculptor was well aware of her distress. When she wiped moisture from her upper lip, in a gesture intended to be unobtrusive, the sculptor mirrored it, mockingly, by sighing, and wiping his forehead on the sleeve of his denim jacket. Then, their eyes met.

No. Not again. Never again.

As the sculptor was about to lunge forward—as Julia sensed he was about to lunge forward—she stood suddenly, snatched up the lamp to defend herself, and stammered, "Thank you! You can leave now! You've said enough! Please take your slides!" The sculptor gaped up at her, all mockery and masculine arrogance drained from his face; the very swarthiness of his skin draining pale.

"Just leave! Now! Quickly! Before there's danger!" Julia cried.

And so, quickly, sweeping his slides into a duffel bag, the sculptor did.

Julia looked around her, at the walls, the windows, the familiar dimensions of the room. Nothing had changed. All was as it had been. She remained where she was. Exactly where she was. (Trembling, behind her desk, the heavy brass lamp pressed against her breasts.)

I am not here, then, am I. Or, if here—who?

* * *

She was sobbing, she had lost all shame opening her heart to one who would help. "Doctor, I'm so frightened of losing my mind! I believe I'm approaching a nervous breakdown—madness!"

Dr. Fitz-James smiled sympathetically, yet doubtfully. "'Approaching,' Julia?"

Julia stared at him, blinking. Was it a poor word choice? One approached a point in time, or in space; one approached, for instance, an abyss. But could one approach anything so intangible as a nervous breakdown? She said, stammering, "Doctor, I have such dreams! Such ugly, hateful, obscene dreams! And now they're spilling over into real life—that's what I fear most." She paused, pressing a tissue against her eyes, conscious of Dr. Fitz-James' thoughtful look. He was a much-admired Queenston doctor; not a psychiatrist, nor a psychoanalyst, but an internist with a reputation for being kindly, informative, up-to-date, intuitively shrewd—with a particular gift for understanding women. Quite coincidentally, Dr. Fitz-James resembled Norman Matterling, in build and physical appearance, though not manner: where Norman was abstract and dreamy, Dr. Fitz-James was alert, almost unsettlingly watchful, Julia felt that he anticipated her very words as she spoke. "And the dreams aren't my own, really—they seem to be the dreams of another person. A madwoman."

"Indeed, Julia! But how do you know?"

"How do I—know?"

Patiently, bringing the tips of his blunt, stubby fingers together, Dr. Fitz-James said, "When human beings dream, they are not conscious; thus they cannot know anything with certainty, not even that they are not conscious." He smiled, as if addressing a young child, or a very slow-witted person. "It's a familiar conundrum—how do we know we *are* awake, when we are awake?—where is the evidence? the material world seems to us real—" He struck the top of his desk smartly with his knuckles, so that Julia, whose nerves were strung tight as a bow, started, "—and so, no doubt, it *is*. But—are we in it, as we think we are? And who are *we?*" He paused, for dramatic effect. Julia was beginning to feel quite helpless, "And when we wake, Julie—excuse me: Julia—and consciousness floods back, the dreaming self vanishes, irretrievable. So—how can we have knowledge of that other self? of the dreams it engenders?"

How like Norman Matterling the man was: the wisps of graying hair, the broad, somewhat heavy face, the pale-blue eyes behind polished lenses, the sense he communicated of absolute and unwavering logic, irrefutable! But Dr. Fitz-James was several years younger than Norman Matterling, his big body more muscular than fatty; there was a masculine edge to his voice that comforted Julia, yet also disturbed her. For, possessed of logic as the internist was, was he also possessed of truth?

Julia wiped at her eyes, and said, weakly, yet stubbornly, "Whatever it is, Doctor, whether I *know* or not, I'm terribly upset. I dread falling asleep; I've had a kind of flu, and have been running a temperature; I had a, a—misunderstanding at the museum where I work, and have taken sick leave for a while. It's all I can do to get through the day—running our household without Norman suspecting that anything is wrong. He'd be devastated if he knew, he depends upon me so completely." Now this fact was uttered, Julia understood it was a fact; perhaps the central fact of her existence as a wife. Dr. Fitz-James nodded, in apparent agreement. Julia said, shuddering, "And what I think I can remember of my dreams—so ugly! Repulsive! Hideous!"

Julia wept. Laughed. Hid her face.

But Dr. Fitz-James said, in the same sympathetic yet skeptical voice, rising from his desk to lead Julia into an examination room, "Now, Julia, you women should remember that certain 'facts' are no more than passing moods, a jangle of neurons—sheer ephemera. Your dreams, my dear, and the disgust they engender, are not 'real'—thus not important."

Julia entered the examination room, which was brightly lit, with a clinical chill. Since childhood she had dreaded physical examinations; even as she understood their necessity. *If I am good, if I obey, will I be helped? loved?* She whispered, "—Not important?"

Dr. Fitz-James laughed. "Not set beside *physical facts*."

To this, Julia could make no objection. She began to undress, with trembling fingers; removing her outer garments, then, shivering, her brassiere and panties—grateful that Dr. Fitz-James was averting his eyes. On the examination table lay an oversized paper smock into which Julia quickly slipped. *If I am good? if I obey?* As she had told the doctor, she was slightly feverish; had not slept more than a few hours in the past several nights; nor had she any appetite. How she hoped Dr. Fitz-James might find a physical disorder underlying her malaise!—for which she might take pills, the most efficient of solutions.

Julia lay on the examination table, her bare feet in the stirrups and her thighs wide spread. Dr. Fitz-James murmured, "Move up just a bit, June,—Julia!" and she felt the warmth of his breath against her skin. *If I am good, good, good. If I obey.* There was no disguising the fact that Julia was shivering with anticipation: excitement, or dread. Her entire pubic region was exposed to the chill, unsparingly bright air of the examination room, and to Dr. Fitz-James' professional scrutiny. (Why was there no nurse in attendance?—but Julia was grateful there was none.) Her eyelids fluttered. The overhead lights and the ceiling beyond shimmered, as if on the brink of dissolution. Dr. Fitz-James murmured, in a muffled, choked-sounding voice, "Now, my dear, this may tickle a little—just a routine check for growths." With rubber-gloved hands he began to press, squeeze, massage Julia's pelvic region, her lower abdomen, her stomach, her breasts; Julia drew in her breath sharply, and held it. "Oh! oh!"—she might have laughed shrilly, or cried. "Oh—Doctor!"

So thorough was the internist, he did the entire procedure a second time, yet more forcibly.

"Oh!—Doctor!" Julia cried, biting her lower lip.

"Very fine, very fine," Dr. Fitz-James said. He was perspiring: his balloon face, looming above Julia, had an oily sheen. "Now, do relax—we'll look at your uterus, and do a Pap smear." Julia made an effort to relax, even as she anticipated discomfort, pain. She saw, to her horror, a tray of glittering instruments on a table close by: several scalpels, one of them the length of a steak knife; a device that uncannily resembled an ice-cream scoop; another that resembled an egg-beater; still another, with an expandable head, to dilate the vagina. *Obey. If I obey. Will I be loved? saved?* She had stiffened, gripping the sides of the examination table tight. Her knees, with no support, were badly trembling; Julia's instinct was to bring them together, even as, gently, yet firmly, Dr. Fitz-James spread them apart.

"Now, my dear, this *may* hurt a little: just a little," he said, selecting, from the tray of instruments, the ice-cream scoop; and disappearing from Julia's view behind her outspread knees.

Julia held her breath. She felt a finger-probe around the lips of her vagina—no pain, really, yet she stiffened at once. Dr. Fitz-James chided her, in a muffled voice, "Dear, do relax! It will be so much better for you, if you do." She could hear his breath, which reminded her of Norman's when his sinuses were congested; she made an effort to obey. *Don't touch. Don't dare. Who am I here?* There was a pause; then the touch of cold metal; then, even as Julia drew breath to scream, yet could not scream, a sudden piercing pain, in her vagina, in the birth canal, of an intensity she had never before felt in her life.

No! no!—Julia tried to slide away from Dr. Fitz-James, but with his left hand he was gripping her buttocks so tightly she could not move. Even as Julia struggled, the cruel instrument plunged deeper; a nova of pain filled her body; and, scarcely knowing what she did, Julia reached out for something with which to defend herself—and there was the knife-sized scalpel suddenly in her fingers, so deftly so lethally fitted to her fingers, she was screaming *Now now! this is happening now!* as, in a frenzy, she slashed and stabbed at the astonished man whose name she no longer knew, bright blood at once splashing his white outfit, blood on his face, blood on his flailing hands, blood pouring from a severed artery in his throat, *I warned you: and now! now!* her assailant stumbling backward with that look of rapt and utter astonishment on his face, colliding with the table bearing the tray of gleaming instruments, and—

And vanished.

And Julia Matterling awoke another time, dazed and terrified, to find herself—where?

In her bed, in her bedroom of many years, amid tangled bedclothes that gave off a reek of panic. Pain throbbed in her loins and the nipples of both breasts were raw—how had it happened?

Night. She was alone. Switching on her bedside lamp with badly shaking fingers (were they bloodstained? no), Julia saw that it was 3:20 a.m. Norman was awake, elsewhere in the house, working.

I am not here, then, am I? Or, if here—who?

It was the night following the day of the embarrassment at the art museum. The misunderstanding involving the Hawaiian-born sculptor who had, or had not, made "threatening" gestures toward Julia Matterling.... All had agreed, a sick leave might be advised.

Shakily, Julia rose from bed (was it bloodstained? no); ran a bath in the adjoining bathroom, water as steamily hot, as cleansing, as she could bear. She could not recall the ugly dream that had wakened her but she seemed to know that her assailant had been someone she knew, clad in white. He had hurt her badly, and then he'd been destroyed: vanished: like the others.

Julia was stiff with pain, but she smiled. *Gone where?*

Startled, then, she glanced up as the door was pushed open, and there stood Norman, perplexed, disapproving, his hair standing up in wispy tufts. "Julia, what are you doing?—at this hour of the morning?" Surely he had every right to be annoyed: Norman Matterling, fresh from the isolation of his work amid galaxies, stars, atoms, quarks, leptons, primal cosmic soup, ready at last for bed. And where was his wife?

How strangely he was staring at her. Julia in her nakedness, a sight he rarely saw. Her shimmering-pale body, her delicate frame, breasts gleaming damp, the shadowy pubic hair at the base of her belly, scarcely visible. And, how strangely too, Julia smiled up at him: a taunting, provocative, sexual smile: lifting her arms to him, yes and her knees raised too.

Julia heard herself say, in a low, suggestive voice. "What do you think I'm doing, Norman?"

The Evening and the Morning and the Night

Octavia E. Butler

Octavia E. Butler sold her first novel in 1976, and subsequently published critically acclaimed novels such as *Kindred, Wild Seed, Dawn, Adulthood Rites*, and *Imago*, these last three assembled in 1989 as *Xenogenesis*. Her newest novel, *Parable of the Sower*, has just been published. She rarely writes short fiction, but when she does her stories are powerful. In the mid-Eighties she published and won awards for two of her stories and was nominated for the Nebula award for "The Evening and the Morning and the Night" (*Omni*, May 1987). It is a moving and chilling novelette about two people consumed by a terrifying disease and their tentative attempts to reach out to each other.

The Evening and the Morning and the Night

Octavia E. Butler

When I was fifteen and trying to show my independence by getting careless with my diet, my parents took me to a Duryea-Gode disease ward. They wanted me to see, they said, where I was headed if I wasn't careful. In fact, it was where I was headed no matter what. It was only a matter of when: now or later. My parents were putting in their vote for later.

I won't describe the ward. It's enough to say that when they brought me home, I cut my wrists. I did a thorough job of it, old Roman style in a bathtub of warm water. Almost made it. My father dislocated his shoulder breaking down the bathroom door. He and I never forgave each other for that day.

The disease got him almost three years later—just before I went off to college. It was sudden. It doesn't happen that way often. Most people notice themselves beginning to drift—or their relatives notice—and they make arrangements with their chosen institution. People who are noticed and who resist going in can be locked up for a week's observation. I don't doubt that that observation period breaks up a few families. Sending someone away for what turns out to be a false alarm.... Well, it isn't the sort of thing the victim is likely to forgive or forget. On the other hand, not sending someone away in time—missing the signs or having a person go off suddenly without signs—is inevitably dangerous for the victim. I've never heard of it going as badly, though, as it did in my family. People normally injure only themselves when their time comes—unless someone is stupid enough to try to handle them without the necessary drugs or restraints.

My father . . . killed my mother, then killed himself. I wasn't home when it happened. I had stayed at school later than usual, rehearsing graduation exercises. By the time I got home, there were cops everywhere. There was an ambulance, and two attendants were wheeling someone out on a stretcher—someone covered. More than covered. Almost . . . bagged.

The cops wouldn't let me in. I didn't find out until later exactly what had happened. I wish I'd never found out. Dad had killed Mom, then skinned her completely. At least, that's how I hope it happened. I mean I hope he killed her first. He broke some of her ribs, damaged her heart. Digging.

Then he began tearing at himself, through skin and bone, digging. He had managed to reach his own heart before he died. It was an especially bad example of the kind of thing that makes people afraid of us. It gets some of us into trouble for picking at a pimple or even for daydreaming. It has inspired restrictive laws, created problems with jobs, housing, schools. The Duryea-Gode Disease Foundation has spent millions telling the world that people like my father don't exist.

A long time later, when I had gotten myself together as best I could, I went to college—to the University of Southern California—on a Dilg scholarship. Dilg is the retreat you try to send your out-of-control DGD relatives to. It's run by controlled DGDs like me, like my parents while they lived. God knows how any controlled DGD stands it. Anyway, the place has a waiting list miles long. My parents put me on it after my suicide attempt, but chances were, I'd be dead by the time my name came up.

I can't say why I went to college—except that I had been going to school all my life and I didn't know what else to do. I didn't go with any particular hope. Hell, I knew what I was in for eventually. I was just marking time. Whatever I did was just marking time. If people were willing to pay me to go to school and mark time, why not do it?

The weird part was, I worked hard, got top grades. If you work hard enough at something that doesn't matter, you can forget for a while about the things that do.

Sometimes I thought about trying suicide again. How was it I'd had the courage when I was fifteen but didn't have it now? Two DGD parents—both religious, both as opposed to abortion as they were to suicide. So they had trusted God and the promises of modern medicine and had a child. But how could I look at what had happened to them and trust anything?

I majored in biology. Non-DGDs say something about our disease makes us good at the sciences—genetics, molecular biology, biochemistry. . . . That something was terror. Terror and a kind of driving hopelessness. Some of us went bad and became destructive before we had to—yes, we did produce more than our share of criminals. And some of us went good—spectacularly—and made scientific and medical history. These last kept the doors at least partly open for the rest of us. They made discoveries in genetics, found cures for a couple of rare diseases, made advances in the fight against other diseases that weren't so rare—including, ironically, some forms of cancer. But they'd found nothing to help themselves. There had been nothing since the latest improvements in the diet, and those came just before I was born. They, like the original diet, gave more DGDs the courage to have children They were supposed to do for DGDs what insulin had done for diabetics—give us a normal or nearly normal life span. Maybe they had worked for someone somewhere. They hadn't worked for anyone I knew.

Biology School was a pain in the usual ways. I didn't eat in public anymore, didn't like the way people stared at my biscuits—cleverly dubbed "dog biscuits" in every school I'd ever attended. You'd think university students would be more creative. I didn't like the way people edged away from me when they caught sight of my emblem. I'd begun wearing it on a chain around my neck and putting it down inside my blouse, but people managed to notice it anyway. People who don't eat in public, who drink nothing more interesting than water, who smoke nothing at all—people like that are suspicious. Or rather, they make others suspicious. Sooner or later, one of those others, finding my fingers and wrists bare, would fake an interest in my chain. That would be that. I couldn't hide the emblem in my purse. If anything happened to me, medical people had to see it in time to avoid giving me the medications they might use on a normal person. It isn't just ordinary food we have to avoid, but about a quarter of a *Physicians' Desk Reference* of widely used drugs. Every now and then there are news stories about people who stopped carrying their emblems—probably trying to pass as normal. Then they have an accident. By the time anyone realizes there is anything wrong, it's too late. So I wore my emblem. And one way or another, people got a look at it or got the word from someone who had. "She *is!*" Yeah.

At the beginning of my third year, four other DGDs and I decided to rent a house together. We'd all had enough of being lepers twenty-four hours a day. There was an English major. He wanted to be a writer and tell our story from the inside—which had only been done thirty or forty times before. There was a special-education major who hoped the handicapped would accept her more readily than the able-bodied, a premed who planned to go into research, and a chemistry major who didn't really know what she wanted to do.

Two men and three women. All we had in common was our disease, plus a weird combination of stubborn intensity about whatever we happened to be doing and hopeless cynicism about everything else. Healthy people say no one can concentrate like a DGD. Healthy people have all the time in the world for stupid generalizations and short attention spans.

We did our work, came up for air now and then, ate our biscuits, and attended classes. Our only problem was housecleaning. We worked out a schedule of who would clean what when, who would deal with the yard, whatever. We all agreed on it; then, except for me, everyone seemed to forget about it. I found myself going around reminding people to vacuum, clean the bathroom, mow the lawn.... I figured they'd all hate me in no time, but I wasn't going to be their maid, and I wasn't going to live in filth. Nobody complained. Nobody even seemed annoyed. They just came up out of their academic daze, cleaned, mopped, mowed, and went back to it. I got into the habit of running around in the evening reminding people. It didn't bother me if it didn't bother them.

"How'd you get to be housemother?" a visiting DGD asked.

I shrugged. "Who cares? The house works." It did. It worked so well that this new guy wanted to move in. He was a friend of one of the others, and another premed. Not bad looking.

"So do I get in or don't I?" he asked.

"As far as I'm concerned, you do," I said. I did what his friend should have done—introduced him around, then, after he left, talked to the others to make sure nobody had any real objections. He seemed to fit right in. He forgot to clean the toilet or mow the lawn, just like the others. His name was Alan Chi. I thought Chi was a Chinese name, and I wondered. But he told me his father was Nigerian and that in Ibo, the word meant a kind of guardian angel or personal god. He said his own personal god hadn't been looking out for him very well to let him be born to two DGD parents. Him too.

I don't think it was much more than that similarity that drew us together at first. Sure, I liked the way he looked, but I was used to liking someone's looks and having him run like hell when he found out what I was. It took me a while to get used to the fact that Alan wasn't going anywhere.

I told him about my visit to the DGD ward when I was fifteen—and my suicide attempt afterward. I had never told anyone else. I was surprised at how relieved it made me feel to tell him. And somehow his reaction didn't surprise me.

"Why didn't you try again?" he asked We were alone in the living room.

"At first, because of my parents," I said. "My father in particular. I couldn't do that to him again."

"And after him?"

"Fear. Inertia."

He nodded. "When I do it, there'll be no half measures. No being rescued, no waking up in a hospital later."

"You mean to do it?"

"The day I realize I've started to drift. Thank God we get some warning."

"Not necessarily."

"Yes, we do. I've done a lot of reading. Even talked to a couple of doctors. Don't believe the rumors non-DGDs invent."

I looked away, stared into the scarred, empty fireplace. I told him exactly how my father had died—something else I'd never voluntarily told anyone.

He sighed. "Jesus!"

We looked at each other.

"What are you going to do?" he asked.

"I don't know."

He extended a dark, square hand, and I took it and moved closer to him. He was a dark, square man—my height, half again my weight, and none of it fat. He was so bitter sometimes, he scared me.

"My mother started to drift when I was three," he said. "My father only lasted a few months longer. I heard he died a couple of years after he went into the hospital. If the two of them had had any sense, they would have had me aborted the minute my mother realized she was pregnant. But she wanted a kid no matter what. And she was Catholic." He shook his head. "Hell, they should pass a law to sterilize the lot of us."

"They?" I said.

"You want kids?"

"No, but—"

"More like us to wind up chewing their fingers off in some DGD ward."

"I don't want kids, but I don't want someone else telling me I can't have any."

He stared at me until I began to feel stupid and defensive. I moved away from him.

"Do you want someone else telling you what to do with your body?" I asked.

"No need," he said. "I had that taken care of as soon as I was old enough."

This left me staring. I'd thought about sterilization. What DGD hasn't? But I didn't know anyone else our age who had actually gone through with it. That would be like killing part of yourself—even though it wasn't a part you intended to use. Killing part of yourself when so much of you was already dead.

"The damned disease could be wiped out in one generation," he said, "but people are still animals when it comes to breeding. Still following mindless urges, like dogs and cats."

My impulse was to get up and go away, leave him to wallow in his bitterness and depression alone. But I stayed. He seemed to want to live even less than I did. I wondered how he'd made it this far.

"Are you looking forward to doing research?" I probed. "Do you believe you'll be able to—"

"No."

I blinked. The word was as cold and dead a sound as I'd ever heard.

"I don't believe in anything," he said.

I took him to bed. He was the only other double DGD I had ever met, and if nobody did anything for him, he wouldn't last much longer. I couldn't just let him slip away. For a while, maybe we could be each other's reasons for staying alive.

He was a good student—for the same reason I was. And he seemed to shed some of his bitterness as time passed. Being around him helped me understand why, against all sanity, two DGDs would lock in on each other and start talking about marriage. Who else would have us?

We probably wouldn't last very long, anyway. These days, most DGDs make it to forty, at least. But then, most of them don't have two DGD parents. As bright as Alan was, he might not get into medical school because of his double inheritance. No one would tell him his bad genes were keeping him out, of course, but we both knew what his chances were. Better to train doctors who were likely to live long enough to put their training to use.

Alan's mother had been sent to Dilg. He hadn't seen her or been able to get any information about her from his grandparents while he was at home. By the time he left for college, he'd stopped asking questions. Maybe it was hearing about my parents that made him start again. I was with him when he called Dilg. Until that moment, he hadn't even known whether his mother was still alive. Surprisingly, she was.

"Dilg must be good," I said when he hung up. "People don't usually . . . I mean . . ."

"Yeah, I know," he said. "People don't usually live long once they're out of control. Dilg is different." We had gone to my room, where he turned a chair backward and sat down. "Dilg is what the others ought to be, if you can believe the literature."

"Dilg is a giant DGD ward," I said. "It's richer—probably better at sucking in the donations—and it's run by people who can expect to become patients eventually. Apart from that, what's different?"

"I've read about it," he said. "So should you. They've got some new treatment. They don't just shut people away to die the way the others do."

"What else is there to do with them?" *With us.*

"I don't know. It sounded like they have some kind of . . . sheltered workshop. They've got patients doing things."

"A new drug to control the self-destructiveness?"

"I don't think so. We would have heard about that."

"What else could it be?"

"I'm going up to find out. Will you come with me?"

"You're going up to see your mother."

He took a ragged breath. "Yeah. Will you come with me?"

I went to one of my windows and stared out at the weeds. We let them thrive in the backyard. In the front we mowed them, along with the few patches of grass.

"I told you my DGD-ward experience."

"You're not fifteen now. And Dilg isn't some zoo of a ward."

"It's got to be, no matter what they tell the public. And I'm not sure I can stand it."

He got up, came to stand next to me. "Will you try?"

I didn't say anything. I focused on our reflections in the window glass—the two of us together. It looked right, felt right. He put his arm around me, and I leaned back against him. Our being together had been as good for me as it seemed to have been for him. It had given me something to go on besides inertia and fear. I knew I would go with him. It felt like the right thing to do.

"I can't say how I'll act when we get there," I said.

"I can't say how I'll act, either," he admitted. "Especially . . . when I see her."

He made the appointment for the next Saturday afternoon. You make appointments to go to Dilg unless you're a government inspector of some kind. That is the custom, and Dilg gets away with it.

We left L.A. in the rain early Saturday morning. Rain followed us off and on up the coast as far as Santa Barbara. Dilg was hidden away in the hills not far from San Jose. We could have reached it faster by driving up I-5, but neither of us were in the mood for all that bleakness. As it was, we arrived at one P.M. to be met by two armed gate guards. One of these phoned the main building and verified our appointment. Then the other took the wheel from Alan.

"Sorry," he said. "But no one is permitted inside without an escort. We'll meet your guide at the garage."

None of this surprised me. Dilg is a place where not only the patients but much of the staff has DGD. A maximum security prison wouldn't have been as potentially dangerous. On the other hand, I'd never heard of anyone getting chewed up here. Hospitals and rest homes had accidents. Dilg didn't. It was beautiful—an old estate. One that didn't make sense in these days of high taxes. It had been owned by the Dilg family. Oil, chemicals, pharmaceuticals. Ironically, they had even owned part of the late, unlamented Hedeon Laboratories. They'd had a briefly profitable interest in Hedeonco: the magic bullet, the cure for a large percentage of the world's cancer and a number of serious viral diseases—and the cause of Duryea-Gode disease. If one of your parents was treated with Hedeonco and you were conceived after the treatments, you had DGD. If you had kids, you passed it on to them. Not everyone was equally affected. They didn't all commit suicide or murder, but they all mutilated themselves to some degree if they could. And they all drifted—went off into a world of their own and stopped responding to their surroundings.

Anyway, the only Dilg son of his generation had had his life saved by Hedeonco. Then he had watched four of his children die before Doctors Kenneth Duryea and Jan Gode came up with a decent understanding of the problem and a partial solution: the diet. They gave Richard Dilg a way of keeping his next two children alive. He gave the big, cumbersome estate over to the care of DGD patients.

So the main building was an elaborate old mansion. There were other, newer buildings, more like guesthouses than institutional buildings. And there were wooded hills all around. Nice country. Green. The ocean wasn't far away. There was an old garage and a small parking lot. Waiting in the lot was a tall old woman. Our guard pulled up near her, let us out, then parked the car in the half-empty garage.

"Hello," the woman said, extending her hand. "I'm Beatrice Alcantara." The hand was cool and dry and startlingly strong. I thought the woman was DGD, but her age threw me. She appeared to be about sixty, and I had never seen a DGD that old. I wasn't sure why I thought she was DGD. If she was, she must have been an experimental model—one of the first to survive.

"Is it Doctor or Ms.?" Alan asked.

"It's Beatrice," she said. "I am a doctor, but we don't use titles much here."

I glanced at Alan, was surprised to see him smiling at her. He tended to go a long time between smiles. I looked at Beatrice and couldn't see anything to smile about. As we introduced ourselves, I realized I didn't like her. I couldn't see any reason for that either, but my feelings were my feelings. I didn't like her.

"I assume neither of you have been here before," she said, smiling down at us. She was at least six feet tall, and straight.

We shook our heads. "Let's go in the front way, then. I want to prepare you for what we do here. I don't want you to believe you've come to a hospital."

I frowned at her, wondering what else there was to believe. Dilg was called a retreat, but what difference did names make?

The house close up looked like one of the old-style public buildings—massive, baroque front with a single, domed tower reaching three stories above the three-story house. Wings of the house stretched for some distance to the right and left of the tower, then cornered and stretched back twice as far. The front doors were huge—one set of wrought iron and one of heavy wood. Neither appeared to be locked. Beatrice pulled open the iron door, pushed the wooden one, and gestured us in.

Inside, the house was an art museum—huge, high-ceilinged, tile-floored. There were marble columns and niches in which sculpture stood or paintings hung. There was other sculpture displayed around the rooms. At one end of the rooms there was a broad staircase leading up to a gallery that went around the rooms. There more art was displayed. "All this was made here," Beatrice said. "Some of it is even sold from here. Most goes to galleries in the Bay Area or down around L.A. Our only problem is turning out too much of it."

"You mean the patients do this?" I asked.

The old woman nodded. "This and much more. Our people work instead of tearing at themselves or staring into space. One of them invented the p.v. locks that protect this place. Though I almost wish he hadn't. It's gotten us more government attention than we like."

"What kind of locks?" I asked.

"Sorry. Palmprint-voiceprint. The first and the best. We have the patent." She looked at Alan. "Would you like to see what your mother does?"

"Wait a minute," he said. "You're telling us out-of-control DGDs create art and invent things?"

"And that lock," I said. "I've never heard of anything like that. I didn't even see a lock."

"The lock is new," she said. "There have been a few news stories about it. It's not the kind of thing most people would buy for their homes. Too expensive. So it's of limited interest. People tend to look at what's done at Dilg in the way they look at the efforts of idiots savants. Interesting, incomprehensible, but not really important. Those likely to be interested in the lock and able to afford it know about it." She took a deep breath, faced Alan again. "Oh, yes. DGDs create things. At least they do here."

"Out-of-control DGDs."

"Yes."

"I expected to find them weaving baskets or something—at best. I know what DGD wards are like."

"So do I," she said. "I know what they're like in hospitals, and I know what it's like here." She waved a hand toward an abstract painting that looked like a photo I had once seen of the Orion Nebula. Darkness broken by a great cloud of light and color. "Here we can help them channel their energies. They can create something beautiful, useful, even something worthless. But they create. They don't destroy."

"Why?" Alan demanded. "It can't be some drug. We would have heard."

"It's not a drug."

"Then what is it? Why haven't other hospitals—?"

"Alan," she said. "Wait."

He stood frowning at her.

"Do you want to see your mother?"

"Of course I want to see her!"

"Good. Come with me. Things will sort themselves out."

She led us to a corridor past offices where people talked to one another, waved to Beatrice, worked with computers.... They could have been anywhere. I wondered how many of them were controlled DGDs. I also wondered what kind of game the old woman was playing with her secrets. We passed through rooms so beautiful and perfectly kept it was obvious they were rarely used. Then at a broad, heavy door, she stopped us.

"Look at anything you like as we go on," she said. "But don't touch anything or anyone. And remember that some of the people you'll see injured themselves before they came to us. They still bear the scars of those injuries. Some of those scars may be difficult to look at, but you'll be in no danger. Keep that in mind. No one here will harm you." She pushed the door open and gestured us in.

Scars didn't bother me much. Disability didn't bother me. It was the act of self-mutilation that scared me. It was someone attacking her own arm as though it were a wild animal. It was someone who had torn at himself and been restrained or drugged off and on for so long that he barely had a recognizable human feature left, but he was still trying with what he did have to dig into his own flesh. Those are a couple of the things I saw at the DGD ward when I was fifteen. Even then I could have stood it better if I hadn't felt I was looking into a kind of temporal mirror.

I wasn't aware of walking through that doorway. I wouldn't have thought I could do it. The old woman said something, though, and I found myself on the other side of the door with the door closing behind me. I turned to stare at her. She put her hand on my arm. "It's all right," she said quietly. "That door looks like a wall to a great many people."

I backed away from her, out of her reach, repelled by her touch. Shaking hands had been enough, for God's sake.

Something in her seemed to come to attention as she watched me. It made her even straighter. Deliberately, but for no apparent reason, she stepped toward Alan, touched him the way people do sometimes when they brush past—a kind of tactile "Excuse me." In that wide, empty corridor, it was totally unnecessary. For some reason, she wanted to touch him and wanted me to see. What did she think she was doing? Flirting at her age? I glared at her, found myself suppressing an irrational urge to shove her away from him. The violence of the urge amazed me.

Beatrice smiled and turned away. "This way," she said. Alan put his arm around me and tried to lead me after her.

"Wait a minute," I said, not moving.

Beatrice glanced around.

"What just happened?" I asked. I was ready for her to lie—to say nothing happened, pretend not to know what I was talking about.

"Are you planning to study medicine?" she asked.

"What? What does that have to do—?"

"Study medicine. You may be able to do a great deal of good." She strode away, taking long steps so that we had to hurry to keep up. She led us through a room in which some people worked at computer terminals and others with pencils and paper. It would have been an ordinary scene except that some people had half their faces ruined or had only one hand or leg or had other obvious scars. But they were all in control now. They were working. They were intent but not intent on self-destruction. Not one was digging into or tearing away flesh. When we had passed through this room and into a small, ornate sitting room, Alan grasped Beatrice's arm.

"What is it?" he demanded. "What do you do for them?"

She patted his hand, setting my teeth on edge. "I will tell you," she said. "I want you to know. But I want you to see your mother first." To my surprise, he nodded, let it go at that.

"Sit a moment," she said to us.

We sat in comfortable, matching upholstered chairs, Alan looking reasonably relaxed. What was it about the old lady that relaxed him but put me on edge? Maybe she reminded him of his grandmother or something. She didn't remind me of anyone. And what was that nonsense about studying medicine?

"I wanted you to pass through at least one workroom before we talked about your mother—and about the two of you." She turned to face me. "You've had a bad experience at a hospital or a rest home?"

I looked away from her, not wanting to think about it. Hadn't the people in that mock office been enough of a reminder? Horror film office. Nightmare office.

"It's all right," she said. "You don't have to go into detail. Just outline it for me."

I obeyed slowly, against my will, all the while wondering why I was doing it.

She nodded, unsurprised. "Harsh, loving people, your parents. Are they alive?"

"No."

"Were they both DGD?"

"Yes, but . . . yes."

"Of course. Aside from the obvious ugliness of your hospital experience and its implications for the future, what impressed you about the people in the ward?"

I didn't know what to answer. What did she want? Why did she want anything from me? She should have been concerned with Alan and his mother.

"Did you see people unrestrained?"

"Yes," I whispered. "One woman. I don't know how it happened that she was free. She ran up to us and slammed into my father without moving him. He was a big man. She bounced off, fell, and . . . began tearing at herself. She bit her own arm and . . . swallowed the flesh she'd bitten away. She tore at the wound she'd made with the nails of her other hand. She . . . I screamed at her to stop." I hugged myself, remembering the young woman, bloody, cannibalizing herself as she lay at our feet, digging into her own flesh. Digging. "They try so hard, fight so hard to get out."

"Out of what?" Alan demanded.

I looked at him, hardly seeing him.

"Lynn," he said gently. "Out of what?"

I shook my head. "Their restraints, their disease, the ward, their bodies . . ."

He glanced at Beatrice, then spoke to me again. "Did the girl talk?"

"No. She screamed."

He turned away from me uncomfortably. "Is this important?" he asked Beatrice.

"Very," she said.

"Well . . . can we talk about it after I see my mother?"

"Then and now." She spoke to me. "Did the girl stop what she was doing when you told her to?"

"The nurses had her a moment later. It didn't matter."

"It mattered. Did she stop?"

"Yes."

"According to the literature, they rarely respond to anyone," Alan said.

"True." Beatrice gave him a sad smile. "Your mother will probably respond to you, though."

"Is she? . . ." He glanced back at the nightmare office. "Is she as controlled as those people?"

"Yes, though she hasn't always been. Your mother works with clay now. She loves shapes and textures and—"

"She's blind," Alan said, voicing the suspicion as though it were fact. Beatrice's words had sent my thoughts in the same direction. Beatrice hesitated. "Yes," she said finally. "And for . . . the usual reason. I had intended to prepare you slowly."

"I've done a lot of reading."

I hadn't done much reading, but I knew what the usual reason was. The woman had gouged, ripped, or otherwise destroyed her eyes. She would be badly scarred. I got up, went over to sit on the arm of Alan's chair. I rested my hand on his shoulder, and he reached up and held it there.

"Can we see her now?" he asked.

Beatrice got up. "This way," she said.

We passed through more workrooms. People painted; assembled machinery; sculpted in wood, stone; even composed and played music. Almost no one noticed us. The patients were true to their disease in that respect. They weren't ignoring us. They clearly didn't know we existed. Only the few controlled-DGD guards gave themselves away by waving or speaking to Beatrice. I watched a woman work quickly, knowledgeably, with a power saw. She obviously understood the perimeters of her body, was not so dissociated as to perceive herself as trapped in something she needed to dig her way out of. What had Dilg done for these people that other hospitals did not do? And how could Dilg withhold its treatment from the others?

"Over there we make our own diet foods." Beatrice said, pointing through a window toward one of the guesthouses. "We permit more variety and make fewer mistakes than the commercial preparers. No ordinary person can concentrate on work the way our people can."

I turned to face her. "What are you saying? That the bigots are right? That we have some special gift?"

"Yes," she said. "It's hardly a bad characteristic, is it?"

"It's what people say whenever one of us does well at something. It's their way of denying us credit for our work."

"Yes. But people occasionally come to the right conclusions for the wrong reasons." I shrugged, not interested in arguing with her about it.

"Alan?" she said. He looked at her.

"Your mother is in the next room."

He swallowed, nodded. We both followed her into the room.

Naomi Chi was a small woman, hair still dark, fingers long and thin, graceful as they shaped the clay. Her face was a ruin. Not only her eyes but most of her nose and one ear were gone. What was left was badly scarred. "Her parents were poor," Beatrice said. "I don't know how much they told you, Alan, but they went through all the money they had, trying to keep her at a decent place. Her mother felt so guilty, you know. She was the one who had cancer and took the drug.... Eventually, they had to put Naomi in one of those state-approved, custodial-care places. You know the kind. For a while, it was all the government would pay for. Places like that ... well, sometimes if patients were really troublesome—especially the ones who kept breaking free—they'd put them in a bare room and let them finish themselves. The only things those places took good care of were the maggots, the cockroaches, and the rats."

I shuddered. "I've heard there are still places like that."

"There are," Beatrice said, "kept open by greed and indifference." She looked at Alan. "Your mother survived for three months in one of those places. I took her from it myself. Later I was instrumental in having that particular place closed."

"You took her?" I asked.

"Dilg didn't exist then, but I was working with a group of controlled DGDs in L.A. Naomi's parents heard about us and asked us to take her. A lot of people didn't trust us then. Only a few of us were medically trained. All of us were young, idealistic, and ignorant. We began in an old frame house with a leaky roof. Naomi's parents were grabbing at straws. So were we. And by pure luck, we grabbed a good one. We were able to prove ourselves to the Dilg family and take over these quarters."

"Prove what?" I asked.

She turned to look at Alan and his mother. Alan was staring at Naomi's ruined face, at the ropy, discolored scar tissue. Naomi was shaping the image of an old woman and two children. The gaunt, lined face of the old woman was remarkably vivid—detailed in a way that seemed impossible for a blind sculptress.

Naomi seemed unaware of us. Her total attention remained on her work. Alan forgot about what Beatrice had told us and reached out to touch the scarred face.

Beatrice let it happen. Naomi did not seem to notice. "If I get her attention for you," Beatrice said, "we'll be breaking her routine. We'll have to stay with her until she gets back into it without hurting herself. About half an hour."

"You can get her attention?" he asked.

"Yes."

"Can she?. . ." Alan swallowed. "I've never heard of anything like this. Can she talk?"

"Yes. She may not choose to, though. And if she does, she'll do it very slowly."

"Do it. Get her attention."

"She'll want to touch you."

"That's all right. Do it."

Beatrice took Naomi's hands and held them still, away from the wet clay. For several seconds Naomi tugged at her captive hands, as though unable to understand why they did not move as she wished.

Beatrice stepped closer and spoke quietly. "Stop, Naomi." And Naomi was still, blind face turned toward Beatrice in an attitude of attentive waiting. Totally focused waiting.

"Company, Naomi."

After a few seconds, Naomi made a wordless sound.

Beatrice gestured Alan to her side, gave Naomi one of his hands. It didn't bother me this time when she touched him. I was too interested in what was happening. Naomi examined Alan's hand minutely, then followed the arm up to the shoulder, the neck, the face. Holding his face between her hands, she made a sound. It may have been a word, but I couldn't understand it. All I could think of was the danger of those hands. I thought of my father's hands.

"His name is Alan Chi, Naomi. He's your son." Several seconds passed.

"Son?" she said. This time the word was quite distinct, though her lips had split in many places and had healed badly. "Son?" she repeated anxiously. "Here?"

"He's all right, Naomi. He's come to visit."

"Mother?" he said.

She reexamined his face. He had been three when she started to drift. It didn't seem possible that she could find anything in his face that she would remember. I wondered whether she remembered she had a son.

"Alan?" she said. She found his tears and paused at them. She touched her own face where there should have been an eye, then she reached back toward his eyes. An instant before I would have grabbed her hand, Beatrice did it.

"No!" Beatrice said firmly.

The hand fell limply to Naomi's side. Her face turned toward Beatrice like an antique weather vane swinging around. Beatrice stroked her hair, and Naomi said something I almost understood. Beatrice looked at Alan, who was frowning and wiping away tears.

"Hug your son," Beatrice said softly.

Naomi turned, groping, and Alan seized her in a tight, long hug. Her arms went around him slowly. She spoke words blurred by her ruined mouth but just understandable.

"Parents?" she said. "Did my parents . . . care for you?" Alan looked at her, clearly not understanding.

"She wants to know whether her parents took care of you," I said.

He glanced at me doubtfully, then looked at Beatrice.

"Yes," Beatrice said. "She just wants to know that they cared for you."

"They did," he said. "They kept their promise to you, Mother."

Several seconds passed. Naomi made sounds that even Alan took to be weeping, and he tried to comfort her.

"Who else is here?" she said finally.

This time Alan looked at me. I repeated what she had said.

"Her name is Lynn Mortimer," he said. "I'm . . ." He paused awkwardly. "She and I are going to be married."

After a time, she moved back from him and said my name. My first impulse was to go to her. I wasn't afraid or repelled by her now, but for no reason I could explain, I looked at Beatrice.

"Go," she said. "But you and I will have to talk later."

I went to Naomi, took her hand.

"Bea?" she said.

"I'm Lynn," I said softly.

She drew a quick breath. "No," she said. "No, you're . . ."

"I'm Lynn. Do you want Bea? She's here."

She said nothing. She put her hand to my face, explored it slowly I let her do it, confident that I could stop her if she turned violent. But first one hand, then both, went over me very gently.

"You'll marry my son?" she said finally.

"Yes."

"Good. You'll keep him safe."

As much as possible, we'll keep each other safe. "Yes," I said.

"Good. No one will close him away from himself. No one will tie him or cage him." Her hand wandered to her own face again, nails biting in slightly.

"No," I said softly, catching the hand. "I want you to be safe, too."

The mouth moved. I think it smiled. "Son?" she said.

He understood her, took her hand.

"Clay," she said. Lynn and Alan in clay. "Bea?"

"Of course," Beatrice said. "Do you have an impression?"

"No!" It was the fastest that Naomi had answered anything. Then, almost childlike, she whispered. "Yes."

Beatrice laughed. "Touch them again if you like, Naomi. They don't mind."

We didn't. Alan closed his eyes, trusting her gentleness in a way I could not. I had no trouble accepting her touch, even so near my eyes, but I did not delude myself about her. Her gentleness could turn in an instant. Naomi's fingers twitched near Alan's eyes, and I spoke up at once, out of fear for him.

"Just touch him, Naomi. Only touch."

She froze, made an interrogative sound.

"She's all right," Alan said.

"I know," I said, not believing it. He would be all right, though, as long as someone watched her very carefully, nipped any dangerous impulses in the bud.

"Son!" she said, happily possessive. When she let him go, she demanded clay, wouldn't touch her old-woman sculpture again. Beatrice got new clay for her, leaving us to soothe her and ease her impatience. Alan began to recognize signs of impending destructive behavior. Twice he caught her hands and said no. She struggled against him until I spoke to her. As Beatrice returned, it happened again, and Beatrice said, "No, Naomi." Obediently Naomi let her hands fall to her sides.

"What is it?" Alan demanded later when we had left Naomi safely, totally focused on her new work—clay sculptures of us. "Does she only listen to women or something?"

Beatrice took us back to the sitting room, sat us both down, but did not sit down herself. She went to a window and stared out. "Naomi only obeys certain women," she said. "And she's sometimes slow to obey. She's worse than most—probably because of the damage she managed to do to herself before I got her." Beatrice faced us, stood biting her lip and frowning. "I haven't had to give this particular speech for a while," she said. "Most DGDs have the sense not to marry each other and produce children. I hope you two aren't planning to have any—in spite of our need." She took a deep breath. "It's a pheromone. A scent. And it's sex-linked. Men who inherit the disease from their fathers have no trace of the scent. They also tend to have an easier time with the disease. But they're useless to us as staff here. Men who inherit from their mothers have as much of the scent as men get. They can be useful here because the DGDs can at least be made to notice them. The same for women who inherit from their mothers but not their fathers. It's only when two irresponsible DGDs get together and produce girl children like me or Lynn that you get someone who can really do some good in a place like this." She looked at me. "We are very rare commodities, you and I. When you finish school you'll have a very well paid job waiting for you."

"Here?" I asked.

"For training, perhaps. Beyond that, I don't know. You'll probably help start a retreat in some other part of the country. Others are badly needed." She smiled humorlessly. "People like us don't get along well together. You must realize that I don't like you any more than you like me."

I swallowed, saw her through a kind of haze for a moment. Hated her mindlessly—just for a moment.

"Sit back," she said. "Relax your body. It helps."

I obeyed, not really wanting to obey her but unable to think of anything else to do. Unable to think at all. "We seem," she said, "to be very territorial. Dilg is a haven for me when I'm the only one of my kind here. When I'm not, it's a prison."

"All it looks like to me is an unbelievable amount of work," Alan said.

She nodded. "Almost too much." She smiled to herself. "I was one of the first double DGDs to be born. When I was old enough to understand, I thought I didn't have much time. First I tried to kill myself. Failing that, I tried to cram all the living I could into the small amount of time I assumed I had. When I got into this project, I worked as hard as I could to get it into shape before I started to drift. By now I wouldn't know what to do with myself if I weren't working."

"Why haven't you . . . drifted?" I asked.

"I don't know. There aren't enough of our kind to know what's normal for us."

"Drifting is normal for every DGD sooner or later."

"Later, then."

"Why hasn't the scent been synthesized?" Alan asked. "Why are there still concentration-camp rest homes and hospital wards?"

"There have been people trying to synthesize it since I proved what I could do with it. No one has succeeded so far. All we've been able to do is keep our eyes open for people like Lynn." She looked at me. "Dilg scholarship, right?"

"Yeah. Offered out of the blue."

"My people do a good job keeping track. You would have been contacted just before you graduated or if you dropped out."

"Is it possible," Alan said, staring at me, "that she's already doing it? Already using the scent to . . . influence people?"

"You?" Beatrice asked.

"All of us. A group of DGDs. We all live together. We're all controlled, of course, but . . ." Beatrice smiled. "It's probably the quietest house full of kids that anyone's ever seen."

I looked at Alan, and he looked away. "I'm not doing anything to them," I said. "I remind them of work they've already promised to do. That's all."

"You put them at ease," Beatrice said. "You're there. You . . . well, you leave your scent around the house. You speak to them individually. Without knowing why, they no doubt find that very comforting. Don't you, Alan?"

"I don't know," he said "I suppose I must have. From my first visit to the house, I knew I wanted to move in. And when I first saw Lynn, I . . ." He shook his head. "Funny. I thought all that was my idea."

"Will you work with us, Alan?"

"Me? You want Lynn."

"I want you both. You have no idea how many people take one look at one workroom here and turn and run. You may be the kind of young people who ought to eventually take charge of a place like Dilg."

"Whether we want to or not, eh?" he said.

Frightened, I tried to take his hand, but he moved it away. "Alan, this works," I said. "It's only a stopgap, I know. Genetic engineering will probably give us the final answers, but for God's sake, this is something we can do now!"

"It's something *you* can do. Play queen bee in a retreat full of workers. I've never had any ambition to be a drone."

"A physician isn't likely to be a drone," Beatrice said.

"Would you marry one of your patients?" he demanded. "That's what Lynn would be doing if she married me—whether I become a doctor or not."

She looked away from him, stared across the room. "My husband is here," she said softly. "He's been a patient here for almost a decade. What better place for him . . . when his time came?"

"Shit!" Alan muttered. He glanced at me. "Let's get out of here!" He got up and strode across the room to the door, pulled at it, then realized it was locked. He turned to face Beatrice, his body language demanding she let him out. She went to him, took him by the shoulder, and turned him to face the door. "Try it once more," she said quietly. "You can't break it. Try"

Surprisingly, some of the hostility seemed to go out of him. "This is one of those p.v. locks?" he asked.

"Yes."

I set my teeth and looked away. Let her work. She knew how to use this thing she and I both had. And for the moment, she was on my side.

I heard him make some effort with the door. The door didn't even rattle. Beatrice took his hand from it, and with her own hand flat against what appeared to be a large brass knob, she pushed the door open.

"The man who created that lock is nobody in particular," she said. "He doesn't have an unusually high I.Q., didn't even finish college. But sometime in his life he read a science-fiction story in which palmprint locks were a given. He went that story one better by creating one that responded to voice or palm. It took him years, but we were able to give him those years. The people of Dilg are problem solvers, Alan. Think of the problems you could solve!"

He looked as though he were beginning to think, beginning to understand. "I don't see how biological research can be done that way!" he said. "Not with everyone acting on his own, not even aware of other researchers and their work."

"It *is* being done," she said, "and not in isolation. Our retreat in Colorado specializes in it and has—just barely—enough trained, controlled DGDs to see that no one really works in isolation. Our patients can still read and write—those who haven't damaged themselves too badly. They can take each other's work into account if reports are made available to them. And they can read material that comes in from the outside. They're working, Alan. The disease hasn't stopped them, *won't* stop them." He stared at her, seemed to be caught by her intensity—or her scent. He spoke as though his words were a strain, as though they hurt his throat. "I won't be a puppet. I won't be controlled . . . by a goddamn smell!"

"Alan—"

"I won't be what my mother is. I'd rather be dead!"

"There's no reason for you to become what your mother is."

He drew back in obvious disbelief.

"Your mother is brain damaged—thanks to the three months she spent in that custodial-care toilet. She had no speech at all when I met her. She's improved more than you can imagine. None of that has to happen to you. Work with us, and we'll see that none of it happens to you."

He hesitated, seemed less sure of himself. Even that much flexibility in him was surprising. "I'll be under your control or Lynn's," he said.

She shook her head. "Not even your mother is under my control. She's aware of me. She's able to take direction from me. She trusts me the way any blind person would trust her guide."

"There's more to it than that."

"Not here. Not at any of our retreats."

"I don't believe you."

"Then you don't understand how much individuality our people retain. They know they need help, but they have minds of their own. If you want to see the abuse of power you're worried about, go to a DGD ward."

"You're better than that, I admit. Hell is probably better than that. But . . ."

"But you don't trust us."

He shrugged.

"You do, you know." She smiled. "You don't want to, but you do. That's what worries you, and it leaves you with work to do. Look into what I've said. See for yourself. We offer DGDs a chance to live and do whatever they decide is important to them. What do you have, what can you realistically hope for that's better than that?"

Silence. "I don't know what to think," he said finally.

"Go home," she said. "Decide what to think. It's the most important decision you'll ever make."

He looked at me. I went to him, not sure how he'd react, not sure he'd want me no matter what he decided.

"What are you going to do?" he asked.

The question startled me. "You have a choice." I said. "I don't. If she's right . . . how could I not wind up running a retreat?"

"Do you want to?"

I swallowed. I hadn't really faced that question yet. Did I want to spend my life in something that was basically a refined DGD ward? "No!"

"But you will."

". . . Yes." I thought for a moment, hunted for the right words. "You'd do it."

"What?"

"If the pheromone were something only men had, you would do it."

That silence again. After a time he took my hand, and we followed Beatrice out to the car. Before I could get in with him and our guard-escort, she caught my arm. I jerked away reflexively. By the time I caught myself, I had swung around as though I meant to hit her. Hell, I did mean to hit her, but I stopped myself in time. "Sorry," I said with no attempt at sincerity.

She held out a card until I took it. "My private number," she said. "Before seven or after nine, usually. You and I will communicate best by phone."

I resisted the impulse to throw the card away. God, she brought out the child in me.

Inside the car, Alan said something to the guard. I couldn't hear what it was, but the sound of his voice reminded me of him arguing with her—her logic and her scent. She had all but won him for me, and I couldn't manage even token gratitude. I spoke to her, low-voiced.

"He never really had a chance, did he?"

She looked surprised. "That's up to you. You can keep him or drive him away. I assure you, you *can* drive him away."

"How?"

"By imagining that he doesn't have a chance." She smiled faintly. "Phone me from your territory. We have a great deal to say to each other, and I'd rather we didn't say it as enemies."

She had lived with meeting people like me for decades. She had good control. I, on the other hand, was at the end of my control. All I could do was scramble into the car and floor my own phantom accelerator as the guard drove us to the gate. I couldn't look back at her. Until we were well away from the house, until we'd left the guard at the gate and gone off the property, I couldn't make myself look back. For long, irrational minutes, I was convinced that somehow if I turned, I would see myself standing there, gray and old, growing small in the distance, vanishing.

His Powder'd Wig, His Crown of Thornes

Marc Laidlaw

Marc Laidlaw is the author of three novels, *Dad's Nuke, The Neon Lotus*, and *Kalifornia*, the latter a very funny and twisted view of popular culture in the not-so-far future. His first published story (a collaboration with Gregory Benford) appeared in *Omni* in 1978 and Laidlaw has subsequently become a regular contibutor to the magazine, with his most recent story, "The Diane Arbus Suicide Portfolio," having appeared in May 1993.

Laidlaw takes a much darker view than Howard Waldrop does in this alternate America story about multiple betrayals.

His Powder'd Wig, His Crown of Thornes

Marc Laidlaw

Grant Innes first saw the icon in the Indian ghettos of London but thought nothing of it. There were so many gewgaws of native "art" being thrust in his face by faddishly war-painted Cherokees that this was just another nuisance to avoid, like the huge radios blaring obnoxious "Choctawk" percussions and the high-pitched warbling of Tommy Hawkes and the effeminate Turquoise Boys, like the young Mohawk ruddies practicing skateboard stunts for sluttish cockney girls whose kohled black eyes and slack blue lips betrayed more interest in the dregs of the bottles those boys carried than in the boys themselves. Of course, it was not pleasure or curiosity that brought him into the squalid district, among the baggy green canvas street-teepees and graffitoed storefronts. Business alone could bring him here. He had paid a fair sum for the name and number of a Mr. Cloud, dealer in Navaho jewelry, whose samples had proved of excellent quality and would fetch the highest prices, not only in Europe but in the Colonies as well. Astute dealers knew that the rage for turquoise had nearly run its course, thank God; following the popularity of the lurid blue stone, the simplicity of black-patterned silver would be a welcome relief indeed. Grant had hardly been able to tolerate the sight of so much garish rock as he'd been forced to stock in order to suit his customers; he was looking forward to this next trend. He'd already laid the ground for several showcase presentations in Paris; five major glossies were bidding for rights to photograph his collector's pieces, antique sand-cast najas and squash-blossom necklaces, for a special fashion portfolio.

Here in the slums, dodging extruded plastic kachina dolls and machine-woven blankets, his fine-tuned eye was offended by virtually everything he saw. It was trash for tourists. Oh, it had its spurts of cheap popularity, like the warbonnets, which all the cyclists had worn last summer, but such moments were fleeting as pop hits, thank God. Only true quality could ever transcend the dizzying gyres of public favor. Fine art, precious stones, pure metal—these were investments that would never lose their value.

So much garbage ultimately had the effect of blinding him to his environment; avoidance became a mental as well as a physical trick. He was dreaming of silver crescents gleaming against ivory skin when he realized that he must have passed the street he sought. He stopped in his tracks, suddenly aware of the hawkers' cries, the pulse of hide drums and synthesizers. He spun about searching for a number on any of the shops.

"Lost, guy?" said a tall brave with gold teeth, his bare chest ritually scarified. He carried a tall pole strung with a dozen gruesome rubber scalps, along with several barrister's wigs. They gave the brave the appearance of a costume merchant, except for one morbid detail: Each of the white wigs was spattered with blood . . . red dye, rather, liberally dripped among the coarse, white strands.

"You *look* lost."

"Looking for a shop," Grant muttered, fumbling Mr. Cloud's card from his pocket.

"No, I mean really lost. Out of balance. *Koyaanisqatsi,* guv. Like the whole world."

"I'm looking for a shop," Grant repeated firmly.

"That all then? A shop? What about the things you really lost? Things we've all lost, I'm talking about. Here."

He patted his bony hip, which was wrapped in a black leather loincloth. Something dangled from his belt, a doll-like object on a string, a charm of some sort. Grant looked over the brave's head and saw the number he sought, just above a doorway. The damn ruddy was in his way. As he tried to slip past, avoiding contact with the rubbery scalps and bloodied wigs, the brave unclipped the charm from his belt and thrust it into Grant's face.

Grant recoiled, nearly stumbling backward in the street. It was an awful little mannequin, face pinched and soft, its agonized expression carved from a withered apple.

"Here—here's where we lost it," the brave said, thrusting the doll up to Grant's cheek, as if he would have it kiss or nip him with its rice-grain teeth. Its limbs were made of jerked beef, spread-eagled on wooden crossbars, hands and feet fixed in place with four tiny nails. It was a savage Christ—an obscenity.

"He gave His life for you," the brave said. "Not just for one people, but for everyone. Eternal freedom, that was His promise."

"I'm late for my appointment," Grant said, unable to hide his disgust.

"Late and lost," the brave said. "But you'll never catch up—the time slipped past. And you'll never find your way unless you follow Him."

"Just get out of my way!"

He shoved the brave aside, knocking the hideous little idol out of the Indian's grasp. Fearing reprisal, he forced an apologetic expression as he turned back from the hard-won doorway. But the brave wasn't watching him. He crouched over the filthy street, retrieving his little martyr. Lifting it to his lips, he kissed it gently.

"I'm sorry," Grant said.

The brave glanced up at Grant and grinned fiercely, baring his gold teeth; then he bit deep into the dried brown torso of the Christ and tore away a ragged strip of jerky.

Nauseated, Grant hammered on the door. It opened abruptly, and he almost fell into the arms of Mr. Cloud.

He next saw the image the following summer, in the District of Cornwallis. Despite the fact that Grant specialized in provincial art, most of his visits to the Colonies had been for business purposes and had exposed him to no more glorious surroundings than the interiors of banks and mercantile offices, with an occasional jaunt into the Six Nations to meet with the creators of the fine pieces that were his trade. Sales were brisk; his artisans had been convinced to ply their craft with gold as well as silver, supplanting turquoise and onyx with diamonds and other precious stones; the trend toward high-fashion American jewelry had already surpassed his highest expectations. Before the inevitable decline and a panicked search for the next sure thing, he decided to accept the offer of an old colonial acquaintance who had long extended an open invitation to a tour of great American monuments in the capital city.

Arnoldsburg, DC, was sweltering in a humid haze, worsened by exhaust fumes from the taxis that seemed the city's main occupants. Eyes burning, lungs fighting against collapse, he and his guide crawled from taxi after taxi and plunged into cool marble corridors reeking of urine and crowded with black youths selling or buying opiates.

It was hard not to mock the great figures of American history, thus surrounded by the ironic fruits of their victories. The huge, seated figure of Burgoyne looked mildly bemused by the addicts sleeping between his feet; the bronze brothers Richard and William Howe stood back-to-back, embattled in a waist-high mob, as though taking their last stand against colonial lilliputians.

Grant's host, David Mickelson, was a transplanted Irishman. He had first visited America as a physician with the Irish Royal Army, and after his term expired had signed on for a stint in the Royal American Army. He had since opened a successful dermatological practice in Arnoldsburg. He was a collector of native American art, which had led him to deal with Grant Innes. Mickelson had excellent taste in metalwork, but Grant had often chided him for his love of "these marble monstrosities."

"But these are heroes, Grant. Imagine where England would be without these men. An island with few resources and limited room for expansion? How could we have kept up the sort of healthy growth we've had since the Industrial Revolution? And without these men to secure this realm for us, how could we have held on to it? America is so vast—really, you have no concept of it. These warriors laid the way for peace and proper management, steering a narrow course between Spain and France. Without such fine ambassadors to put down the early rebellion and ease the co-settling of the Six Nations, America might still be at war. Instead its resources belong to the Crown. This is our treasure house, Grant, and these are the keepers of that treasure."

"Treasure," Grant repeated, with an idle nudge at the body of an old squaw who lay unconscious on the steps of the Howe Monument.

"Come with me, then," Mickelson said. "One more sight, and then we'll go wherever you like."

They boarded another taxi, which progressed by stops and starts through the iron river of traffic. A broad, enormous dome appeared above the cars.

"Ah," said Grant. "I know what that is."

They disembarked at the edge of a huge circular plaza. The dome that capped the plaza was supported by a hundred white columns. They went into the lidded shadow, into darkness, and for a moment Grant was blinded.

"Watch out, old boy," Mickelson said. "Here's the rail. Grab on. Wouldn't want to stumble in here."

Grant's hand closed on polished metal. When he felt steady again, he opened his eyes and found himself staring into a deep pit. The walls of the shaft were perfectly smooth, round as a bullet hole drilled deep into the earth. He felt a cold wind coming out of it, and then the grip of vertigo.

"The depths of valor, the inexhaustible well of the human spirit," Mickelson was saying. "Makes you dizzy with pride, doesn't it?"

"I'm . . . feeling . . . sick . . . ." Grant turned and hurried toward daylight.

Out in the sunshine again, his sweat gone cold, he leaned against a marble podium and gradually caught his breath. When his mind had cleared somewhat he looked up and saw that the podium was engraved with the name of the hero whose accomplishments the shaft commemorated. His noble bust surmounted the slab.

BENEDICT ARNOLD
FIRST AMERICAN PRESIDENT-GENERAL,
APPOINTED BY KING GEORGE III
AS REWARD FOR HIS VALIANT ROLE
IN SUPPRESSING THE PROVINCIAL
REVOLT OF 1776-79

David Mickelson caught up with him.

"Feeling all right, Grant?"

"Better. I—I think I'd like to get back to my rooms. It's this heat."

"Surely. I'll hail a cab, you just hold on here for a minute."

As Grant watched Mickelson hurry away, his eyes strayed over the circular plaza, where the usual hawkers had laid out the usual souvenirs. Habit, more than curiosity, drove him out among the ragged blankets, his eyes swiftly picking through the merchandise and discarding it all as garbage.

Well, most of it. This might turn out to be another fortunate venture after all. His eye had been caught by a display of absolutely brilliant designs done in copper and brass. He had never seen anything quite like them. Serpents, eagles, patterns of stars. The metal was all wrong, but the artist had undoubtedly chosen them by virtue of their cheapness and could easily be convinced to work in gold. He looked up at the proprietor of these wares and saw a young Indian woman, bent on her knees, threading colored beads on a string.

"Who made these?" he said, softening the excitement he felt into a semblance of mild curiosity.

She gazed up at him. "My husband."

"Really? I like them very much. Does he have a distributor?"

She didn't seem to know what he meant.

"That is . . . does anyone else sell these pieces?"

She shook her head. "This is all he makes, right here. When he makes more, I sell those."

In the distance, he heard Mickelson shouting his name. The dermatologist came running over the marble plaza. "Grant, I've got you a cab!"

Grant gestured as if to brush him away. "I'll meet you later, David, all right? Something's come up."

"What have you found?" Mickelson tried to look past him at the blanket, but Grant spun him around in the direction of the taxis—perhaps a bit too roughly. Mickelson stopped for a moment, readjusted his clothes, then stalked away peevishly toward the cars. So be it.

Smiling, Grant turned back to the woman. His words died on his tongue when he saw what she was doing with beads she'd been stringing.

She had formed them into a noose, a bright rainbow noose, and slipped this over the head of a tiny brown doll.

He knew that doll, knew its tough, leathered flesh and pierced limbs, the apple cheeks and teeth of rice.

The cross from which she'd taken it lay discarded on the blanket, next to the jewelry that suddenly seemed of secondary importance.

While he stood there unspeaking, unmoving, she lifted the dangling doll to her lips and daintily, baring crooked teeth, tore off a piece of the leg.

"What . . . what . . ."

He found himself unable to ask what he wished to ask. Instead, fixed by her gaze, he stammered, "What do you want for all of these?"

She finished chewing before answering. "All?"

"Yes, I . . . I'd like to buy all of them. In fact, I'd like to buy more than this. I'd like to commission a piece, if I might."

The squaw swallowed.

"My husband creates what is within the soul. He makes dreams into metal. He would have to see your dreams."

"My dreams? Well, yes, I'll tell him exactly what I want. Could I meet him to discuss this?"

The squaw shrugged. She patiently unlooped the noose from the shriveled image, spread it back onto its cross and pinned the three remaining limbs into place, then tucked it away in a bag at her belt. Finally, rising, she rolled up the blanket with all the bangles and bracelets inside it and tucked the parcel under her arm. "Come with me," she said.

He followed her without another word, feeling as though he were moving down an incline, losing his balance with every step, barely managing to throw himself in her direction. She was his guide through the steaming city, through the crowds of ragged cloth, skins ruddy and dark. He pulled off his customary jacket, loosened his tie, and struggled after her. She seemed to dwindle in the distance; he was losing her, losing himself, stretching into a thin strand of beads, beads of sweat, sweat that dripped through the gutters of Arnoldsburg and offered only brine to the thirsty. . . .

But when she once looked back and saw him faltering, she put out her hand and he was standing right beside her, near a metal door. She put her hand upon it and opened the way.

It was cool inside and dark except for the tremulous light of candles that lined a descending stairway. He followed, thinking of catacombs, the massed and desiccated ranks of the dead he had seen beneath old missions in Spanish Florida. There was a dusty smell, and far off the sound of hammering. She opened another door and the sound was suddenly close at hand.

They had entered a workshop. A man sat at a metal table cluttered with coils of wire, metal snips, hand torches. The woman stepped out and closed the door on them.

"Good afternoon," Grant said. "I. . . I'm a great admirer of your work."

The man turned slowly, the stool creaking under his weight, though he was not a big man. His skin was very dark, like his close-cropped hair. His face was soft, as though made of chamois pouches; but his eyes were hard. He beckoned.

"Come here," the man said. "You like my stuff? What is it that you like?"

Grant approached the workbench with a feeling of awe. Samples of the man's work lay scattered about, but these were not done in copper or brass. They were silver, most of them, and gleamed like moonlight.

"The style," he said. "The . . . substance."

"How about this?" The Indian fingered a large eagle with spreading wings.

"It's beautiful—almost alive."

"It's a sign of freedom." He laid it down. "What about this one?"

He handed Grant a small rectangular plaque inscribed with an unusual but somehow familiar design. A number of horizontal stripes, with a square inset in the lower right corner, and in that square a wreath of thirteen stars.

"It's beautiful," Grant said. "You do superior work."

"That's not what I mean. Do you know the symbol?"

"I . . . I think I've seen it somewhere before. An old Indian design, isn't it?"

The Indian grinned. Gold teeth again, bridging the distance between London and Arnoldsburg, reminding him of the jerked beef martyr, the savage Christ.

"Not an Indian sign," he said. "A sign for all people."

"Really? Well, I'd like to bring it to all people. I'm a dealer in fine jewelry. I could get a very large audience for these pieces. I could make you a very rich man."

"Rich?" The Indian set the plaque aside. "Plenty of Indians are rich. The tribes have all the land and factories they want—as much as you have. But we lack what you also lack: freedom. What is wealth when we have no freedom?"

"Freedom?"

"It's a dim concept to you, isn't it? But not to me." He put his hand over his heart. "I hold it here, safe with the memory of how we lost it. A precious thing, a cup of holy water that must never be spilled until it can be swallowed in a single draft. I carry the cup carefully, but there's enough for all. If you wish to drink, it can be arranged."

"I don't think you understand," Grant said, recovering some part of himself that had begun to drift off through the mystical fog in which the Indians always veiled themselves. He must do something concrete to counteract so much vagueness.

"What I'm speaking of is a business venture. A partnership."

"I hear your words. But I see something deeper in you. Something that sleeps in all men. They come here seeking what is lost, looking for freedom and a cause. But all they find are the things that went wrong. Why are you so out of balance, eh? You stumble and crawl, but you always end up here with that same empty look in your eyes. I've seen you before. A dozen just like you."

"I'm an art dealer," Grant said. "Not a . . . a pilgrim. If you can show me more work like this, I'd be grateful. Otherwise, I'm sorry for wasting your time and I'll be on my way."

Suddenly he was anxious to get away, and this seemed a reasonable excuse. But the jeweler now seemed ready to accommodate him.

"Art, then," he said. "All right. I will show you the thing that speaks to you, and perhaps then you will understand. Art is also a way to the soul."

He slipped down from the stool and moved toward the door, obviously intending for Grant to follow.

"I'll show you more than this," the Indian said. "I'll show you inspiration."

After another dizzying walk, they entered a derelict museum in a district that stank of danger. Grant felt safe only because of his companion; he was obviously a stranger here, in these oppressive alleys. Even inside the place, which seemed less a museum than a warehouse, he sensed that he was being watched. It was crowded by silent mobs, many of them children, almost all of them Negro or Indian. Some sat in circles on the cement floors, talking quietly among themselves, as though taking instruction. Pawnee, Chickasaw, Blackfoot, Cheyenne, Comanche . . . Arnoldsburg was a popular site for tourists, but these didn't have the look of the ruddy middle-class traveler; these were lower-class ruddies, as tattered as the people in the street. Some had apparently crossed the continent on foot to come here. Grant felt as if he had entered a church.

"Now you shall see," said the jeweler. "This is the art of the patriots. The forefathers. The hidden ones."

He stopped near a huge canvas that leaned against a steel beam; the painting was caked with grease, darkened by time, but even through the grime Grant could see that it was the work of genius. An imitation of Da Vinci's Last Supper, but strangely altered . . .

The guests at Christ's table wore not biblical attire but that of the eighteenth century. It was no windowed building that sheltered them but a tent whose walls gave the impression of a strong wind beating from without. The thirteen were at supper, men in military outfits, and in their midst a figure of mild yet radiant demeanor, humble in a powdered wig, a mere crust of bread on his plate. Grant did not recognize him, this figure in Christ's place, but the man in Judas's place was recognizable enough from the numerous busts and portraits occurring in Arnoldsburg. That was Benedict Arnold.

The Indian pointed at several of the figures, giving them names: "Henry Knox, Nathanael Greene, Light-Horse Harry Lee, Lafayette, General Rochambeau . . ."

"Who painted this?"

"It was the work of Benjamin Franklin," said his guide. "Painted not long after the betrayal at West Point, but secretly, in sadness, when the full extent of our tragedy became all too apparent. After West Point the patriots continued to fight. But this man, this one man, was the glue that held the soldiers together. After His death, the army had many commanders, but none could win the trust of all men. The revolution collapsed and our chance for freedom slipped away. Franklin died without finishing it, his heart broken."

"But that man in the middle . . . ?"

The Indian led him to another painting. This was much more recent, judging from the lack of accumulated soot and grease. Several children stood gazing at it, accompanied by a darkie woman who was trying to get them to analyze the meaning of what was essentially a simple image.

"What is this?" she asked.

Several hands went up. "The cherry tree!" chimed a few voices.

"That's right, the cherry tree. Who can tell us the story of the cherry tree?"

One little girl pushed forward. "He chopped it down, and when He saw what He had done, He said, 'I cannot let it die.' So He planted the piece He cut off and it grew into a new tree, and the trunk of the old tree grew, too, because it was magic."

"Very good. Now, that's a fable, of course. Do you know what it really means? What the cherry tree represents?"

Grant felt like one of her charges, waiting for some explanation, innocent.

"It's an English cherry," the teacher hinted.

Hands went up. "The tree! I know, I know! It's England."

"That's right," she encouraged. "And the piece he transplanted?"
"America!"
"Very good. And do you remember what happened next? It isn't shown in this painting, but it was very sad. Tinsha?"
"When His father saw what He had done, he was very scared, he was afraid his son was a devil or something, so he tore up the little tree by the roots. He tore up America."
"And you know who the father really is, don't you?"
"The . . . King?" said Tinsha.

Grant and his guide went on to another painting, this one showing a man in a powdered wig and a ragged uniform walking across a river in midwinter—not stepping on the floes but moving carefully between them, on the breast of the frigid water. With him came a band of barefoot men, lightly touching hands, the first of them resting his fingers on the cape of their leader. The men stared at the water as if they could not believe their eyes, but there was only confidence in the face of their commander—that and a serene humility.

"This is the work of Sully, a great underground artist," said the jeweler.
"These . . . these are priceless."

The Indian shrugged. "If they were lost tomorrow, we would still carry them with us. It is the feelings they draw from our hearts that are truly beyond price. He came for all men, you see. If you accept Him, if you open your heart to Him, then His death will not have been in vain.

"Washington," Grant said, the name finally coming to him. An insignificant figure of the American Wars, an arch-traitor whose name was a mere footnote in the histories that Grant had read. Arnold had defeated him, hadn't he? Was that what had happened at West Point? The memories were vague and unreal, textbook memories.

The jeweler nodded. "Yes, George Washington," he repeated. "He was leading us to freedom, but He was betrayed and held out as an example. In Philadelphia He was publicly tortured to dispirit the rebels, then hung by His neck after His death, and his corpse toured through the Colonies. And that is our sin, the penance which we must pay until every soul has been brought back into balance."

"Your sin?"

The Indian nodded, drawing from the pouch at his waist another of the shriveled icons, Christ—no, Washington—on the cross.

"We aided the British in that war. Cherokee and Iroquois, others of the Six Nations. We thought the British would save us from the Colonists; we didn't know that they had different ways of enslavement. My ancestors were master torturers. When Washington was captured, it fell to them—to us—to do the bloodiest work."

His hands tightened on the figure of flesh; the splintered wood dug into his palm.

"We nailed Him to the bars of a cross, borrowing an idea that pleased us greatly from your own religion."

The brown hand shook. The image rose to the golden mouth.

"First, we scalped Him. The powdered hair was slung from a warrior's belt. His flesh was pierced with thorns and knives. And then we flayed Him alive."

"Flayed..."

Grant winced as golden teeth nipped a shred of jerky and tore it away.

"Alive...?"

"He died bravely. He was more than a man. He was our deliverer, savior of all men, white, red, and black. And we murdered Him. We pushed the world off balance."

"What is this place?" Grant asked. "It's more than a museum, isn't it? It's also some kind of school."

"It is a holy place. His spirit lives here, in the heart of the city named for the man who betrayed Him. He died to the world two hundred years ago, but He still lives in us. He is champion of the downtrodden, liberator of the enslaved." The jeweler's voice was cool despite the fervor of his theme. "You see... I have looked beyond the walls of fire that surround this world. I have looked into the world that should have been, that would have been if He had lived. I saw a land of the free, a land of life, liberty, and happiness, where the red men lived in harmony with the white. Our plains bore fruit instead of factories. And the holy cause that of the republic, spread from the hands of the Great Man. The King was dethroned and England, too, made free. The bell of liberty woke the world; the four winds carried the cause." The jeweler bowed his head. "That is how it would have been. This I have seen in dreams."

Grant looked around him at the paintings, covered with grime but carefully attended; the people, also grimy but with an air of reverence. It was a shame to waste them here, on these people. He imagined the paintings hanging in a well-lit gallery, the patina of ages carefully washed away; he saw crowds of people in fine clothes, decked in his gold jewelry, each willing to pay a small fortune for admission. With the proper sponsorship, a world tour could be brought off. He would be a wealthy man, not merely a survivor, at the end of such a tour. The Indian watched him, nodding. "I know what you're thinking. You think it would be good to tell the world of these things, to spread the cause. You think you can carry the message to all humanity, instead of letting it die here in the dark. But I tell you . . . it thrives here. Those who are oppressed, those who are broken and weary of spirit, they alone are the caretakers of liberty."

Grant smiled inwardly; there was a bitter taste in his mouth.

"I think you underestimate the worth of all this," he said. "You do it a disservice to hide it from the eyes of the world. I think everyone can gain something from it."

"Yes?" The Indian looked thoughtful.

He led Grant toward a table where several old books lay open, their pages swollen with humidity, spines cracking, and paper flaking away.

"Perhaps you are right," he said, turning the pages of one book entitled *The Undying Patriot*, edited by a Parson Weems. "It may be as Doctor Franklin says. . . ."

Grant bent over the page and read:

"Let no man forget His death. Let not the memory of our great Chief and Commander fade from the thoughts of the common people, who stand to gain the most from its faithful preservation. For once these dreams have fad'd, there is no promise that they may again return. In this age and the next, strive to hold true to the honor'd principals for which He fought, for which he was nail'd to the rude crucifix and his flesh stript away. Forget not His sacrifice, His powder'd wig and crown of thornes. Forget not that a promise broken can never be repair'd."

"I think you are right," said the jeweler. "How can we take it upon ourselves to hide this glory away? It belongs to the world, and the world shall have it."

He turned to Grant and clasped his hands. His eyes were afire with a patriotic light. "He brought you to me, I see that now. This is a great moment. I thank you, brother, for what you will do."

"It's only my duty." Grant said.

Yes. Duty.

And now he stood in the sweltering shadows outside the warehouse, the secret museum, watching the loading of several large vans. The paintings were wrapped tightly in canvas so that none could see them.

He stifled an urge to rush up to the loading men and tear away the cloth, to look just once more on the noble face. But the police were thick around the entrance.

"Careful, Grant," said David Mickelson at his elbow.

News of the find had spread throughout the city and a crowd had gathered, in which Grant was just one more curious observer. He supposed that it was best this way, although he would rather have had his own people moving the paintings. The police were being unwontedly rough with the works, but there wasn't anything he could do about that.

Things had gotten a little out of hand.

"Hard to believe it's been sitting under our noses all this time," said Mickelson. "You say you actually got a good look at it?"

Grant nodded abstractedly. "Fairly good. Of course, it was dark in there."

"Even so... what a catch, eh? There have been rumors of this stuff for years, and you stumble right into it. Amazing idea you had, though, organizing a tour. As if anyone would pay to see that stuff aside from ruddies and radicals. Even if it weren't completely restricted."

"What... what do you think they'll do with it?" Grant asked.

"Same as they do with other contraband, I'd imagine. Burn it."

"Burn it," he repeated numbly.

Grant felt a restriction of the easy flow of traffic; suddenly the crowd, mainly black and Indian, threatened to change into something considerably more passionate than a group of disinterested onlookers. The police loosened their riot gear as the mob began to shout insults.

"Fall back, Grant," Mickelson said.

Grant started to move away through the crowd, but a familiar face caught his attention. It was the Indian, the jeweler; he stood near a corner of the museum, his pouchy face unreadable. Somehow, through all the confusion, among the hundred or so faces now mounting in number, his eyes locked onto Grant's.

Grant stiffened. The last of the vans shut its doors and rushed away. The police did not loiter in the area. He had good reason to feel vulnerable.

The jeweler stared at him. Stared without moving. Then he brought up a withered brown object and set it to his lips. Grant could see him bite, tear, and chew.

"What is it, Grant? We should be going now, don't you think? There's still time to take in a real museum or perhaps the American Palace."

Grant didn't move. Watching the Indian, he put his thumb to his mouth and caught a bit of cuticle between his teeth. He felt as if he were dreaming. Slowly, he tore off a thin strip of skin, ripping it back almost down to the knuckle. The pain was excruciating, but it didn't seem to wake him. He chewed it, swallowed.

"Grant? Is anything wrong?"

He tore off another.

Covenant of Souls

Michael Swanwick

Michael Swanwick made his debut in 1980 with two powerful stories, "The Feast of St. Janis" and "Ginungagap," both of which were nominated for the Nebula that year. Since then, he has published short fiction in a variety of genre and mainstream markets. *Omni* has published several science fiction or fantasy stories by Swanwick, but increasingly his time has been taken up with novels, the most recent of which, *Stations of the Tide,* won the Nebula for Best Novel in 1992.

"Covenant of Souls" (*Omni,* December 1986) is a novelette about the end of civilization as we know it, and much of the background is taken from Swanwick's former job as church secretary for Tabernacle Church in West Philadelphia (the same church in which he got married).

Covenant of Souls

Michael Swanwick

Something ugly was growing in the air above the altar. Peter Wieland didn't notice it at first. He'd entered the sanctuary from the rear, through the Thirty-seventh Street narthex, and gone to the front pew without once glancing at the altar. He set his brown paper bag beside him and removed a cup of black coffee, a bottle of grapefruit juice, and an egg-and-sausage sandwich. He flattened the bag and set the bottle and cup atop it. Stray drops of coffee and juice mingled in its folds.

Downstairs the nursery school was coming in from the play yard—Peter could hear the children's voices. He loosened his coat and reached into his shirt pocket for the leads to his Sony-Toshiba "Soundless." The magazine was loaded to capacity with forty-some thumbnail discs. He looped the bone-inductor mike around his neck and, eyes closed, switched it on. Full, rich music flooded his body—Peter had set the *Worcester Fragments* first in the stack so he could have Gregorian chants to go with breakfast and the beginning of the workday. He leaned back and let the noiseless sound thunder up his spine. Then slowly, lazily, he opened his eyes.

Light through the east window glinted yellow off a carved wooden angel at the tip of one rafter support. Peter's gaze wandered to the front of the chancel and down the arch of organ pipes recessed into the stone behind the darkly shadowed presbytery.

He saw the thing.

Peter squinted, shook his head in an involuntary shiver. He saw . . . something, he was not sure what. It was as if he'd stared into the sun until the rods and cones of his eyes began to burn out. It shimmered. Gingerly, he stretched out a thumb at arm's length and found he could hide it from view. But it was still there when he lowered his arm, a small, crawling . . . nothingness in the air.

He shifted his head, forcing his gaze away. The thing did not move. It remained over the altar, whether he was looking that way or not.

Peter's mouth tasted sour. He wrapped his unfinished sandwich in a paper napkin, shoved it into his pocket, and gathered up the trash. He left the sanctuary with only one backward glance at the strange presence he was *not quite* sure was there.

Peter dumped the trash in a basket in the parish hall and then reset the thermostat timer for the Social Action Committee meeting that night. He went downstairs to the smaller furnace room off the kitchen to check the boiler's water level. It was low today, and he ran a few gallons in. Back through the staircase landing, with its line of padlocked storage cabinets, Peter climbed the four steps to the dirt-floored half-basement under the sanctuary. He unlocked the door. The *Fragments* were still playing within him, though he had long forgotten their presence.

Peter peered into the dark, cold basement. A few miserly glints of light seeped from windows inadequately boarded up. He flicked the light switch, and a string of bare electric bulbs lit up in a sparse line to the sanctuary boiler in the far rear. Their light barely seemed to reach the ground; darkness huddled around them.

Taking the unfinished sandwich from his pocket, Peter unwrapped it and set it down on the dirt, atop its napkin. "Listen," he called into the darkness. "There's a bite of food here, and if you stop by the church office, I'll write you out a meal letter. You can take it to the Emergency Center down the street, and they'll give you a meal. But I want you out of here or I'll call the cops. You understand that? Do you?"

There was no answer.

He locked the door behind him and took the steps in two leaps. The momentum stayed with him, and when Sheila from the nursery stepped onto the landing, he almost collided with her. She flinched away with a small shriek.

"Jesus!" he said, "you startled me." The music switched off, and suddenly the world seemed empty and silent.

Dark, curly hair framed Sheila's thin face. "I'm sorry." She laughed and made a clutching motion at her heart. Then, serious again, she nodded toward the door. "So what's the verdict? Do you still think there's someone living in there?"

"Yeah, one of the vent people, I think. Probably just some harmless old wino who kicked in a window, but I'd hate to go wandering through there looking for him. It's like a maze, all broken furniture and old walls for rooms that don't exist anymore."

"Well, couldn't we just call the police and let *them* throw this guy out?"

Peter shook his head. "I wouldn't want to unless I was absolutely sure. You realize they're charging fifty bucks for a false call?"

"I can remember when the police would come for free."

"You should—they only started charging six months ago."

Sheila looked at him reproachfully. "That was a joke."

"Oh." There was something terribly woebegone about her expression, her tone of voice, that was completely out of sync with their conversation. Peter looked more carefully at Sheila and saw that she was actually trembling at the brink of tears. "What's the matter, then?" he asked gently.

"Have you seen Sam lately?"

The question took him by surprise. "No, not lately—I'd assumed he was mostly working in this part of the building."

"Oh, Peter, I just talked with Sam yesterday, and I think he's dying!"

Jennifer came out of the coal bin, where she had made a nest for herself. Furtively, she made her way to first the one door (sniffing at the sandwich there but not touching it), then the other. The second door's frame was weak. She put a shoulder to it and heaved and gave the door a shove with one hand. Still locked, it popped open. She was in the children's bathroom now, all yellow-painted stalls and a single sink. It was warm here and smelled pleasantly of decay. She paused at the back landing to listen before going through the main room and into the kitchen. She could hear the children and their teachers out in the play yard again.

Jennifer hit up the refrigerator first, stealing a swallow of milk from a plastic gallon there and an open jar of spaghetti sauce with a circle of blue-green mold growing atop it. In one of the cupboards was a tin of cookies, sealed against the mice, and she lifted a handful of cookies from it.

With a spoon she found in the stainless-steel sink, Jennifer carefully scraped off the mold. She retreated back to her nest, temporarily satisfied, alternating butter cookies with spoonfuls of sauce.

She still could not remember arriving at the church or what—if anything—had come before. Her mind was like a body coming out of surgery, numb but with unfamiliar pains waiting under the anesthetic. She was not consciously aware that her memories had fled, and she was driven by no desires, aims, or goals.

But she knew that she had to eat.

* * *

When Peter arrived at his office in the old manse (which was attached to the church but had no connecting passage *with* it), he found a note from the pastor on a piece of Covenant letterhead: ON STUDY LEAVE THRU TUES WEEK-WILL LEVE TYPING, TAKE MSSGES EVES. Beside it was a stack of work: routine correspondence, the November *Peace Letter*, next Sunday's service, last month's council minutes.

With a disgusted sigh, Peter slapped on the typewriter. His Toshiba began playing a decade-old Touchstone album: hard-driving electric folk. He set the council notes to one side of the typewriter and an ashtray to the other, lit up, and began typing:

Council APPROVED the trustees' recommendations that (1) we will need to terminate our existing contract with the sexton effective January 1 of the new year. We will provide letters of recommendation and provide assistance in seeking out other churches for Sam if he is interested.

Peter let the cigarette dangle from his mouth, like Bogart, occasionally drawing it up with his lips and sucking in a long drag. He paid little attention to what he was typing, still worried about the thing over the altar, wondering whether he'd gotten caught in the weekend drugs trap and taken his hallucinations with him into the workweek. The outer door slammed, the office door flew open, and Sam stormed into the office. "Listen," he said, "you call the curator, call Mr. Alverson, and tell him that the coffee urn in the kitchen is broke. It's broke, and *I* can't fix it 'cause I don't got the parts. Now I've shut off the water to the urn and I've disconnected the pipes, but I don't know whether I can lift it down or not. I can't move this arm too well, 'cause they just operated on it."

The old sexton's face and neck were swelled and puffy, and his skin was unnaturally gray. His breathing was harsh.

"I could help you take the urn down," Peter offered.

"I didn't ask for no help!" the man snapped. "I can do it. Never said I couldn't. I just want you to call Mr. Alverson and tell him I'll need me some money for parts."

A quick flip through the Rolodex brought up Alverson's work number, and he punched it into his phone. A secretarial voice said, "Rosen and Weiss," and Peter said, "Yes. Hello. I'm calling from Midlands Investment Corporation, and I'd like to speak with Mr. Alverson."

A moment later Alverson's voice said, "Hello, Mr. Wexberg? I—"

"No, this is the church," Peter said. "The reason I'm calling is . . ."

"Peter," Alverson said tiredly, "there is not the *money* for whatever it is.

How can I make you understand that?"

"Look," Peter said, "I'm not calling you about the roof or the toilets or the pipes that are going to burst one of these days and take out half the church with them. I just want you to talk with Sam." He thrust the receiver at the sexton. "Here."

He snatched up the *Peace Letter* and scanned a pious rant on radiation-burn victims for grammatical errors. When Sam was gone, he reread the last paragraph on the typewriter. *I'll bet that nobody's actually told Sam any of this,* he thought. He went on to the next paragraph.

(2) When a new sexton is hired, a warm, sensitive supervisory relationship should be developed which has not existed in recent years with Sam.

It was night when Jennifer next came out, and because she dared not return to the refrigerator so soon, food was harder to find. The kitchen cupboards yielded only a chunk of old cheese, hard as a rock and ignored even by the mice. Gnawing off one tasteless flake at a time, Jennifer went up the back stairs to the top floor.

The room over the parish hall was originally a chapel, and it still retained the rose windows and oak balconies. But the floor space had been partitioned into three rooms at a time when the nursery school had been larger. Now they were used exclusively for storage. Jennifer climbed over a partition and systematically rifled old supply cabinets until finally she found a box of noodles among the crayons, paper scissors, and glue. She took two handfuls down to the kitchen and threw them into a pot, which she filled with water and set on the ancient, black gas stove to boil.

The nursery room across from the kitchen had been left unlocked, and Jennifer peeked within. It was a room for hobbits, filled with child-scaled tables and chairs and lit only by a fluorescent bulb over the fish tank. Chains of paper loops and shadowy crayoned pictures festooned the walls. Low shelves were tumbleful of toys. She tapped a bit of fish food to the guppies and watched them flurry over it. There was a plastic brush on one table. She picked it up and sat down in a munchkin-size chair and began combing out her straight, midback-length hair. It glinted auburn in the fish light.

She was about to go check on the noodles when the lights blazed on and an old black man walked in the door.

Jennifer flinched back in the chair, half blinded and afraid. Her heart scudded wildly, and her large-knuckled hands clenched white. The sexton stopped when he saw her. "I got to clean this room *tonight,* missy," he said defiantly.

But when Jennifer started to stand, the man waved her down. "No, don't you get up; that's all *right*—I'll mop around you. No need for you to get up." He lifted a bucket of soapy water into the room and shifted a few chairs and toys, shaking his head at their being in his way. He plunged the mop into the bucket and began swabbing.

"You with the nursery school?" Sam asked. When she said nothing, he nodded, taking her silence for assent. He mopped vigorously, with the habit of years. But the effort it cost him was obvious, and his breathing soon grew ragged and harsh. He took a gulping breath and leaned against the mop, closing his eyes for strength. "Then you ought to know that I can't come in during the day," he said. "A little bit in the morning, but I got chemotherapy and radiotherapy during the day. I don't want to come in at night, but I got no choice."

"Why?" She was startled by her voice—it was totally new to her. It frightened her, and yet almost immediately she wanted to say something again, for the question had caught her by surprise, and she still had no sense of how her voice sounded.

"There's a mass on my lungs," he said, "but that's not all. There's more wrong than that. They found the mass, but they're not sure about the other." Gingerly he sat down on one of the low tables. "There's something the matter with my heart."

Jennifer searched for words, found some: "You'll get better." Their sound thrilled and elated her.

The old man opened his eyes, stared off into the middle distance sightlessly. "I'm not going to get better, young miss. I'm going to die." Tears trembled at the corners of his eyes, and he shook his head, sending them flying. "But you know what, I don't *want* to die. I realize that everybody got to die *some*time, but that don't make it any easier. I don't *want* to die!"

"You won't die," Jennifer said.

Sam clutched the mop handle, staring bitterly at the floor. The tears began falling, large, slow, one at a time.

Quietly Jennifer left. In the kitchen she found the noodles had overboiled and the water had put out the flame in the gas burner. Before she returned to her nest she saw Sam put his key ring away in one of the cupboards on the front basement landing. He covered them over with an old rag, but she knew where they were.

Coming up the walk to his office, Peter tripped and dropped his breakfast. The bottle of juice shattered into the sandwich, and he was able to save only half the coffee. He entered his office in a foul mood, dumped the food into the trash, and plugged in the electric heater he kept in the leg well of his desk.

He pulled the paperback copy of *Moby Dick* from his hip pocket (he was one-third through, his usual bog-down point) and slammed it onto the desk top. Impatiently he drew up his chair. Among the papers on his desk was the Xeroxed council minutes sheet he'd left in the pastor's mail slot the night before. He'd circled the sexton items and written HAS ANYBODY TOLD SAM? in the margin. Now it had been returned with NO. DO IT, PLEASE printed below in the pastor's calm, neat lettering.

Angrily, Peter scrawled ARE YOU AWARE THAT SAM IS *DYING*? below the pastor's note and returned the minutes to the slot. That bought him a day. He picked up his paperback, ignoring the phone that started ringing just then, since he wasn't yet officially in. Then the doorbell buzzed, and that he couldn't possibly ignore.

"Yes?" He opened the door partway, blocking entry with his body. It was one of the vent people, a short, fat man with his hair done up in greasy dreadlocks. His clothes were rotting on his body. Peter could smell them. The man was the color of the city—clothes, skin, hair, all the same grimy industrial gray—and Peter recognized him. "Oh, it's you, Ashod."

Ashod clutched a broken plastic rosary in one fist held up before him, crucifix dangling at the end of a single string. It was bright pink. "I gave you a meal letter two weeks ago," Peter said. "I can't give you another for at least a month. Come back when it gets really cold, and nobody'll mind."

Ashod waved his fist back and forth in negation, the crucifix swinging wildly. "No, no, it's not that. I want to see the lady."

"Lady? Somebody in the nursery school?"

Ashod nodded his head vigorously. "No. I want to see the *Lady*. I want her to make the voices go away."

The telephone was ringing again. It was almost certainly time he was at work. "Come back when it's cold," Peter said, closing the door. "Understand? *Cold.*"

Jennifer was learning the building's rhythms, the daily ebb and flow of people. She emerged when the nursery school children were outside in the yard. Moving quickly, efficiently, she stole another handful of noodles and set them to boiling. Then she took a double handful of colored crayons, being careful to choose only the largest, near-unused ones, and husked them of their paper shells. She set a second pot of water to boil and placed a slightly smaller pot within to make a double boiler. She dumped the crayons into the smaller pot and watched them soften and wilt—periwinkle blue folding over aquamarine, goldenrod yellow over bittersweet brown.

When the noodles were done, she strained them and dumped them onto a plate. The crayons were all melted by then, and she briskly stirred them into a brown swirl and then a chocolate mess. She poured the crayons over the noodles, took up a spoon, and began eating.

Sheila found Peter just inside the sanctuary door. One hand rested on a stone arch, and a trace of steam curled up from his nostrils. "Peter," she said, "the nursery rooms are *freezing*. Isn't there anything you can do about it?"

"Already taken care of," he answered abstractedly. "The water was low in the boiler, so the automatic shutoff cut in. I bled in water, and the radiators should be heating up soon."

"Everything seems to be going wrong now that Sam isn't here in the daytime anymore. Why does the heat keep going off?"

"Well, you could say it's because there's a leak where the radiator pipes loop under the sanctuary. When the water heats up, the pipe expands and dumps onto the dirt floor there until the system shuts itself off. Or you could say it's because most apprentice plumbers were of draft age, so the master plumbers have to do the scut work themselves; so there's more demand than they have time for, and they charge accordingly. Or you could say that as long as I can correct it by adding water, it's not an emergency, and they won't allocate money to fix it."

"But—"

"The thing to keep in mind," Peter said, "is that this kind of problem is normal with a system this old."

"I guess so, but—oh! Do you want to hear the latest? The children have seen a ghost!"

"A ghost?" Peter said blankly.

"Yes, a girl ghost—they say she's very pretty. They're all excited, and now they're trying to set up ghost traps for her. They're so cute!"

Peter was giving her his undivided attention now, and Sheila found his steady, green gaze disconcerting. He said nothing, but she had no difficulty following his thoughts.

"Oh," she said. "You think the person in the basement . . . Peter, you've got to call the police and get her *out* of there!"

"As long as the nursery school guarantees the false-call fee."

"They wouldn't hurt her, would they?" Sheila asked, suddenly apprehensive.

Peter smiled cynically. "They'd beat the crap out of her for sure. The police have been taking a real tough line on street people lately."

"Then there must be some other way!"

"No," Peter said calmly, "it's the police or else let her stay." His expression was distant, abstracted again. He reached out and took her hand, placed it against the stone arch. "Feel this, would you?"

The stone was as cold as ice. It throbbed ever so slightly under her touch. Now that she was aware of it, too, it hummed subliminally, like a machine or a high-tension power line. Attuned, it seemed as if the entire building were full of the almost inaudible vibration. "What is it?" she asked.

Peter shrugged.

It must have something to do with how cold it is, she decided.

Peter turned from locking up the church to see that someone was standing before the manse door, futilely waiting for someone to come answer the bell. He walked up behind the man, keys out, said, "Can I help you?" in a tone that implied he couldn't, and began unlocking the door.

"Yes," the man said, "I'd like to see the inside of your church." He was well dressed and clean-shaven and good-looking in a perfectly forgettable sort of way.

"Services are ten-thirty Sunday mornings," Peter said, stepping inside and preparing to close the door.

"It's not about that, sir!" the man said quickly, bringing his hands up before him. He proffered a wallet badge—badly printed allegorical figures with a shield, Latin slogan, space for name typed in and signature squiggle—and put it away when Peter shrugged. "I'm from the Cancer Research Center at Philadelphia Medical College—perhaps you've heard of us?" Of course Peter had; the college was only a few blocks distant. "We're doing a building-to-building canvass in this area."

"We give through the church's national headquarters."

"Oh, it's not that, sir." The man gave a short, insincere laugh. "We're searching for some stolen—and very valuable—research materials, and we have good reason to believe that the thief has hidden them in this area. If you could only—"

"No," Peter said.

The man smiled plausibly. "I believe you will find it *easier*, sir, if you—"

"I'm halfway through the week, and already I'm two days behind schedule. I've got a bulletin and two mailings to get out, and I can't spare the time to nursemaid visitors. Now if you want to go through channels, the pastor here is associated with PMC through the chaplain's office. If you can get him to agree that you are more important than my usual work—fine. If not, you can always come to services. Ten-thirty Sunday mornings." He shut the door in the man's face.

But my *God*, that man's eyes were cold.

* * *

Jeremy was playing hide-and-go-seek. Normally, it was hard to get away from his teachers, but today Debbie was sick and the substitute never showed up, and neither did one of the parent volunteers; so they were short on adults. And then Gregory's mother had called because he'd forgotten his lunch, and Ming-su had started crying because she always cried at that time of day, and there was someone banging on the door to get in; so for a minute there was no one in the room but kids. So Jeremy told Heather, who was his girlfriend and who was going to marry him when they grew up, to close her eyes and count real slow; and he ran into the kitchen looking for a place to hide.

The kitchen was full of cupboards and stuff, but they were either locked or else the knobs were too high to reach. It was too narrow behind the refrigerator and too open under the sinks. Then he noticed that someone had left the oven door open.

Jeremy knew that ovens were dangerous, so he put his hand in first to make sure it was off and not hot. Then he crawled in. It was roomy inside and easy to shut the door after him, because it was springy and light. You just tapped it and it closed on its own. It was dark. Lying on the floor, Jeremy stifled a giggle at the thought of Heather looking for him. There was a little hole near his nose, and a funny smell came out of it that made him feel sleepy. He had just closed his eyes for a minute or two when the oven door opened and the ghost looked in. She was real pretty and real skinny, too. She did not look surprised to see Jeremy, and he was too sleepy to be surprised himself. "Shhh," he said. "I'm hiding."

"Oh," the ghost said. Then, "Is it fun?"

Jeremy thought about that for a moment, then said, "No." It had been fun, but now it was mostly just dull.

The ghost smiled then and said, "Well why don't you come out?" She reached in her arm—a long, long way—and gently tugged him out.

For an instant he felt dizzy and funny and cold, but then he was standing blinking on the kitchen floor, and the ghost was gone. The kitchen looked funny because the shadows had shifted and the light had changed since he had crawled inside. It was all of a sudden a lot later in the day.

He ran off to find Heather.

Peter was the only attendee from the church staff at the monthly tenants' meeting. They sat around a table in the old manse's conference room, in front of the fireplace with its glazed tile and tinned-up front, swapping gossip and sharing news. Peter listened and nodded and answered questions and con-

structed the month's complaint list:
1. Heat! (leak under sacristy—fix?)
2. Mice
    —more traps?
    —poison not working?
3. Light bulbs (*if* can find source will extend credit)
4. Toilet paper (tell Sam)
5. Building Security
    —more padlocks
    —everyone more care
6. Dupe key for WomensRights
7. Rent Schedule
    —can wait another week, nursery school?
    —can wait another *month*, STPPRCDC?

The afternoon volunteer for the Stop the Point Pleasant Radio-Chemical Dump Coalition complained that the Latin American campaign was drawing off most of their volunteer labor and wanted to know why there were so many derelicts around the building of late. Peter shrugged, promised to find out, and made a note:

8. Why winos?

Mrs. Untiedt, of WomensRights—a relatively successful organization that rented the entire basement floor of the old manse and mostly used the door directly out through the nursery school play yard—asked why they hadn't gotten their doorbell fixed yet. Peter explained that their usual handyman didn't like working for churches, which were notoriously slow to pay, and made another note:

9. Nudge Jack—doorbell!

Sheila told about one of the nursery school children, who had been lost for several hours that morning, and who claimed to have hidden in the kitchen oven. "He couldn't have hidden there," she said, "or he'd have suffocated." Then, thoughtfully, "I don't think that oven is safe, though, Peter. You've really got to *do* something."

"Do you want the door welded shut?" Peter asked.

"No, don't do *that*," Sheila said. "We need the oven because sometimes we bake for the children."

Peter nodded and wrote:

10. Make oven safe for children.

Before Sheila could think to ask how he intended doing this, he rose and broke up the meeting.

Sam was waiting at the desk. "Listen," he said, "I got to talk with Mr. Alverson." His neck was still puffed out beyond his chin, and his skin was a gruesome color gray. Peter nodded, dialed, and told the secretary: "This is Harry's brother—Fred Alverson? I'm in town unexpectedly and thought I could have lunch with Harry."

When Alverson's voice cried out, "Fred! You old son of a bitch, what are you—?" Peter handed the phone over to Sam and walked out of the room.

Sheila was waiting in the hallway. She nodded toward the room and in a low voice said, "How is he?"

Peter shook his head. "He's going to die."

"Don't say that!"

"He's going to die," Peter said stubbornly. "And he's going to keep working here until he drops. Every time I go to the bathroom I expect to open the stall door and find him sitting dead on the crapper."

There were a lot of different paints in the cabinet, and some were good to drink and others were not. There was a thunderstorm going on, and as Jennifer crouched in the dark and tasted, she could hear distant rumblings and stone-rattling *cracks* in the air overhead. There was also the sound of pouring water and a few snaps of blue electricity from the steel cable of one lightning rod that ran through the cellar into the earth. Sated at last, she fetched the sexton's keys and went exploring.

The door to the organ room was off the sacristy, and it didn't open all the way. Jennifer slid inside, closing the door after her, and waited for her eyes to adjust.

Everything was gray and dark and dusty. The organ works were mostly tier upon tier of wood pipes and electrical fixtures, with two long rows of leather bellows-hinges, all hammered together a lot looser and more haphazardly than one would expect. They towered up and up, behind the metal arch of the treble pipes, and Jennifer found a wooden ladder nailed to the works and clambered up to the first landing.

The dust was finger thick there, and other than a half-burnt candle stub or two, there was nothing of interest. She found the next set of rungs off to one side and went up.

As she climbed she became aware of a strange, expectant feeling in the air, a crackly sense of static electricity. Glancing over a shoulder, she saw pale, pastel lights shimmer on the treble pipes—Saint Elmo's fire. With a surge she heaved herself onto the top level. She could see all of the sanctuary from here, through the pipes; and the electrical fires blazed up brighter, shifting in quicksilver fashion. She saw the thing afloat over the altar too, but to her untutored eye it was of no greater interest than any other part of the building.

Jennifer's hair lifted lightly upward, the ends trailing blue sparks so that it formed an aura about her face. *Fata morganas* drifted through the floating mass.

The flames leapt from organ pipe to organ pipe, blazing up and subsiding like a Bach mass played on a color organ. There was sparkling electricity everywhere, in the cables and fixtures and wires. The stops began opening and shutting of their own accord, in a silent, electric symphony. Jennifer stretched up on her toes. Her auburn hair afloat, the world crackling with color and energy, thin electrical flames sizzling about her, she danced.

Later she found a burned-out light bulb there, on the upper catwalk, and ate the filament at its heart. She had to break the inside to get at it, but she fixed it up afterward, as good as new.

The minutes were waiting for Peter on his desk, with a new notation in the pastor's hand: SALARIES MUST BE CUT SOMEWHERE—PLEASE NOTIFY SAM. It was as close to an explicit threat as he was going to get.

Peter lit up a cigarette, realized that he already had one going in the ashtray, and stubbed it out. He rubbed the back of his neck, then restlessly strode to the chancel kitchen, off of the conference room. It was tiny and contained a broken refrigerator, a rusting gas stove that no one dared fire up, and a dozen empty cupboards. The linoleum was browned and buckling.

Taking a glass from the strainer, Peter washed it thoroughly under the tap and drew a drink of water. He tapped his cigarette's ashes into the old porcelain sink and washed them down the drain with a long spurt of water. Then, back at his desk, he rummaged through the small-emergencies drawer until he found a bottle of aspirin among the tampons and the lollipops.

Where, he asked himself, was the loophole? He popped the aspirin dry, thought a minute, took a sip of water. Finally he slapped on the typewriter. The pastor hadn't actually ordered him to fire Sam in person. It took three tries to come up with a final draft of the memo. He typed up a clean copy, read it through, and was satisfied. He forged the pastor's signature to it and dropped it in Sam's mail slot.

Done, he lit up a cigarette, noticed the previous one burning in the ashtray, and—exasperated—let them both burn. He was too wired to type now, so he scooped up a box of old clothing that had been donated to the church weeks ago and that he'd been meaning to store in the church with the rest. Outside, en route to the church, he noticed several clutches of wine bottles against the church wall and made a mental note to lift some more padlocks from the hardware store, to firm up security. He passed through the sanctuary without once looking at the altar and went to the front narthex, where the staircases to the balcony were.

He was halfway up one set of stairs when a pale face appeared at the top. A slender young woman in denim—a redhead. "The church is closed, miss," he called to her, and the face disappeared. A cold touch of fear in his stomach, he jogged up the stairs, looked around. "If you need some help . . . " he called. Something stirred off to one side, a ripple of stained-glass light over red hair, and the woman shifted into the shadows of the far stairway.

"Hey!" He dropped the box and stumbled over the piles of dusty cartons crammed with donations for the annual rummage sale. At the foot of the stairs the door between the narthex and the sanctuary was swinging shut. He pushed through. He was just in time to see the woman disappear behind the presbytery beyond the altar. A door closed gently.

Peter didn't try to follow. The thing over the altar was swirling madly, like a pinwheel. He couldn't understand how the woman could have moved so quickly, and he yelled after her, "I wasn't going to hurt you! What do you think I am, some kind of fucking monster?"

The children were playing a run-around game, so Sheila felt secure in leaving them to the supervision of parent volunteers while she went up to the old chapel for supplies. She retrieved the library paste first, paused, then went into the toddlers' room for the construction paper.

The toddlers' room had been part of the Sunday school program when Covenant was still an expanding congregation. A good dozen cribs stood serene in the soft light. They were arranged neatly against the walls, sidebars up and plasticized mattresses growing dusty. At the near corner a stairway rose to the west balcony. The stairs were so cluttered with broken furniture and toys that only a narrow, twisting pathway led upward.

Sam sat on the third step up. His eyes were dry and hard, and he was staring sightlessly at the cribs.

"Sam?" Sheila said. "Is everything all right? Why aren't you at the hospital?"

He didn't answer, didn't even move.

"Sam!" She was genuinely alarmed now and reached out to touch his arm.

It was as if her touch broke a spell. Sam snapped his head her way, eyes startled, and scrambled awkwardly to his feet. "I was just taking some things upstairs," he said defensively. "That's all I was doing."

"I believe you, I believe you!" Sheila protested. The old man scooped up a broken hobbyhorse, cradled it in his arms.

"It ain't no question of believing or *not* believing," he said. "I was just going upstairs." He turned and ascended.

Sheila stared after him for a long moment before hoisting her supplies and turning to go. As soon as she was far enough down the stairs that he wouldn't hear her, she threw back her head and said aloud, "I do not believe that man! He is so *exasperating*." It made her feel a lot better.

Halfway down the stairs she was stopped again, this time by a near-subliminal noise. She cocked her head. It was almost like the vibration in the sanctuary the other day, or— she raced down the stairs, cut across the parish hall and out to the Thirty-seventh Street narthex. Someone was outside, leaning on the buzzer.

"Who is it?" she called. Putting down her supplies, she peered through the peephole. There was a man outside, dressed in a suit. "You'll have to speak up," she yelled.

". . . from the hospital," the man was saying. "We're running a canvass of all the buildings—"

"You'll have to go to the church office," she called back. "We don't open this door during school hours." She picked up her box and headed downstairs. Almost to her surprise, the man went away.

The acid was in the glue backing of a Mickey Mouse decal. Mickey was dressed as the Sorcerer's Apprentice, gesturing up stars, and you were supposed to lick off the LSD and then slap the decal onto your forehead. Too cute by half, Peter thought, and when he'd done up the tab, he crumpled the little mouse and swallowed it.

While waiting for the drug to pass into his bloodstream, Peter did first some typing and then some filing.

When he found himself obsessively going back to each piece of filing to be sure it was retrievable and not placed away in some nonsensical, drug-generated location, he quit and went up the stairs to the second floor. Hands behind his back, Peter stood before the hall window, looking down into the play yard. Children were scurrying about busily, swinging on the old tire hung from the oak tree, scrambling over the wooden monkey bars some parent had built years ago. Foam-rubber mattresses had been tied around the oak's trunk to protect the children.

As he watched, a sudden wind blew through the tree and filled the air with yellow leaves. For an instant they hung motionless, defining the space between ground and sky, receding into infinite perspective. Then they swirled away.

Years before, he'd worked for an inner city corporation, in a room with a window view of a church's slate roof and nothing else. Ordinarily the roof was a barren, featureless stretch, but this one time it had snowed the night before, and the snow was loosened by a warm winter sun so that occasionally patches would let go and slide away in a puff of powdery white. Kim Soong, the only other typist in the room at that moment, had leaned over her machine and stared, entranced. The room filled with silence.

The acid was hitting. He felt a painful twinge in his stomach from the minute trace of strychnine that was a by-product of the drug's manufacture.

Slowly and carefully he descended the newly challenging stairway and, remembering to lock up behind him, went outside and to the church door.

Two men lay across the step, passing a paper-bagged bottle back and forth. The dark one beamed at Peter's appearance, and they both scrambled to their feet.

"This my friend Walter," Ashod said. His companion, a sallow, half-shaven beanpole of a man, nodded several times. He had haunted eyes, with ring upon ring of darkness beneath them. "He's come to meet the lady, too."

Peter looked blankly first at the one man, then the other, and then away from both. He saw that there were a dozen or so more vent people—shopping-bag ladies among them—scattered about the churchyard. Some wandered slowly, aimlessly about, and others sat huddled in decaying blankets and chunks of squashed-down cardboard boxes. One was pissing against the wall. It was a regular little Reaganville, and they looked as though they had come to stay. *Fuck it*, he decided suddenly, *I'm on drugs, I don't have to cope with this*. He retreated into the church, slamming the door after him.

The stone ribs of the sanctuary were still humming softly to themselves, but now—with the acid in him—Peter was not bothered by the phenomenon. After all, things were *supposed* to be strange on acid. And one way or another, Peter was determined to return things to the way they were supposed to be.

The sanctuary was cold. Peter shivered, convulsively stared upward, and was shocked motionless by the wooden angels above. They glinted gold and then silver shards of ice. They multiplied, like the leaves had earlier, and filled the church—angel upon angel, as regular and unvarying as an Escher print.

The empty spaces were angels too, and the images flashed from solid angels to negative angels and back in a flickering dance. The air was filled with music, words, and notes transformed into a solid, calligraphic tracery in an alphabet he did not know. There was something familiar about the music, and with a start Peter recognized it as Vangelis's *Heaven and Hell*. His Toshiba was still playing, and that realization was a jarring intrusion of reality.

The thing over the altar was larger now, much larger, the size of a clenched fist or of a coiled snake. The angels that intruded upon it were seized as if by overwhelming gravitational forces, crumpled to nothing, and swallowed up by it.

The angels went on dancing. In a flash of insight Peter realized that they were all mechanical. Identical, perfect—they were machines, creatures of a purely deterministic universe, entirely devoid of free will. They danced their machine dance in the air, and it meant nothing.

There were fewer angels now, as one by one they were devoured by the thing over the altar. They kept on dancing, though, and if they were aware of the thing—if they were even capable of awareness—it did not matter, for all was meaningless, all was a dance. Blind forces ground them down, and joylessly they danced.

And the thing over the altar continued to slowly grow.

He fled—from the angels' cold dance, from the acid-etched sense of total futility, but mostly from the horrible, nasty *eating* obscenity afloat in the church. Out of the sanctuary and down, into the basement, away from the light, into obscurity and darkness. When he had stopped he found himself huddled into a cold, lightless corner. The ghost was there. He could feel her breath on his face, sense a near-visual glimmering of warmth from her body.

Sam was eating lunch. He sat with the makings spread out before him in the old chapel, by the unused chimney where the rat had taken up residence. He started with an apple, chewing it slowly and thoughtfully as he considered the job he had done on the trap.

The rat trap was dark and smoky. Rats were clever; they didn't like new smells, chemical smells, human smells. He'd built a small fire of twigs and old leaves out by the trash cans in the play yard and charred the trap over it, holding the trap in a clamp he had made of an old coat hanger.

The apple finished, Sam unscrewed the peanut butter jar, plunged a knife in and stirred the oils around real good. He began spreading it onto a slice of Wonder bread, paying close attention to the act, involving his whole mind in it, because the alternative was to think about what the doctors had told him that morning. He paused and smeared a dab of peanut butter onto the trap for bait, then returned to spreading the sandwich thick. Peanut butter made good bait because rats liked that kind of greasy stuff, oily and rancid.

He was sitting in a patch of colored light from the south rose window, and for some while it had flickered gently, as if interrupted by the shadows of a lightly tossing tree branch. But there was no tree outside there, and Sam looked up, puzzled, to see what was interfering with the light.

There was a white girl in front of the window, glory light streaming about her, and she was sitting cross-legged in the air.

Sam could not blink, could not look away. His sandwich was frozen in front of him. He knew this girl, had met her once before in the basement. She had been wearing the same denim jeans and jacket then, and her hair was as red as it had ever been.

Footsteps sounded on the stairs, and Sam ignored them. But when the door slammed open, the suddenness of the sound made him glance without thinking back toward the hallway, and he saw Sheila enter the room. The light about him cleared, and he didn't have to look up again to know that the girl was gone.

"Sam." The nursery school teacher was before him now, and she peered into his face, concerned. "Sam, I'm very worried about you, about the way you've been acting today Have I offended you? Should I be apologizing for something?"

He looked away, could not answer. But she would not go away.

"Sam, what's *wrong* with you today?"

Sooner or later, he knew, he would have to tell somebody. "I think I'm cured," he said slowly. And burst into tears.

The vent people were roasting a dog in one of the window wells. By pure good fortune they'd chosen one of the few wells that had been cinder-blocked up. The skinned carcass was hung on a spit, turned erratically by an enthusiastic, hunchbacked individual. The church wall was black with smoke and grease. They offered Peter a leg, but he shook his head and wandered away. There were over a hundred vent people in the churchyard, and their trash and scattered possessions made the yard as cluttered and filthy as a battlefield. One toothless old hag lifted her skirts and squatted, to the profound disinterest of her fellows. Her piss steamed as it hit the ground. A convulsive alky, looking like a skinny black spider, swooped great circles in the walkway dust with both hands, babbling of demons in his head.

And all the while there were at least five radios playing, battered and ugly things scavenged from garbage bags but with a good decade's life left in their permablast batteries. They were tuned to three separate newscasts, and the fragmentary snatches of global hysteria tumbled and cascaded one over another.

—*warned that unless American troops withdraw from Burma—escaped from the Rocky Mountain arsenal—survivors' reports of CBW warfare were denied—troops called up from—martial law declared in five midwestern states—*

Peter stopped before an old scissors grinder, who had set up his cart on the sidewalk. It was an ancient thing, hammered together from scraps and pushed about by hand. The whetstone was run by a vintage 1922 electric motor in black enameled housing, which fed off of a tangle of car batteries hooked up in series.

—*reported shot down over Sinkiang*—

"You and I," shouted the scissors grinder, "*heedlessly* deserted God some many years ago to join vain Satan's *vain* revolt against God's *temporary laws.* All *truths* emanate from God, and we will reap what we have sown. This is *why* we are now in human bodies. *To reap what?*"

A fat woman waddled past, going "Quackquackquack," like a cartoon duck on amphetamines. She drew Peter's eyes away from the orator, and he saw that the yard was as abuzz with divergent theologies as the Middle Ages were before the Inquisition.

—*meanwhile tensions escalated in the Middle East and Africa in a bizarre*—

A deadpan little man in very clean clothes stood on the steps and shouted, "The Bible tells of the *scarlet whore* that is *Babylon* that is the *beast* that has put her *foot* on the serpent! She has *swallowed up* the seventh seal and has loosed the horrors of the *Rocky Mountain arsenal.* If you have *faith* the size—"

And somehow in the confusion of voices, Peter realized he did not have to be here—did not, in fact, even know how he had gotten here—and went inside, to his office.

—*limited use of tactical nuclear*—

There were three cigarettes afire in the ashtray by the time Sheila came into the office. One by one, Peter had lit them up and put them down, unsmoked. She cheerfully waved a hand in the bluish smoke and said, "Phew! It smells like a train station in here."

Her presence was an anchor he could hang on to. "Hi," he said.

"Peter, it's wonderful," she bubbled. "Have you heard the news? Sam's doctors say he's going to be okay. He's had a spontaneous remission—isn't that wonderful? It was a miracle, they said—a one-chance-in-a-billion miracle!" She banged her fists together and bounced up and down on her toes in elation.

"A miracle," Peter said numbly. He should have felt happy for Sam, and yet he didn't. All he could think of was the memo firing the old man, and that Sam wasn't going to die in time for him to avoid receiving it.

"Yes, but Peter"—her mood shifted again—"you have to do something about all these dirty, filthy vagrants who are hanging around the church. The parents are going to be coming by to pick up their children in a couple of hours, and they are going to have a *fit.* Really."

"They're not really dangerous," Peter said. "They're none of them capable enough to be dangerous."

"Peter, I want you to get rid of them! Call the police or something. If we don't get them out of here, we're going to lose half our students!" She leaned forward, examining his face. "Are you *on* something?"

"Not anymore," he said, and belatedly realized that it was true. He was perfectly straight. Just tired—extremely tired, almost stunned with weariness. There was a strange blank area in his memory between when the acid had peaked and he'd come to among the vent people. Something flickered there, bright and ungraspable. He shrugged mentally. Chalk it up to the drugs and forget it.

Taking a deep breath to settle himself, he picked up the phone, dialed, and when Alverson's secretary refused to put him through, snarled, "Listen, sister, this is Sergeant Blindwood of the Pennsylvania State Police, and I am right in the middle of a fucking *shoot-out*. We have a psychotic individual holding this fucker's wife and fucking *kids* and shouting slogans about the fucking Hard Anarchy Liberation *Army*, and you are holding me *up*. How'd you like to have your sex life investigated with a fucking *crowbar*?"

A moment later a very small and hesitant voice said, "Peter . . . this *is* you, isn't it?"

Peter tossed the receiver to a horrified Sheila. "All yours," he said.

She held it as if it were a poisonous snake that would bite her if she let go. Then she said, "Peter, you can't evade responsibility by having someone else say the words." There was compassion in her voice.

Slowly—reluctantly—Peter reached for the phone, closed his fingers about it, took it. "Harry? Listen, I'm sorry about all this. I dialed the wrong number." He listened in silence for a time, said, "Yes, I know," and listened some more. The outside door closed gently as Sheila left.

When Alverson hung up, Peter jabbed down on the plunger, cutting the connection. He took a deep breath and dialed the number for the police. "Hello," he said, "I'm calling from the Church of the Covenant on Thirty-seventh Street . . ."

Time was short, and Jennifer was hungry again. She had scoured the church from top to bottom, passing by many things—cookie dough, Ivory soap flakes, Brillo pads, clay—that she might normally have lingered over. But she could no longer spare the time to build from precursor elements. The chemical dump counter advocacy group's office was originally the choir director's, a century ago when the position was full-time. It had a skylight with plastic sheeting stapled to its underside and a row of narrow, lead-glass windows that looked into the storage rooms of the top floor. Jennifer had climbed through one of these and was going through a carton of bumper stickers when the thing in the sanctuary stirred.

The sense of its movement rose through shafts and vents left over from an early, unsuccessful attempt to retrofit a forced air heating system to the church. Jennifer shuddered as if a jolt of electricity had shot up her spine. For an instant she thought it was about to happen, and she was racked by terror and bleak despair. It was too early. She was not ready. Then the movement ceased—there was yet a chance, however slim. She was on her feet and through the window almost immediately.

Fear drove her down the stairs, running silently, wanting to hide but not daring to do so. Inspiration made her nab the key ring from the sexton's closet. As sly and furtive as a shadow, she slipped back up the stairs, through the narthex, and into the parish hall. She could hear the sexton working in the chancel, but the connecting door was shut, and he couldn't see her. One key of the ring fit into the communion cabinet. She opened the doors and found what she needed.

There were a lot of linen napkins, which she shoved aside, and a tray with slots for perhaps a hundred tiny little glasses to fit into. The bread was carefully wrapped in white paper. It was half gone from the previous Sunday and stale and hard as wood. but it would do—it would do!

Triumphantly she shoved the bread under one arm and cradled the two bottles of communion wine in the other. She ran.

There was a dark storm gathering outside. The thunderhead piled up, charcoal blue, over the surrounding buildings. Faint lightnings shimmered within its heart. The vent people danced happily on the saturated, green lawn. On every side the blind and featureless walls of the high rises blocked out large chunks of the sky. It felt like being enclosed in a box.

Peter stared glumly out the window, waiting, all pretense of working gone. He shifted papers to either side of his desk to make room for his elbows and rested his chin on his arms.

Fast flashes of red and blue light struck and rebounded off the church walls, and Peter saw that police cars were pulling up, blocking off the surrounding streets. There were more of them than he had expected, some twenty or so, and they arrived eerily silent—flashers on and sirens mute.

Three cars—one unmarked—nosed through the blockade and parked by the curb. Their inhabitants conferred, formed a party, and moved briskly up the walk. One man craned his neck interestedly as they passed by the scissors grinder's old cart, which had been pulled apart and made into an altar of sorts What might have been a crucifix canted crazily atop it, with several broken plaster Madonnas—scavenged from God knows where—lashed to its arms.

Peter stood as the deputation neared the door. Outside, police lounged against their cars, the visors of their black glass helmets flipped up. They were held in check by neocortical implants, like dogs on a leash, and several were gently tapping their truncheons into open palms.

The doorbell rang. Answering, Peter found himself facing three police officers. Their faces were impassive and might well have been carved from the same block of ice. Standing with them was the smooth and plausible man from the Cancer Research Center "Hello," the Cancer Research man said to Peter pleasantly. "I see we're on the same team now."

The door from the chancel to the back stairway was badly warped out of shape. There were splits through the center, and it was so badly bowed that it wouldn't even shut properly. Sam had removed it from the frame and set it down on two sawhorses. To do the job properly, he should soak the oaken door in water for a few days and then weight it down between flat metal plates, to warp it back into shape. Lacking the time and tools, though, one did the best one could. So . . . first you move the hinges down an inch, to rehang the door lower. Then you sand down the edges where it's sticking. A little putty in the cracks, some weather-stripping around the edges, and the job is done.

Sam whistled an old Motown tune as he sanded, enjoying the shift and feel of his muscles. He felt good, stronger than he had been in years, and all the swelling around his neck had gone down.

The doctors wanted him to go through another battery of tests, but under close questioning by his sister—she was a sharptongued woman, was Sophia!— they admitted that he didn't actually need them. They were just curious to know why he wasn't dead. He was healed, though. They said so themselves.

He could feel—subliminally—the thing growing in the sanctuary, but he felt no need to do anything about it.

There was enough trouble in the world without borrowing more. And like they always said, you don't open the oven door until the cake is done. Fine oak dust whispered down to the floor as he handled the paper, sliding it along the door's edge in long, firm, even strokes.

The communion wine was cheap stuff, with a metal cap that unscrewed instead of a cork. Jennifer took only a taste, but that first sip went down *real* smooth. It jolted through her brain like lightning, snapping synapses open and shut, setting off a cascade of images from her past:

She was back in the hospital, strapped onto a gurney. Everything was white and smelled of disinfectant and hospital food. They had cropped her long, blond hair and were shaving the stubble that remained. When she opened her mouth to scream, someone shoved the side of his hand in, saying, "Hush, pretty baby, we're just going to fine-tune that pretty little brain of yours." She bit down hard and his hand tasted—

His hand tasted like her husband's when they made love. He would touch her face gently, wonderingly, and she'd twist her head sideways to catch his hand in her teeth. Feeling like some kind of wild, free animal, she'd bite down into the flesh. It tasted of salt and sweat and curly black hairs. He was on leave from the Air Force but scheduled to rotate back to Mauritania soon, to fly more bombing missions. He was an officer—

He was an officer, and when she saw him coming up the walk, stalwartly expressionless, she knew her husband wasn't coming back, and she wished so hard for it to be all a mistake that it seemed the world must shudder to its core for the sheer intensity of her desire. But the officer walked right up to her door anyway, rang the bell, delivered the news. It was as he was turning away that the air seemed to shimmer and the young officer fell to the ground, blood gushing from his nose and mouth. Half embedded in the walkway, he struggled. She knew that he wasn't to blame, but still the blood came out—

The blood came out the same way it did later when she left the hospital, her skull abristle with tiny silver wires and implants that were supposed to control her but did not. All the guards fell down, hemorrhaging, even those who did not try to stop her but turned to run. The red hair and the clothing formed around her because on some cunning animal level she knew she needed them to escape. She walked—

They were good memories, and they filled up the empty spaces. The pain was real and good and brought her a step closer to being human again. She tilted the bottle and chugalugged it all down. Bubbles *blork*ed to the top, and the bottle was empty, and her head was full of thoughts.

She uncapped the second bottle.

"I shouldn't be letting you in without the pastor's explicit permission," Peter fretted.

—*half of Houston up in flames. We're trying to get a reporter in now to confirm*—

The vent people parted for the group, stepping back a pace from the intensity of the Cancer Man's eyes. Ashod came bustling forward and waved his pink plastic rosary in Peter's face. "Save yourself!" he shouted. "Get down on your knees—pray for forgiveness!"

One of the police officers reached out to touch Ashod gently on the chest, and he went stumbling back, face contorted with pain.

"Peter," the Cancer Man said. They were at the church door now, and Peter had his keys out. "Let me introduce myself. My name is William Oberg. I'd be pleased if you called me Bill." He shook Peter's hand. "Now," he said, not letting go, "we're friends, yes? I'm sure you wouldn't mind showing your old chum where you work, would you?" He tightened his grip, and Peter gasped in pain. The police looked on with interest.

"No," Peter said quickly "No objection." The pain ceased.

"Good." Oberg let Peter open the church door, then led the troop through the narthex and into the sanctuary. He stopped in amazement.

"Jesus Christ," one of the cops said. Another crossed himself.

The thing over the altar had grown. It was the size of a basketball now, so large that it was almost possible for the eye to fix on it and assign it some definite shape and image. But not quite. It was oddly compelling, even hypnotic. Peter seemed to remember—

"Okay, it's pretty far gone," Oberg said, "but we can still handle it if we can get hold of the girl."

Peter started and for the first time actually *looked* at Oberg. He could half-see into the man, see the whirling wheels and cams embedded just below the plastic flesh, the fine gold wires and wheat-seed monitor lights. Oberg glanced fleetingly Peter's way, and Peter's breath froze within his throat. The man had no eyes! Only deep metal funnels that led from his face into a cold and lightless stacking of cryonic plates. Peter exhaled, and Oberg shifted into a thin surface image, with no interior, as insubstantial as a hologram or a soap bubble. His movements left long, bright trails. *Oh God, no,* Peter thought. He was flashing back. These fuckers were not going to show him any mercy if they discovered he was on drugs.

Luckily, they were scurrying about like automatons and hadn't noticed yet. Oberg was laying out elastic cords and metal restraints on the communion table. One policeman unhooked a flashlight from his belt and clambered over the presbytery. He poked the light between the organ pipes and peered within. The two other police went into the balconies. One shimmied up a loose pew to the steeple door. From within he called down, "Ugh. It's ankle-deep in pigeon shit here."

"The windows have been broken for years," Peter said inanely. It was hard to fake a straight response.

"Check it anyway," Oberg called back. He tightened a cinch on the communion table and stepped back, satisfied. The altar had become a restraining table, with devices to hold the legs spread wide *here*, the arms up and to the side *there*. Directly above, the thing whirled madly.

The table lacked only a victim. Oberg laid a fatherly hand on Peter's shoulder. "Perhaps you have some idea where she might be?" he suggested.

The second bottle of wine was on its way to her lips when the passage suddenly convulsed. The walls turned blue and lurched over on their sides. Jennifer jerked, and the floor came smashing up into the side of her face. The empty bottle fell away, shattering into a thousand cobalt fragments. The half-eaten communion loaf burst into cold, blue flames.

The surviving bottle was pouring purple wine into Jennifer's lap. Frantically she stoppered it with her thumb. The glass was scalding cold; it stung like hornets. But she clutched it to her and did not let go.

Sick with uncertainty and pain, she stood. Her head was abuzz with blue sparks, and the carbon smoke from the burning loaf was billowing up to fill the room. All the passages were atilt; they steepened when she tried to climb them. She had to grab one-handed at pillars and moldings and doorjambs to pull herself upward, into the icy flames.

The arm cradling the bottle spasmed with cold, and the bottle fell away. It bounced twice, spraying wine, but miraculously did not break. Jennifer stretched out, trying to retrieve it. She almost fell from her fingerhold trying, but—too far! Too far! She reached again, nearly dislocating her shoulder and wrists with the effort.

Her knuckles whitened, weakened. Involuntarily, she let go of the door frame and slid four yards down the hall. The wine bottle rested on the floor curling above her, in the center of a spreading purple stain. A full quarter of its contents remained within the bottle—she could see it.

But she could not reach it. The floor lifted away from her too steeply and could not be scaled. It was easier—much easier— to let gravity pull her down the hall, into the redness. Into the warmth.

"No," Peter said. "I couldn't guess."

But he was afraid of Oberg. And Oberg was a man who understood fear, knew its every touch and nuance, could read its track on the human face. "Is she on this floor?" he asked. "No? Upstairs, then? Downstairs? *Where* in the basement?"

Outside, the vent people were suddenly still. The silence was startling.

Then a quick series of soft explosions went *pop-pop-pop.* Tear gas. Pandemonium broke out, shrieks of pain or rage mingling with incoherent cries of fear as the police moved in. Like most urban dwellers, Peter had seen his share of riots in the past few years. He could picture in his mind what was happening: There would be an outer circle of police, to prevent fugitives from escaping and force them back into the fray, and two or more flying wedges to move through the mob, clubs flashing.

Oberg touched Peter gently, caressingly. His fingers scuttled up Peter's neck like a spider and stroked softly below one ear. "Why don't you lead us there, hmmm?"

It was hard to concentrate. Peter trembled in confusion, caught between the vision of the riot and the touch of Oberg's hand. He was no longer sure which was real. Something crashed against one of the windows, an early Tiffany the congregation had always held in reserve against final bankruptcy. It smashed a small piece of emerald glass, sending splinters flying. The entire window echoed and reverberated with the blow.

"Shall we go?" Oberg said.

Miserably, Peter led them downward.

Sam was lifting the door into place when the call came. He paused in his work and cocked his head, listening. Outside, the vagrants were stirring up a fuss, but he ignored them. The call came from closer in, somewhere below.

He leaned the door carefully against the sheet music cabinet and went down the stairs. He paused at his supply closet to pick up the flashlight. It was a long, heavy thing, encased in a black rubber sheath. He flicked it on, to make sure it worked. He was unlocking the door to the basement when a small white boy caromed into his legs. "Whoa," he said. "What's this?" He put his hands on the boy's shoulders.

"I got to see the ghost!" the child cried. Sam hoisted him into the air, let him rest in the crook of his arm. It had been a long time since he had held a child like this; not since his own son was a little boy, in fact. A long, long time.

They were not the only two to hear the call. Sheila joined them at the lady's side.

Peter had an awful feeling. He unhappily led Oberg and the policemen down. Twice he tried to turn them away, and each time Oberg had read the tension in his neck, his shoulders, and turned him back to the right path. He didn't even know how he knew it was the right path. It was getting harder to keep track of what was and what was not. His vision split fuzzily in two, and he glimpsed briefly through the eyes of a nursery school child and then one of her teachers. Alternate scenes overlay one another.

It was an awful, choking sensation. Peter was dizzied by shifting visions through the eyes of others—Sam, Jeremy, Sheila, even the police. Sometimes one, sometimes several at once. He felt their breaths in his lungs, the touch of their clothes on his skin, their thoughts running through his head, briefly there and then gone. It confused him, made him foggily unsure which of these many people he actually was.

The only light in the coal bin came from Sam's flashlight, shining like an orange moon in her eyes, which were green, and Sam wanted to crouch and raise her from the dirt, but somehow (Sheila didn't know how she knew) it was understood that she was not to be moved. Jeremy stared down with large, solemn eyes and dug an elbow into Sam's ribs—the sexton understood and put him down—and Sheila fretted because she had children to tend to, a door to rehang, and none of them knew what was actually going on.

A voice came from out of the darkness.

"Children, there is a new world growing," it said. "It was planted by mistake and it grows like a weed—without direction. But it can be tamed and pruned—it can be reclaimed by the proper authorities."

Now Oberg loomed out of the darkness, amusement predominant on his face. "What is growing," he said, "is a viewpoint more than anything else. It has been contaminated by your presence, by everyone here in the church that this young lady has met. Left alone, it would become a perfect reflection of your true selves. It would be a judgment on you."

He paused. Nobody spoke or moved. "There is a war on," he said. The police were pale blobs behind him, clustered loosely about Peter (he glimpsed himself multiplied through their eyes). "Our government is locked in a death struggle with the evil empires of the earth. This young woman has the potential to win that war for us. Under our direction the world can be . . . *turned.* It can be made safe for us forever." He sauntered forward, in no particular hurry. "Please stand back," he said. "This woman is government property."

When Sam saw the man reach for Jennifer, he acted swiftly, without thought. His flashlight swung in a great arc at Oberg's face as Sheila shrieked and grabbed for Jeremy, who was knocked, laughing, to the floor. Oberg didn't even flinch. One of the police seized Sam and swung him about; another forced his hands behind his back and snapped handcuffs on them—Sheila saw them glint in the light cast by the flashlight that fell, forgotten, to the floor. There was a foot right by Jennifer's eyes; it loomed enormous, and she ignored it.

The boy from the church office was with them. His face was slack and bewildered. "Why didn't you help?" Sam asked bitterly. "You could have done something!"

"Sam..." Peter said. "They wanted me to fire you, Sam." His eyes were all dazzled with tiny, glittery stars. "I didn't, though; I wouldn't do it."

The government man was bending over the lady in the dirt. He lifted her up in his arms. A policeman yanked Sam backward, away from them. But he was staring at Peter, puzzlement in his face.

"What did you *do* to him?" Sam demanded. Then, angrily, "*Look* at him! What did you *do*?"

It was like a procession. First came Oberg, carrying the ghost, limp and helpless, in.his arms. She stared vacantly upward. Then came the first cop, pushing Sam, handcuffed, before him. Then the second, leading Peter by the arm, and the third, with both Sheila and the child.

That was not how Peter saw it. His vision was flashing from person to person, first through a patrolman's eyes, then out Oberg's, then—simultaneously—his own and Sheila's. The shifting was growing faster, and multiple views more common so that if he could only hold it in his mind—he was seeing a comprehensive *gestalt* view, each person through several sets of eyes and his own.

There was a wine bottle lying on the stairs, in the midst of a spreading stain, and Oberg casually kicked it aside. It went spinning and bounced down two steps. Sam nearly stumbled over it, and Peter (seeing it happen in five overlapping viewpoints) snatched it up in an ungainly, newborn-clumsy swoop. Peter had no intention of doing anything with the bottle. He was just being automatically, obsessively neat. But his guard reached out and slapped it away, out of his hand, as a potential weapon. It flew downward, spraying wine in all directions. Peter watched it slowly fall through several sets of vision, bounce, and disappear behind them all.

He felt a strange sense of bereavement, and permanent loss.

Outside, the roaring of the riot was rising and falling, regular-irregular, like ocean waves or streams of cars on the freeway. "Almost to the sanctuary," Oberg commented lightly. There were people being beaten on the doorsill outside. Insanely, at least one still held a blaring radio.

—vehemently denied. Spokesmen said the nuclear strike was a preventative retrodestabilization effort.

There were wet, maroon stains on Peter's slacks and shirt, and a bit of wine still clung to his free hand. Absently he raised it to his mouth, licked it off.

And the taste of it jolted him like an electric shock. It snapped his mind back together, reassembled it from scattered fragments, cut off the visions through the others' eyes. He was himself again.

And he remembered.

When he had stopped running, he found himself huddled into a cold, lightless corner. The ghost was there. He could feel her breath on his face, sense a near-visual glimmering of warmth from her body.

What do you want? she asked him. He was not surprised that he could hear her, even though she had not spoken, because he was still wearing his Toshiba, and his thoughts were not rational enough for any further reasoning.

But what *did* he want? It was a question he could never have answered straight. But in his hallucinogen-saturated state, he found that the answer came out easy and lucid and straightforward, as if it arose from the center of his being, where there were no lies and evasions, no confusion and no misunderstanding, but simply what was.

"I want to understand what's going on," he said, "and I want to know what to do about it." The blackness waved around him, ran its fingers through his brain.

Her answer came—again—not in words but in a sense of delighted amusement, of pleased recognition: *So be it.*

Standing there in the lightless cellar, amid dirt and broken furniture, his ears singing acid songs, head bowed slightly to avoid hitting it against the low overhead beams, he received his gift. It was an understanding so pure and complete, so detailed and comprehensive, undeniable, and true that no human mind could have contained a fraction of it without being destroyed completely. Faced with this overload, his mind shut down to avoid handling it.

He found himself being dragged roughly through the narthex by a policeman. This was bewildering. He had only faint shadow memories of the events since his visit to the lady in the basement, and they seemed . . . unconvincing. Nor did he retain his illumination; all that remained of it were three words, running like a mantra through his head.

"What was that?" Oberg paused before the sanctuary door. He cocked his head, trying to listen over the riot noises. "That sound . . ."

Children burst all around them, cascading up from the stairs, bubbling out into the narthex. As the startled cops drew their guns, they came whooping, crowding about them, shreeping and chirping with excitement.

"Shoot the little bastards!" Oberg commanded. The policemen all stared at him in horror and disbelief. "*Shoot* them!" he insisted, and still they disobeyed.

Peter was so preoccupied by the words running through his thoughts that he did not at first realize that his guard had released him. The children—and the parents and teachers who came running after—had separated him from the group; he realized now that he was leaning against the door to the outside.

Open the door. Open the door. Open the door. The words tumbled over and over, one upon the other—*open the door*—urgent and overwhelming. *Suppose,* he thought, *just suppose they meant something. Suppose you were supposed to take them literally.*

He put his hand on the door. Outside, the riot was in progress. Hundreds of vent people were being forced against the door. Some were beating on it with their hands; it shivered and vibrated in sympathy.

Open the door.

Oberg had noticed him now. He was pointing at Peter and shouting some angry command that could not be heard over the children and the riot. One of the policemen turned toward him.

He opened the door and stood to the side.

Vagrants and derelicts, vent men and shopping-bag ladies—the insane and confused, the outcast and discarded, the filthy and vile, the crazy and crippled, and those haunted by religious or political visions that made no sense to anyone but themselves . . . all flooded through the door, a great wash of stinking humanity, excited and fearful, some shouting cries of joy or triumph, many badly injured, at least one attempting to sing. They swarmed over police and captives and children, teachers and Oberg and parents and all, and swept them into the sanctuary.

Oberg was slammed against the doorsill, his head cracking sharply against the wood. He slumped.

The lady, falling from his arms, was snatched up by Sam, who carried her within. The flows of children and derelicts converged around the altar.

Jennifer's eyes were bright and alert and serenely calm.

—*advising all inhabitants of nuclear targets—that includes all residents of the BosWash corridor, any port cities*—

The thing still hovered over the altar.

"It's *pretty!*" Sheila gasped by Peter's ear.

It was. It glimmered slightly where it floated, and there were hints of bright colors and far places in its light. It whirled and spun, as if to some unheard music. It seemed full of promise and possibility.

Just as Jennifer was lowered onto the altar, though, fierce light bloomed outside the windows. The unseen skies turned brilliant with nuclear fire, and the stained glass grew intensely, unbearably bright. It was the beginning of the war they had all been expecting for so long.

A horrified silence fell, and then—shocked by that awful hush—several of the children began to cry.

Jennifer gasped and convulsed—at last her time had come. She stretched out a hand over her head, and the thing above her pulsed. Three times it expanded and contracted, and then it exploded.

The explosion engulfed them all in an instant, swallowing up the church and expanding outward, ever more rapidly, still growing. The last coherent thought Peter had before he was transformed entirely was that perhaps Oberg was right. Perhaps it was a judgment on them all.

Rapid circles, of reality and light, raced one another around the globe.

—Mark 4:30-32

Includes six new, never-before-published stories and four reprints from Omni magazine

With stories by:
Bruce McAllister, Elizabeth A. Lynn,
Richard Kadrey,
Neal Barrett, Jr., Tom Maddox,
Robert Silverberg,
Paul Park, Jack Dann, J. R. Dunn,
Suzy McKee Charnas

Ask at your local bookstore or order direct from Omni

_____ Copies of *OMNI Best Science Fiction One* at $8.95 each. **Total** _____

_____ Residents of NC, NJ, and NY add appropriate sales tax _____

_____ Shipping and handling (U.S. $2.50; Canada $4.00;
Foreign $6.00 for first book $1.00 each additional) _____

Grand Total _____

_____ Check or money Order _____ MC _____ VISA

Signature _____
(Required)
Account Number _____ Exp. Date _____
Name _____
Street Address _____
City _____ State _____ Zip _____

Send this entire coupon to: **OMNI Books
c/o CCC
2500 McClellan Ave.
Pennsauken, NJ 08109**

Please allow four to six weeks for delivery. Offer good while supplies last.
All orders must be paid in U.S. funds drawn on a U.S. bank.

Includes six new, never-before-published stories and four reprints from Omni magazine

With stories by:
Lucius Shepard, Tom Maddox,
Gregg Keizer, George R. R. Martin,
Bruce McAllister,
Pat Cadigan, Maggie Flinn,
Dan Simmons, Garry Kilworth,
Elizabeth Hand

Ask at your local bookstore or order direct from Omni

_____ Copies of *OMNI Best Science Fiction Two* at $10.00 each. **Total** _____

_____ Residents of NC, NJ, and NY add appropriate sales tax _____

_____ Shipping and handling (U.S. $2.50; Canada $4.00;
Foreign $6.00 for first book $1.00 each additional) _____

Grand Total _____

_____ Check or money Order _____ MC _____ VISA

Signature _____
(Required)
Account Number _____ Exp. Date _____
Name _____
Street Address _____
City _____ State _____ Zip _____

Send this entire coupon to: **OMNI Books**
c/o CCC
2500 McClellan Ave.
Pennsauken, NJ 08109

Please allow four to six weeks for delivery. Offer good while supplies last.
All orders must be paid in U.S. funds drawn on a U.S. bank.

Includes ten new, never-before-published stories and one reprint from Omni magazine

With stories by:
*Bruce McAllister,
Simon Ings, Thomas M. Disch,
Ursula K. Le Guin,
Gahan Wilson, John Crowley,
Pat Cadigan, Ian McDonald,
Scott Baker, Pat Murphy*

Ask at your local bookstore or order direct from Omni

_____ Copies of *OMNI Best Science Fiction Three* at $10.00 each. **Total** _____

_____ Residents of NC, NJ, and NY add appropriate sales tax

_____ Shipping and handling (U.S. $2.50; Canada $4.00; Foreign $6.00 for first book $1.00 each additional)

Grand Total _____

_____ Check or money Order   ____ MC   ____ VISA

Signature _____
(Required)
Account Number _____ Exp. Date _____
Name _____
Street Address _____
City _____ State _____ Zip _____

Send this entire coupon to: **OMNI Books
c/o CCC
2500 McClellan Ave.
Pennsauken, NJ 08109**

Please allow four to six weeks for delivery. Offer good while supplies last.
All orders must be paid in U.S. funds drawn on a U.S. bank.